LADY GOD

BY LESA LUDERS

NEW VICTORIA PUBLISHERS

Published by New Victoria Publishers Inc., a feminist, literary, and cultural organization, PO Box 27, Norwich, VT 05055-0027.

Acknowledgments
I am grateful to Ursula Hegi and Tina Foreyes for their friendship and encouragement.

Acknowledgement is made to the publisher for permission to quote from the Alfred A. Knopf edition of *The Bluest Eye* (Copyright © 1970 by Toni Morrison) granted by International Creative Management, Inc.

Printed and Bound in the USA
1 2 3 4 5   1999 1998 1997 1996 1995

Library of Congress Cataloging-in-Publication Data

Luders, Lesa, 1958-
    Lady god / by Lesa Luders.
        p.   cm.
    ISBN 0-934678-59-6
    I. Title.
PS3562. U257L3   1995

813'.54- - dc20

95-19139
CIP

For Connie

But to find out the truth about how dreams die,
one should never take the word of the dreamer.
Toni Morrison
The Bluest Eye

Chapter One

Outside of Pike, I hitched a ride on a logging truck and studied my road map, trying to decide where I'd get off. I could have picked any town on the trucker's route, but I chose Willow. It had a nice sound to it. I would settle in a town named after a tree.

Sheets of heat rose from the tarred streets of Willow. My feet were sweating inside my hiking boots, my flannel shirt was damp, and my hair felt hot against my back. I considered taking my boots off and going barefoot as I explored my new town, but I was leery of the sidewalks on Main Street. Silver-colored particles, intermixed with the concrete, glittered like shards of glass.

I bought a pair of thongs from a drugstore, pulled my boots off and tied them to the strap of my duffel bag. I'd never worn thongs before. I liked the slapping sound they made against the heels of my feet. We didn't wear thongs back home in Pike or on the mountain overlooking the town. There, spiked brush crept across the mountainside and into the city; it would cut you if you didn't cover your feet in shin-high boots and your legs in bluejeans.

My mother had been different from anyone else who walked the trails. She said the brush couldn't cut her because she was blessed with thick skin. The timber opened at her legs as she ran down the deer paths. Rarely was she cut, despite her scant covering. On the mountain overlooking Pike, she wore white gowns. In the summertime, she often wore nothing at all.

She died in the summer of my fifth year. August fifteenth. Only twenty-two years old, she was my present age when she died. My mind paints pictures of her last summer which resist completion. Year by year the lines have become sharper, the colors deeper, the dimensions broader. Memory reconstructs her from the outside in. Draw a woman. Give her eyebrows the shape of crescent moons, her hair the color of onyx. Give her breath a reddish tint, drifting from her lips like smoke. Let her lifeline be unbroken, let her palms be gold. When you've given all there is to give, give her eyes.

For seventeen years I've tried, but I can't complete the picture. I cannot draw the eyes, because they're always changing; they switch from intense pleasure to overwhelming pain. The picture grows larger with each passing year.

She took me with her to the mountain, singing as she hiked the dirt road that led from the city to the sky. Every time she sang, she sang a new song. I grew up believing that songs were conversations set to melody.

In her arms she carried me to the top of the mountain where the meadow spread before us like a heaven, skirted by white clouds. Lowering herself to the ground, she drew me to her lap. Wild grass surrounded us, buttercups, Indian paintbrush, daisies. And dandelions. They were flowers too, my mother insisted. "It's all in the naming, Landy," she said, calling me by the nickname she created. She didn't want me to go by my given name of Alexandra, thinking it would be truncated into "Alex," not fit for a woman. The name was given in memory of Dad's father, Alexander. But "Landy" is the name that stayed.

My mother removed the white head from a dandelion and wove its stem into my hair without breaking the star-like threads. My hair was nearly as long as hers, as dark. "Call them weeds and you'll see them as weeds," she said. "Call them flowers and that's what they become. It's all in the naming, Landy." A startled look came to her eyes as the threads of the dandelion flew into the air, blown by her breath.

Her gown fluttered in the breeze, revealing legs limber as wind. My father said of them, "They go all the way to her neck." But they did not. They stopped at her hips and her waist took over, slender, then her breasts, round, and her eyes…as changeable as the songs she sang.

Holding me on her lap, she blew a wispy thread of the dandelion from my cheek. In a smoky voice, she spoke of a god who gave her no comfort, this day. "God hates us, Landy. But that's all right, because we hate God."

Sadness was a color in her eyes—black—as overpowering as the darkness falling around us. She seemed as tall as the trees as she wrapped me in her arms and ran down the deer path. Covering my head with her hands, she brushed through the low-slung limbs of a black pine. A branch scraped her face and sprung free. Passing her hand across her forehead, she leaned into a cedar tree and tipped her head toward the sky. A trickle of blood seeped out of a cut above her left eyebrow. I had rarely seen her bleed. The color of her blood frightened me. When I traced the jagged edges of the cut, she said, "It's just a scratch, baby."

The blood, bright as a rose, continued to course above her eye. Red blood, she was a red woman. Indian. But not enough, she said, not enough to matter. I once asked her how much, and she tossed me a quarter, saying, "That much."

The blood dried in a thin line over her left eye, as if two eyebrows were there. Stepping out of the boughs of the cedar, she stared at the trees spearing the sky. Clusters of stars fell into her eyes. "Did you know that the phosphorous material in a star is duplicated in our bones?" she said. "Think of that."

She began to shake her head and then her head fell, dropping so low her chin brushed against her collar bone. The tremor filtered down her neck, settling within her spine. Her voice came out of a cave: "Moses came from a different mountain top than this one, Landy." The gown trembled at her knees as she stepped over a fallen pine. She didn't speak for a long time as we walked the trail; when she did her voice was clear, chiming. "Let's sing, Landy, a nursery rhyme. You pick."

Would she sing a nursery rhyme? They were the only songs that didn't change each time she sang them, so I could memorize them and understand them, sing myself to sleep with them.

"Which one, Landy?" A wreath of branches from a fir tree encircled her head like a crown. "Which?"

"Mockingbird."

"Mockingbird it is." Taking my hand, she walked slowly down the path. "Hush little baby don't say a word...." Her voice was hypnotic. I loved her voice. I loved her. "Mama's going to buy you a mockingbird...." I loved her and I believed her.

We lived our real lives on the mountain, shaping the mornings and the afternoons to her will, the day-life that existed outside of Pike's shadow. The mountain rose three miles from the town's boundaries, three miles from everything but the two of us. My father inherited it from his father who bought it when land was cheap and plentiful. Logging companies scattered timber along its borders, but didn't go further on the mountain.

"We don't need the money now," she would say to my father. "When the two of us are gone, Landy can decide if she wants to sell the timber."

He looked at her with such tenderness—he was a gentle, gentle man. "It's *your* mountain."

"My mountain?" She raised his hand and kissed his palm. "Do you also plan to give me the river?"

"Can't give away what I don't own."

"That's right," she whispered.

His hands roamed her waist as she leaned her hips between his legs. "You want every tree still standing?" he asked.

"Every tree."

"All right," he said. "We don't need the money now."

Her fingers slid down his chest, opened his belt buckle. "But this, I think you do need."

Hiding behind the railing, I watched them from the top of the stairs, then closed my eyes so tight I could see nothing but black. In my imagination, she wasn't with him anymore. He was at work in the saw mill, and she was where she belonged—on the mountain with trees she would not cut towering above her. I, with my arms spread like wings, walked in her heel prints.

The mountain became hers. It was her mountain.

***

On her mountain, the sun made me drowsy, and the shadow from my mother crossed upon me. I walked with my eyes half shut in the darkness of her shadow.

"Here," she said. "You're a tired, tired girl."

She picked me up. I rested my head against her neck as she jogged toward Pike, cradling me to her front. Silence filtered around us. I listened to it—a woodpecker rapped in the tree above, a fir beat against the wind, and the twigs rustled as a white tail leapt away. There was too much noise in that silence.

"A rhyme," I said, staring at her chin. "You could say a rhyme?"

"All right." Her voice was the color of redwood; her voice could make brown leaves green. "Little Miss Muffet sat on a tuffet eating

4

her curds and whey. Along came a spider and sat down beside her and frightened Miss Muffet away." As she looked down at me, her lips curved into a half-smile, the same nearly imperceptible smile her son—my younger brother Stevie—would wear years later, after she was gone. "If I were Miss Muffet, I wouldn't have let a spider ruin my meal," she said. "But then we'd have a different story, wouldn't we?" Her lips brushed my ear and her breath rustled inside my head. "Little Miss Muffet sat on a tuffet, eating her curds and whey. Along came a spider and sat down beside her." Holding me tight, her fingers tickled my sides. "And Miss Muffet said, 'Get away from me you measly old spider, I'm trying to eat.'"

Laughing, I squirmed beneath her fingers.

"Get away, spider," she said. "Don't you eat my food." Her lips were soft against my cheek. "Do you know that I love you, Landy?" When I nodded, her hair fell into my eyes; it carried the scent of the wild.

On the sidewalk leading to our house, she set me down. Next door, the Widow Kyle watched us from her picture window. My mother flipped her head and pointed her middle finger into the air. The Widow drew her curtains shut.

"Nosy bitch," my mother said, and began to knead her fingers through my hair, searching for woodticks. She did this every night after we came off the mountain. She said she didn't want to lose me to Rocky Mountain fever, the woodtick disease that kills the children of negligent mothers.

As she knelt before me, her eyes met my own. "We're two of a kind, you and I." Arching her back, her hair cascaded past her waist. "Lady Godiva."

I heard the words I could understand, embedded within the whole: *Lady God.* "Lady Godiva was a heroine," she explained. "Do you know what a heroine is, Landy?"

I shook my head.

"For a child who's nearly half-way to a decade, it's a word you should know." She nodded at me. "Heroine."

"Heroine."

"It has the same meaning as hero," she said. "Do you know the meaning of hero?"

I nodded. "Dad is a hero."

"That's right," she said. "Because he's keeping the loggers off our land." She ruffled my hair. "Heroine is used to describe women. Hero—heroine. Lady Godiva rode naked down the streets to lower the county taxes. Can you imagine such a thing? Riding down the streets simply because her husband told her to? Nearly a thousand years later, we still remember her name. We don't give a damn about her husband's name. Why? Because he lost. He lost."

I stared up at her long black hair. "Heroine."

"You were a good girl today. I want to thank you for that." She smiled, resting her forehead on mine. My breath mixed with hers, inseparable. There was no mine or hers. There was only ours.

I believed I could see inside her pupils, straight into her mind. She was a lady, and she was as powerful as God. She was Lady God.

"God is a heroine," I said softly.

She cocked her head toward me, gave a low smile. "God, I hope so." She lifted her hair over her head and let it fall, strand by strand, down her back. "Let's get dinner ready for your father. He'll be home soon."

***

After she was gone, on nights when sleep was a brass ring I couldn't catch, I would talk to her. It was the closest thing to praying that I knew.

***

Now that I had chosen the town of Willow, I had to find a place to live, but the housing was scarce. Willow was a college town, and all the apartments were leased to student renters. The beginning of summer, students were away from college, and their parents *paid* for them to keep a place to live. Not only that, but they subleased those apartments until the students came back. Now, why would you rent one bed knowing that you had to leave it tomorrow? The rentals that were left were taken over by college students looking for roommates. They were marked in the classified section of *Willow Times* : women or men, two bedrooms, non-smoker, no pets, studier. *Studier?* A studier of textbooks—not me. The houses were just as bad as the apartments. When they were available, the rent was way, way over my head. That is until I found a house advertised with contradictory descriptions: "a mansion" and "cheap rent." The fact that it was cheap drew me to its door.

From the sidewalk, I stared up at it. The chimney towered above the rooftop like a big black arm. Scratches scarred the base of the front door; I guessed they were left by dogs and cats begging to come inside.

Patchins, the landlord, pointed his chin toward the front lawn where the grass was yellow as straw. "As a renter, you'd be responsible for watering. Got five rooms, all empty at the moment, so you get your pick." I pressed my shoulder into the door, springing it open. When Patchins joined me in the hallway, something darted from one of the rooms and flew over our heads. I thought it was a bat. When I ducked, I nearly knocked my jaw into Patchins' fists as he shadow-boxed with the figure above us.

"Can you make it out?" he asked.

As my eyes adjusted to the darkness, I saw that it was a robin, trapped inside for god knows how long. Its body was shrunken and the red on its breast was covered with dust. "It's a bird," I said. "It looks half starved."

"This ain't no birdhouse." Patchins clapped his hands. "Shoo." Perched on a shelf at the end of the hallway, the robin tipped its head and preened its feathers. "I got a no pet policy," Patchins said. "That includes dogs, cats, and birds. Only pet I allow is the kind that makes its messes inside a fish bowl."

"Let me try to get it out of here." Standing in the threshold, I cupped my hands to my mouth and gave the only birdcall I knew how to reproduce, the sound a grouse makes as it flaps its wings in a mating dance—thrumming. Lured by my voice, or frightened by it, or simply attracted to the light beyond the door, the robin fled the mansion.

"That's the ugliest birdcall I ever heard," Patchins said.

"It doesn't have to be pretty as long as it works."

Patchins gave me a tour of the rooms on the first floor. Fingerprints of previous renters smudged the walls. "Got some others up the stairs." He led me to a tunnel-shaped room on the upper level. "She's my favorite, this one." The bathroom marked one end of the room, the kitchen the other; no point between them was wider than fifteen feet. The ceiling turned inward like an inverted V. I had to stay in the center of the room to avoid hitting it.

"This is the kind of place makes a fellow feel tall," Patchins said. "But I suppose you're used to such a feeling, huh?"

"I guess so." I was two inches shy of six feet tall, but I'd never had to worry about bumping my head on a ceiling before.

When I opened the bathroom door and saw the claw-foot bathtub,

I settled on the mansion despite its low ceiling and sense of decay. So entirely deserted, it wouldn't take much effort to make it mine.

Patchins pulled a receipt book from the kangaroo pocket of his overalls. He sat on the couch and instantly sunk to mid-chest within its innards. I offered my hand and pulled him free. "Another good thing, there ain't no deposit," he said, finding a solid seat on the arm of the couch.

"There ain't nothing left to damage."

"And she's got a bed, and a stove with a working oven, and a 'fridge with a working freezer. You go anywhere else in town that's got all those extras and you'll be paying out of your nose. A hundred twenty-five."

"I won't pay a hundred twenty-five."

"What will you pay?"

I stared at the carpet and wondered where I'd go if I couldn't talk him down in price. I didn't want to end up sleeping on a park bench blanketed by a newspaper that didn't contain a single story about anyone I knew. That fear made me brave like fear can when it's all you have to rely on.

"I'll pay seventy-five."

"A hundred."

"Eighty-five."

"Ninety."

"Eighty-five tops, Patchins."

He bit the cap off his pen and wrote the figure on the receipt. "Your name would be what?"

"Sorenson."

"What am I supposed to write down for a first name?"

"Just plain Sorenson will do."

"Girl Sorenson." Patchins chuckled. "You come here to go to college? We got a registered college right there up the hill."

"That's good to know." Schooling wasn't for me, not the kind where they keep you locked inside four walls. When I made it through high school, I did what was asked of me, not a smidgen more. My real schooling came from my mother.

"Well if you ain't a student, what might you be?"

As I studied the cobwebs dangling from the light fixture, I thought that here in this new town with no old faces, I could be just about anything I wanted to be. "I'm a grocery checker. I checked in with the manager at the IGA down the street and he says he'll put me on in September."

"Being how this is only July, that'd leave lots of days before a paycheck, huh?" When I didn't respond, Patchins shrugged and headed for the door. A stocky five-foot-five, he didn't have to worry about bumping into the ceiling. "Welcome to Willow."

I changed out of my highland clothing and put on cut-offs and a t-shirt and walked around my new house, listening to the thongs slapping against my feet. I pressed my palms to the windowpane and looked at the houses dotting the streets below me. On the western horizon the sky was a soft pink, like the nose of a newborn calf. As I watched the sun dip out of sight, I remembered something my mother once told me when we were in the meadow on the mountain. She said that those who believe the sun sheds light do not understand the way of the universe. She said that each morning the sun inhales and captures the darkness, draws it into its center, and each night the sun exhales and frees the darkness. Darkness is the constant, the stable state. It is the true entity. Light is merely what is left behind when darkness vanishes. My mother said that the perception of the sun as a benign globe shedding light on the world is false, for the sun sheds nothing—it steals the dark. The sun is a masked man, a false identity, the prime player in a celestial scam. My mother loved the sun because it could pull off such a grand illusion.

In high school, for a science project, I wrote an essay explaining my mother's theory. It came back to me with a red F. "Interesting," the teacher wrote, "But utterly ridiculous."

The sun as a thief of darkness did not hold up against the logic of science, but in relation to the logic of my mother's mind, it was as sound as $e = mc^2$.

Chapter Two

In the silver light of dusk, I kicked a stone down Main Street, past the jagged storefronts set against the sky: Betty's Jeans and Things, the Willow Grange, the Christian bookstore, Ernst Hardware. At the end of the block, two fast food restaurants were keeping competition with each other—McDonald's and Wendy's. Behind me, from the edge of town, the train bellowed; a lonesome dog mistook the sound as animal and echoed it with howls. Sometimes, on the mountain, I'd be like that dog, answering the wails of the coyotes. Knowing that I couldn't unleash my voice in the middle of Willow made my throat begin to ache, made me more homesick than I would have thought possible earlier that morning when I hitched a ride on a logging truck, leaving my father, my brother, my mother's mountain and her grave behind.

At the IGA I wandered the aisles, studied the goods stacked across the shelves. Back home, we had what we needed, but the selection was not as wide, the store not nearly as big as this. A blind man could shop in Pike's IGA without assistance, the same goods stacked across the shelves from year to year. In its way, Pike was traveling toward the end of the twentieth century, but folks still lived by the cover of *Field and Stream*. In the paperback section, we had rows of romance novels—stories of nurses falling in love with doctors, patients falling in love with doctors, and doctors falling in love with their medicine. In reality, we didn't have a single doctor in Pike. If you needed a healer, you wound your bandages tight and drove to the hospital in Colville.

In Pike's IGA, we had stacks of leafy-eared *True Confessions*, *Hunting Digests*, and *Beautiful Hairstyles*. Next to them were some out-dated issues of *Time*. We never got the issues on the date marked on the front cover; they were always one week late. The whole world outside of Pike could have exploded and we wouldn't have known it. Of course, those with televisions would know of the end of civilization, but Stevie and I didn't have a working television. It sat in the corner of our house and acted like an end table, holding matchsticks and empty beer bottles. Dad promised us he would get it fixed or buy another, and he always drank the money.

Whenever I took my break at Pike's IGA, I pushed aside the *True Confessions*, found a copy of *Time*, and brought it with me to read in the backroom. In that short ten minute break, I learned of the other side of the world, the world that existed outside of Pike, Washington—an enigma of drugs and crime, of the crew burning as their space shuttle exploded, of the wall going down in Germany, of the unrest in the Soviet Union, of Iran, of South Africa, of the Palestinians, of Desert Storm, of corruption in the Republican party, of corruption in the Democratic party, of corruption in politics altogether, of Rodney King, of earthquakes, of the battle against AIDS.

Ten minutes of being exposed to all that—not my world, but the other world—left me aching to climb a tree and see the whitetailed deer, the red-winged blackbird, the coyotes beneath me. Ten minutes was all I could handle.

As I walked back to my checkout counter, I read *MAD* magazine to get the other stuff out of my mind. It was like this every time I worked—the part of me that needed to be exposed to life outside my mother's mountain in deep battle against the part of me that needed to know the amount of wind I'd face in hiking up to her mountain. I read *Time* and *MAD*. Two extremes—that was me.

Everything I learned about my part of the world came from my mother. Life, love, death. She said we were better than the rest of the women in town, that they did not know the meaning of life, love, and death. But we did, and we were superior to them. The reason we are alive, she said, is to be a part of the natural world. Not a controlling part, but a part where the limb of a tree is your limb, where every creature is your creature, where the earth is your earth. Everything is spiritual in nature. *Everything on the mountain.* When we were surrounded by trees, she said, it was like praying with our eyes wide open.

But the other part, when she spoke of God—"God hates us, Landy, but that's all right because we hate God."—left me searching her face. Was she, a Lady God, in battle with the God of the Bible?

God of the Bible is a bad God? That God would kill us if he could? But aren't there many Gods in the world, good Gods and bad Gods? The God on the mountain is but one God, and when we become one with the earth we are safe?

To her, the God of the mountain existed on the mountain. Dazed on the meadow, surrounded by wild grass, she said, "Feel it? God damn, it is beautiful."

From her I learned everything. I learned that we were superior because spirituality resided in the weeds beneath her, in a white tail, in a tree. From her, I learned God Damn.

After she died, I carried my superior self to school, to the IGA, and I never made a friend outside my brother Stevie. Underneath the charade of walking down the street mimicking my mother's posture—head straight, chin in the air—I did not feel superior at all. Her death left me empty. The only thing that could fill me was her mountain.

Now, wandering Willow's IGA, the mountain was just a refuge in my mind. In the magazine section, I checked the date of *Time*. It was no more than a day old.

I bought cleaning supplies, bread and cheese, and jogged to the mansion. I brushed the cobwebs from the ceiling, washed the fingerprints from the walls and swept the skeletons of spiders from the corners, then tried to fall asleep in my new home. Home. What is home? The song says it's anywhere you hang your hat; my floppy straw hat was perched on the bedpost above me, but home wasn't here. Maybe it's closer to the truth to say that home is where you hang yourself.

***

I woke with the resolve to find work. My savings were low, I didn't have nearly enough money to hold me over until my job at the IGA came through. Facing empty days in a land that had no mountains frightened me.

A restaurant on Main Street, The Saddle Inn, had a sign up: "Waitress Wanted." Not even noon and the owner, Lyman, was hunched over a Bloody Mary in the dining section. "Come in tomorrow night at six. Hank'll show you the ropes." Gesturing toward the adjoining room, Lyman said, "Tell him I could use another." He handed me his red-stained glass.

I followed the voices to the bar where a couple of men were drinking coffee with quivering hands. The undisguisable scent of whiskey

12

overpowered the scent of the coffee in their mugs.

The man behind the bar had his back to me, reading the morning paper. His shoulders were wide and relaxed, and his sandy-colored hair slipped beneath the collar of his chamois shirt. Six feet tall or thereabouts, his body held him comfortably.

Unnoticed, I stared at him for a long while before I finally said, "Excuse me."

He turned to me with something like surprise, and not a bad surprise. I wasn't the habitual clientele of the bar; I was young and my eyes were clear. His eyes were clear also, brown, like good earth, meeting my own.

"Lyman sent me over. I guess I'll be working with you."

"Hank Chapman," he replied.

I passed my knuckles over my brows and tried to find a name to give him in return. Landy? Not here in this new town. Alexandra? The name belonged to my birth certificate, not to me. Alex? A man's name, yes, but maybe I could make it right for a woman.

"Alex Sorenson," I said.

"Glad to have you with us."

"I'm just happy I found work." I set Lyman's empty glass on the counter. "He said he'd like a refill."

Hank slipped the glass beneath the bar, set a coffee cup in front of me and filled it. I tried to pay for the coffee, but Hank wouldn't take my money. "Coffee's free from now on. Fringe benefit."

***

Friday night when I came in for work, Blue Dog, a country band, set up and began to play. No one seemed to notice them until after nine, the same time they began to notice me.

"Hey honey, two beers over here."

I turned to the voice, pointing my finger at myself.

"You the new waitress?" he asked.

"Yes, sir, I am."

"Call me Henry, honey. Sir is for the president. You got a name?"

"Alex."

"Alex, honey, you better make that a pitcher." As I walked away, he said to his friends, "Check out that girl's legs, would you?"

I wished I'd worn a flannel shirt and jeans instead of the short sleeved blouse and cotton skirt I'd picked up at the Goodwill on the edge of town. Beneath the hem of the skirt, my legs were taut, the way legs look when they're used to running long distances. I hadn't worn nylons. I hated the way they clung to my skin, and my legs were a natural dark color without them, the color I was born with, passed from my mother. I saw my reflection in the mirror behind the bar and studied myself in the clothing I'd never wear in Pike. Bluejeans, boots, long-sleeved shirts—those were my clothes, not these. People didn't call me Honey in Pike or tell each other to look at my legs.

"How's it going?" Hank asked.

I folded my hands behind my back, shaking my head. My hands knew how to chop wood, clean game birds and cook them tender, fend off mean dogs and taunting boys, but they didn't know how to treat Henry and his mouthful of sugar.

"I kind of lied about my experience. I've never waitressed before."

"I guessed," Hank replied. "The only way to deal with the customers is to tell them what you want from them."

"Or don't want."

Hank smiled. "Or don't want."

Holding the pitcher with both hands, I returned to Henry's table. "Thanks honey," he said, and then he reached out and patted my behind.

"My name is Alex and if you touch my ass again you're going to wish you hadn't."

Henry stared up at me for a long moment before he dipped his head in a nod of agreement. "All right," he said. "I have a feeling you could whup me if you got mad enough, Alex. I ain't going to chance it." He set a two dollar tip in my hand.

At closing time, I helped the people who needed it out the door. One man needed it badly. Earlier in the evening, he'd ordered a fifth of tequila from the bar and had been drinking straight shots with beer chasers all night. He'd introduced himself as Mike McPherson, saying that if I ever mistakenly called him Mikey he would promptly act like someone who is addressed so and piss his pants.

His hair came to the middle of his back and he had a neatly trimmed rust-red beard. A dash of silver hair spread from the left corner of his bottom lip to the edge of his chin, like a lightning bolt shooting from his mouth. He was drunk in a dangerous way, alone, and surveyed me with low-lidded eyes as he'd done all evening, an unnervingly detached gaze, as I cleared the empty beer bottles from the table next to his.

A gold earring dangled from his right ear. Shaped in the form of a pyramid, it rested against the side of his neck. No more than an inch of tequila remained in his bottle; floating in it was a brown worm. He lifted the bottle over his head and the worm slid into his mouth. "Magic," he said and headed for the door.

Hank and I set the chairs on top of the tables, swept the floor, and locked the door behind us as we stepped outside. My hair flew out behind me as the wind came off the wheat fields with an indivisible force. In Pike, the wind was not so unified. Broken by towering trees, it lashed like a finger separated from the hand.

"You're not from Willow," Hank said.

"I'm from a town called Pike. It's far north, the Washington side of British Columbia. Loggers mostly." I smiled. "You know, Willow is a big town compared to Pike."

"How'd you end up here?"

"Luck of the draw." I met his eyes and held them, and knew that's what it had been—luck. Good luck to happen upon this town for no other reason than the sound of its name, Willow, a good-sounding name to pick out of a map, a good town with good people who will listen when you say what you mean.

"Do you need a ride home?" Hank asked.

"I like to walk." He got in his car and went wherever people go when the day's about to break. Home maybe, to his wife. He wore her on the third finger of his left hand.

Inside my room, I sprawled across the bed, stared at the ceiling. The breeze rustled in the maple outside my bedroom window, the branches tapped the roof, and creaking noises rose from the first floor as if the mansion were shifting under my weight. New sounds, in time I hoped they would become as familiar as Pike's noon whistle.

Before the sun had time to wipe the sleep from its eyes, someone was knocking on my door. Pulling the covers to my neck, I thought the intrusion was within my dream. I was still unsure as my bedroom door opened. Patchins stood over me jangling a set of keys in his hand.

"Brought you a present." From behind his back he revealed a pint-sized jar of milk. A frothy layer of cream was on the top; beneath it, the milk was the color of a blind dog's eyes. "From my own milk cow," he said. I inched higher in bed, so angry at him for walking into my room that I couldn't speak. "She's a mean one," he said. "More sour than twisted owl crap, but her milk is sweet."

"You...you just let yourself into my room?"

Patchins shrugged. "You didn't answer."

"I want a chain lock."

"What for? Willow's safe as a mama's womb."

"I want you to go out and buy me a chain lock. Today, Patchins."

A gold band pressed into his ring finger like the tie that separates sausage links. "One thing about me," he began, "I always take care of my renters."

***

He seemed to have believed it when he said it, but he didn't show up again for two weeks. No one did, no people checking out the rooms, no mailman to deliver "Occupant" letters. No one showed.

I put myself on a schedule, getting up early every morning and heading for the IGA for a word with the manager—showing him how interested I was in getting on with him. The manager's name was Tiny, and no joke intended. I never got over the feeling that I was being derogatory when I called him that. All of him was tiny—sapling arms, spindly legs—and his head was shaved in a crewcut with no pompadour style to make him seem an inch taller than what he was. His little body would get smaller when I asked if anything had opened up unexpectedly. Nothing, not until September when one of his checkers was getting married with plans to stay at home.

Leaving him, I hiked the five miles to the wildlife refuge. Loneliness was one of the reasons I went there, being an inch away from flat broke had a lot to do with it, and getting fired from the Saddle Inn for pouring a pitcher of beer over a customer's head played another part. The customer deserved what he'd gotten, trespassing on my body without my permission. I tried to justify myself to Lyman ("He pinched me here," crossing my arm over my left breast), but Lyman was drunk and unreasonable, and fired me on the spot. Even Hank couldn't get through to him. Mike McPherson had watched the whole thing, the streak of lightning in his beard shimmering as he clenched his jaw. He stormed out of the bar and a moment later I turned in my apron and followed him, but we didn't share the same sidewalk on our separate ways home.

All those reasons brought me to the refuge each day. But the over-riding reason was that the silence reminded me of the mountain. I sat

on a downed pine and sipped the Coke I'd picked up at the IGA, shook
my hair free of the sweat on my neck and repeated a nursery rhyme
under my breath: *If I'd as much money as I could tell, I never would
cry: Old Clothes To Sell, Old Clothes To Sell. I never would cry: Old
Clothes To Sell.*

My mother used to chant the rhyme like a prayer as she sold her
clothing for nickels and dimes to the poor families who lived on Mill
Creek Road. She used the money to buy different clothing from flea
markets—lacy gowns, hoop skirts, hats with veils—and wore the
second-hand clothing on the mountain where no one could accuse her
of putting on airs, because no one saw her. We would dance in box-
steps across the meadow. "You're a fine dancer," she would say. "Fred
Astaire."

Sometimes at night, I would watch the way my father stood
behind her, his arms wrapped around her waist, as she prepared dinner.
He moved as she moved, a kind of dance across the kitchen floor. But
after she left us, his steps became clumsy from the presence of drink.
Tiny red lines, like the legs of spiders, overtook the whites of his eyes.
There were no secrets in his eyes, only grief. Grief is not a secret.
Everything it touches shares the pain.

Every morning he went to the mill where the sawdust etched
yellow lines in his face and every night he went to the bars. I would
go through his wallet as he was passed out on the couch, taking money
to buy groceries for my brother Stevie and me, and would hoard the
money through the month until the next paycheck came. One frigid
January morning Stevie woke with a chest that was filled with syrup.
Our ration money was gone, every last cent, and Dad was nowhere to
be found. Drunk, gone four days. "God damn drunk," Stevie hissed as
I massaged Vicks across his chest and wrapped one of Dad's wool
socks around his neck. I left Stevie to sleep and found Dad's wedding
ring stashed in a dresser drawer where he'd buried it years before. I
thumbed a ride into Colville where no one would know me and sold
the ring to a pawn shop, and tried not to feel guilty for doing such a
thing because there was nothing else to do.

But in Willow, my money ran out after I gave Patchins his second
month's rent and I had nothing to sell—no wedding rings, no clothing,
nothing anyone would give a dollar for. The fear rose slowly, stronger
every day, of being in a house with sounds I didn't recognize, in a
town where I didn't know when noontime came because no whistle

blew. Willow bent me as low as its valleys and made me search the sky and try to believe what my mother once said: that the phosphorous material within a star is duplicated in my bones.

***

When Patchins finally brought me the chain lock for my door, I took it to Ernst Hardware and exchanged it for cash. I spent half of the lock money on bulk rice and beans; the rest jingled in my pocket as I walked to Jake's Pit, a tavern on First Street. Jake's Pit and the Saddle Inn were my kind of bars—you could walk inside and hear yourself think at the same time. Main Street had some other bars which were not for me; the sound of rap blared out their open doors, and students—fresh back from the summer with their families—were inside revving it up.

I'd passed Jake's Pit often on my nightly walks, watched the people coming and going, yet had never ventured inside. But this night the thought of returning to the mansion sent a shiver up my spine. I was beginning to hear voices inside the walls. They carried a tone I remembered yet couldn't place, slow as the accents of home.

The entrance to the tavern was cavernous, leading toward the main drinking area. In the far end of the room, above the Red Ball machine, the head of a trophy buck was mounted. Magnificent, the pose, so natural the buck seemed alive.

I edged to the bar and slid a stool out quietly so it didn't scrape against the wooden floor. A few stools separated me from a handful of locals who wore ball caps with insignias: John Deere, CAT, Skoal. The man in the CAT hat gave a nod in my direction and called to the bartender who was tending to an order of chicken and jo-jos. "Mat, this girl seems to be needing a beer."

As the bartender turned to me, strands of greased hair fell over his left eye like a pirate's patch. Youngish, sharp-edged thin, his cheekbones were slowly being brushed with patches of red. "I hate to ask, but you wouldn't have a driver's license would you?"

I didn't have a driver's license, but I did have an I.D. card with the street address of my house up in Pike. They make the cards for retarded people who can't drive, the elderly who shouldn't drive, and for folks like me—people who certainly *can* drive, but don't feel like putting in the time or energy to get a license.

Mat took the card and broke into a grin as he slapped it in my hand. "You're from Pike? I go hunting up there every year. Beautiful country. That buck over there..." He pointed at the far wall. "My dad got it at Ruby Creek. You know Ruby?"

"You know Pike?"

The CAT man put a dollar on the counter before I could reach for my money. "This one's on me."

"Oh," I said, "I've got money."

"It's Stan's law to buy a drink for a new one," Mat replied.

"That's the truth," Stan, the man in the CAT hat, said. "My law."

I set my chin in my palm and smiled as Mat exchanged hunting stories with Stan. They spoke in the rehearsed way of hunters who begin each story with the same line every time it is told ("Couldn't hardly see the buck come out of the brush, the fog was so thick.") and end each story with the same line every time it is told ("One shot and he fell."). Stories of good hunts told to each other so often that, when they were both old and white, they'd probably cease being able to distinguish their own tale from the other's. This night, the stories were for me, of bear hunts, elk, deer; I fell headlong into their voices. Tale after tale, beer after beer, I listened so closely I went away.

Stan took his cap off and struck it across his knee. His forehead was two-toned, tanned below where the brim had been, white above, the face of a man who lives in wheat fields. Stretching his arms over his head, he said: "It's past my bedtime."

With Stan gone, the bar was empty; just Mat, the buck on the wall, and me. I asked Mat for paper and a pen so I could write a letter home, and took them to a table in the back of the bar, stared at the blank sheet and tried to find words to say.

After *Dear Dad*, the words stopped. Then the month came: *August*. August what? The days strung together like beads of a single color, not one separate.

Mat gave me a nod and turned to the television set ledged in the corner of the ceiling. Jay Leno was harping about the Bobbitts' knife. A monologue, mixing with my own:

How are you Dad? You two are eating okay? Not just TV dinners, I hope. I got a job as a cocktail waitress. I found a nice apartment too. All in all this is a pretty good little town. I even made a few friends.

I fanned the tablet and closed my eyes as the false breeze brushed my skin. Behind the tavern, the train rumbled past and the floor vibrated. The sound of the wheels drew me alert as they always would back home—like a camel to water Dad used to say. I wondered if camels ever got their fill. I thought I'd gotten mine one day when a howling sound traveled down the line. It was a coyote. He'd been walking the tracks in the early morning. As the sun grew strong, the sections of the rail expanded with a clicking sound up the line. In the fraction of time when the rail whipped into connection, the direction of the coyote's life was forever altered. Two sections of rail drew together on the tip of his tail. He couldn't pull himself free and couldn't understand I wouldn't hurt him no matter how I tried to show him that I would not, offering him a sniff of my outstretched hand. I watched him through my fingers as the train approached. The coyote sprung and bit at his tail. I prayed that in the very last moment, he would become free.

What could that coyote have done to prevent an attack from such a one-in-a-million occurrence, and what could he possibly have done to deserve falling to such odds? I buried the pieces of him. But I couldn't pry the tip of his tail from the railroad track.

Well, Dad, I just wanted you to know where I was so you wouldn't worry. And Stevie, sorry I keep calling you that, but it's a hard habit to break—Steven, Steven. Tell Shannon I say Hello. I think you're both very lucky to have found each other so young, but I guess you know that without me saying. I guess you also know all about how easy it is to get pregnant, so I suppose you don't need me talking to you about it.

Twirling the pen between my fingers, I called to Mat for another beer. "You look tired," he said, as he brought the beer over.

"I am kind of. Tired."

"You sure you want this beer?"

My head spun from too much beer with too little food with too little sense. "Yeah, I do."

"Boyfriend?" He pointed at the letter.

"A Dear John. Not that I don't have love. I do."

"If you need help spelling words or anything, just ask." He laced the bar towel around his neck and returned to his spot behind the counter, and I returned to mine.

How's Hepburn? Right now she's probably asleep under the armchair, kicking her legs in a grouse hunt. Does she look for me?

When I swallowed a mouthful of beer, it came back up, boiling nearly. "Mat? I don't know what day it is."

"Tuesday."

"The date, Mat, the date."

"August fifteenth."

Taking a long drink of beer, I thrust the pen into the page.

Dad Dad Dad DAD. Does this day have any meaning for you? Do you know it's the day she died? Do you even remember the day I left and do you care why? You fucking better care because it's the day I hiked to my mother's mountain and found the loggers driving the bulldozer across her grave. Her grave! Did you forget she was there? After you had her buried on her mountain, the whole fucking town turned their backs so that her grave wouldn't be charading with the graves of Pike Washington's founding fathers and mothers. "Put her on the mountain", they said, looking the other way, "Keep her out of our cemetery."

It hasn't even been two months since I was there, but it feels like an eternity, and the same question keeps running through my mind: Could it have been so simple for you to sell the mountain, to sell her grave? Those loggers will rip up everything until there's nothing left but scars. They won't keep her grave up. They won't care about her at all. No one will remember. You loved her once, I know you did. Then I try to understand, but I can't. If you loved her, if you really loved her once, how could you have sold the only thing left of her?

I stared at the letter a half-hour, a half-life, I didn't know. The brown bottle of beer was cold against my palm. Dark brown, my mother's skin is dark brown, she is brown from forehead to feet, Mama is earth brown. And now she is only earth.

"Alex?"

I looked up and saw someone standing next to me saying my name. This wasn't in my mind. It was Hank and he was holding my shoulder and saying my name. I tore the letter from the tablet and ripped it into pieces, set them in the ashtray. I wished I smoked, for then I'd have a match and could light the pieces on fire. Then it would all go away and I would know the voices I heard were not of ghosts crying in the mansion walls, in the streets, in the refuge and the sky.

I huddled over the tablet and wrote in scrawling sentences that didn't fit between the lines. *Don't worry about me. I'm fine. I live in wheat country now.*

Hank swayed left and right. I thought I'd be sick to see him go away, left or right, go away. I closed my eyes and reopened them, but still he swayed. When my hand found its way to the beer bottle, Hank took it in his own and helped me to my feet.

"Let me drive you home," he said.

"I think I can walk."

"I don't think you can."

The floor rolled like an ocean. "I don't think I can."

As we drove up the street, the world spun and didn't settle. The mansion was black and lonely, and there was nothing more in the world that I wanted than not to be alone another night in those shaking walls. I heard my voice as I would hear a stranger's. "I wouldn't mind if you'd like to come to my room. I have…coffee." Hank shook his head, then stopped the motion, meeting my eyes as I asked: "Does your wife wait up?"

"We're separated," he answered. "In a sense."

"How so…sense. No sense?"

"None to me."

"You still live with her?"

"I'll be finding another place before too long."

"So then why don't you want my coffee?"

He freed his hand from the wheel and laced it across the back of the seat. "How old are you?"

"Don't fool yourself, Hank. I'm old as water." I threw open the car door and fell to the sidewalk as I got out. Grabbing the door handle, I pulled myself to my feet. "I'd rather scratch with the chickens than go home again," I said. "Do you know that?"

"I'll help you up the stairs."

"You will not." Finding my sea legs on the rollicking field of yellow grass, I walked away.

He waited until I got to the door. "Take care of yourself, Alex."

Entering the dark hallway, I replied, "Back home they call me Landy."

Chapter Three

Half drunk and heart sick, I remember my name.

Somewhere in the time after my mother went away I decide to buy a calf and raise it for beef, so we'll have food in the freezer no matter what shape my father happens to be in. Dad gives me the money one night when he's home early, clear-eyed with another resolution to quit drinking and be a father to Stevie and me.

"So you're going to be a rancher, Landy?"

"No sir. Just the one cow."

The calf's nose is pink and the fur on her forehead is white. I know I'll never be able to eat something I care enough about to name: Bell.

After two hours separated from her herd, Bell begins to bellow. I follow her around the pasture and try to block her as she walks into our barbed wire fence. Bawling, she knocks me to the ground.

Stevie runs out of the house and stares at Bell tossing her head into the barbed wire. "She going to die, Landy?"

"*No.*"

Hepburn, our black lab, falls to her haunches in submission as if I'd yelled the word at her. "Not you, good dog, good good dog," I assure her, until she jumps up joyously, flipping her tail against my leg. I grab her the moment before Bell's hoof lands between her eyes.

I set Stevie far from the fence so the calf can't harm him and order Hepburn to his side. Grabbing Bell by the haunches, I try to pull her from the barbed wire, but can't budge her. As long as she stays with us, Bell won't jump over any moon.

"She's going to die isn't she, Landy?"

I take her haunches and pull until it seems my arms will snap out of their sockets; slowly Bell comes free of the wire. She struggles to her feet and begins to walk in circles, bellowing.

Hepburn follows as I take Stevie's hand and run toward Parson's place. Parson sold me the calf. He'd know what to do. Stevie is nearly flying behind me as we race down the streets and cut through the pasture bordering Parson's land. Parson is out back, throwing feed to his cattle. "Hey Ripper, sa sa sa, Hey Whitey, sa sa sa." He can name his cows and eat them too.

In their front yard, Mrs. Parson chases after her son Jessie, a pair of hair-cutting scissors in her hands. "Can't avoid it, monkey," she says as she catches him in her arms. She sets him on the front step and begins to cut his hair. As the scissors scoot above his ears, I put my hand on top of my head, remembering the bald spots that used to be there. After my mother was buried on the mountain with no headstone to mark her grave, I chopped my hair off in handfuls, a foot of it, until my skull was covered with a bristly black mat. My hair grew back in patches. Strands of it kept finding their way into my fists.

Stevie tugs on my pants. When I don't respond, he steps on my foot. "You going to trade Bell for a better one?"

"Stay here." I crawl between the barbed wire and run toward Parson, dodging piles of dung.

Stevie tries to follow me and gets stuck on the barbed wire. He isn't skilled at snaking through fences or forests, and often gets caught on low-hanging limbs or barbed wire hidden in the brush. Poison ivy follows him. Cow dung and dog crap are land mines under his feet.

His pants rip as he tries to pull away. "God damn fence."

"Steven." As he turns to me, his eyes are a solid marble black. "Calm down or you'll rip your whole leg off." I unlatch his pants from the barbed wire and lift him over the fence, away from the dung scattered across the pasture that carries a million cow diseases. "Stay put," I say. Parson nods at me as I approach. "Bell's sick. She won't get up, Mr. Parson."

He pulls a worn tobacco pouch from his pocket and begins to roll a cigarette. "Calf's in shock, Landy. Blind staggers. Couple days she'll be fine."

"I'll sell her back same price I paid."

"You might want to reconsider, wait it out."

Gazing at the green-colored dung drying on his boots, I say, "I'd just as soon give her back to you today."

"Let's bring her home, then." He lifts Stevie over the barbed wire and sets him down at his side. "Should have let him come inside my pasture if he wanted," he says to me. "Little cow shit never hurt no boy."

Mrs. Parson is still on the front steps; Jessie, with his new haircut, is on her lap. She waves the scissors toward us. "I'm all warmed up if you two are willing."

Stevie shakes his head and his eyes disappear beneath his hair. As I set my arm on his shoulder, it takes an enormous effort for me to move my head in the sign of No.

Parson throws open the door of his truck. "Come along." He hoists Stevie into the cab and I crawl up after, propping my elbow out the window. Parson places Stevie's hand on the gear shift and sets his own hand on top. "Throw her into first, son." As we pull out of the drive, Stevie can't keep his eyes off Parson and I can't keep mine off Mrs. Parson who lifts her hand to me. I drop my head and when I look up again we are passing by her, close enough for me to see her eyes; I have to find the oil stains on the floorboards quickly so that I won't see what I often see when I make the mistake of looking into my neighbors' eyes: pity for me and Stevie, for my Dad.

After Parson returns Bell to the herd, Stevie follows me to the house where we find the basket of eggs left on our doorstep by Widow Kyle, our next-door neighbor, our best friend lots of times. I handle the eggs delicately because I know the risk it takes to snatch them. The Widow's hen will pierce your eyes as soon as look at you. Holding a club over the hen, the Widow would say, "Act like a lady, you mean old fool," in the same tone she used to take with her husband, with a single change of words: "Act like a man, you mean old fool." When her husband ran off in the dead of night four years before, Mrs. Doyle Kyle took the name of Widow Kyle.

Trailing me to the kitchen, Stevie stretches himself as tall as he can make his body take him; even on his tiptoes he's only half my size. "I'm hungry for some popcorn," he says.

"Sure." I set my hand on his brow, clearing a path for his eyes. "I could cut your hair good as Mrs. Parson cut Jessie's. I watched how she did it."

"I'm going to Dad's barber. Dad said so."

Our father is a Santa that Stevie still believes in, coming in with promises of paid-for haircuts and new shoes. I'm not about to take the belief from him; it'd be like telling someone there is no God, no nothing, no hope, just you to set it all right or wrong.

"Tonight, maybe," Stevie says.

I set the pan on the wood stove, waiting for it to get hot enough to pop corn, glance at the clock on the wall. Five p.m. If Dad isn't home in an hour, he won't be home. "We'll put lots of butter on it," I say. Stevie loves butter like others love ice-cream. He would eat it out of the tray with a spoon if I let him.

He pushes the footstool next to the wood stove. "Hot enough, you think?" he asks. He leans over the pan and spits into it. The pan hisses like a snake as he delivers another stream of spittle into it.

"I'd say it's hot enough, Stevie." I pour oil into the pan and hand him the bag of popcorn. I hold the corners, guiding him, as he pours a thick layer into the pan. "Spit flavored popcorn," I say. "Yum."

Stevie grins, leaping to the call of a game we play lots of nights as I scan the cupboards, trying to figure out what to cook us for dinner. "Spider sandwiches," he says.

"Macaroni and ants."

The heat of the wood stove glows on his cheeks; he shines like a polished penny. "Dog poop burgers." His bangs fall over his brows like a curtain as he butts his head into my side; when he looks up at me his eyes are like the amber marbles we call clearies. "Booger pie, Landy, let's have us some booger pie."

That Saturday morning, Stevie and I decide to build a log cabin on the mountain. From my father's shed, we steal an axe, handsaw, hammer and nails, and carry them with us as we hike the dirt road to the mountain top. Stevie picks out the first tree we'll chop down. It looks like a Christmas tree. "Go at 'er," he says. My hands sting as the axe connects; it springs away and nearly hits me on the shins.

As I get a solid grasp on the axe handle, I imagine the tree is the face of Dirk Ramstead, the leader of the group of boys from Mill Creek road; he calls me Landy Dandy and composes insults that rhyme with 'head.' Head, dead, led, fed, bed, wed. "Landy Dandy ain't right in the head, Landy Dandy will never be wed." Dirk Ramstead's mom used to take care of Stevie while my mother and I went to the mountain, and was paid with coins stolen from Dad's collection. I'm glad Stevie got out of their house before Dirk had a chance to rub off on him. There is only one honorable thing about Dirk that I'm aware of. He never calls Stevie names when we come off the mountain, just me. Maybe he leaves Stevie alone because he really believes what he says of me—that I'm not right in the head—and thinks I might just be crazy enough to hit him in the skull with my walking stick, rather than the back, if he made any rhymes to go with Stevie's name. There is a kind of power that comes when people perceive you as crazy. My mother had it, much greater than I; people leave you alone.

When the axe connects with the sapling, it is like hitting a pencil into a taut rubber band. I'm not about to give up on that tree, but Stevie does. He rambles around in the meadow sticking his nose into the tunnels where the ground squirrels live. The muscle in the fleshy part of my palm, below my thumb, is cramping by the time the sapling starts to give. It doesn't fall in a way that gives me any kind of moral victory, it just starts to lean over backwards without breaking.

Stevie finds me sitting on top of the half-down tree. "Maybe we ought to just build a deer blind instead," Stevie says.

We bring in any kind of cover we can find: fallen logs, branches, moss, sticks, leaves, rocks. Stevie places a long branch into Hepburn's mouth and she drags it to the meadow. We sit inside our blind and eat our raw hotdogs.

"You know..." Stevie's voice is thoughtful. "Something I been meaning to ask you."

I press my back into the rocks and musty-smelling sticks of our deer blind. "Yeah."

"Dad says, he says when you were little, you used to wet your pants at night."

"I did," I say. "A few times, I guess."

"Dad says, he says you used to have nightmares, too."

I pull up a handful of wild grass and fill the gap between two branches of the deer blind. I feel angry, not at Stevie but at Dad, for using me as a way of making Stevie feel better about himself. Stevie looked up to me. It wasn't fair of Dad to hold me out as proof that everyone is fallible. Better, I thought, to hold himself out as example. He'd had plenty of his own nightmares and spent enough time puking up whiskey in the kitchen sink to serve an example of fallibility.

My head hurts as Stevie continues. "He says you had this thing—he called it the night terrors. He says it's like you'd be awake, your eyes would be open and sometimes you'd even be walking around the house, but you'd really be asleep. Dreaming like, but you'd be walking around with your eyes open. I know he doesn't always tell the truth. But would he be lying about that, Landy?"

"He wasn't lying," I say. The bad dreams came right after my mother went away and stayed for a couple of years.

"Sometimes," Stevie says. "I wake up at night and Hepburn's there and I think she's a bear. That's the times...I wet my bed."

I put my hand over my lips so he won't see me smile. Nightmares about bears—I am not worried for him.

"You ever dream about bears biting you in the head?" he asks.

I have a policy to lie to Stevie only when a lie is more helpful than the truth, as it is now. "Sure," I say. I don't tell him that after my mother went away my dreams were in one color—red—filled with butcher knives, ropes, suffocation, strangulation, and blood. I don't tell him that years ago my dreams simply stopped. I knew that others dreamt at night—I'd watched Stevie's eyes shifting under the nearly transparent filter of his eyelids as he slept; I'd seen my father's lips move as he pressed his face against the couch; I'd seen Hepburn's legs kick and heard her whine. Others dreamed but I didn't, or at least I couldn't remember my dreams, not for a long, long time.

Stevie nibbles his hotdog, leaving the last bite for Hepburn. She licks it off his palm. "There was this one time I was at the Widow's helping her collect her eggs," he says. "That's a mean old hen she's got, you know it? Dad drives up, drunk like usual. The Widow tells me to stay put and she goes over to him. I can hear her talking to him, you know how she does when her top lip crinkles up like that? She was steaming mad. You know what she says to him?" Stevie lowers his voice as he leans toward me. "She says it wasn't his fault Mom was crazy. She called her that, Landy—she called her crazy in the head. Was that why she killed herself, Landy, because she was crazy in the head?"

"No." My head feels crazy. Like it's full of water. "She was...she was a lady."

"Then why do you think she did it?"

It feels as if my brain is sloshing around, bumping against my skull. "If I tell you, will you stop asking me all the time?" I tell Stevie the truth that had come to me after years of praying at her grave, after months when sleep was like a killer in my head. When the truth finally came to me, my dreams stopped being colored with red. "There was this woman who was her mother—she'd be our grandmother, and she died. Mama missed her so much she wanted to be with her, but the only way to be with her was to be…dead. So she decided to let herself be dead." My eyes drift to the lilac tree that I had planted years ago to mark her grave. At the foot of the lilac tree, among the wild grass, was a dandelion.

"Some folks think that's a bad thing, what she did. But you see, it's all in what you call it, Stevie, it's all in the naming. Some folks call it wrong. But you could just as well call it right. She didn't want to be here any more. She wanted to be with her Mama. I don't see how that's wrong."

Stevie stares at the ground. He speaks so softly I have to lean toward him to hear. "You miss her?" he asks.

"Yes."

"Everyday?"

"Mostly," I say.

He looks up at me. A thin white path breaks through the dirt on his cheek; at the bottom of the path is a tear. "Does that mean you'll decide to be dead too?"

"No, Stevie." His nose his running. I bring my shirt tail up and tell him to blow. After he blows himself dry, he leans into me and I hold him to my front. "You worry about too many things," I tell him. "I'm not going anywhere."

Stevie is silent for a long while. He is so little in my arms, I wonder if he will ever grow. It doesn't take long for Stevie to feel all right again. That's something I envy in him—he may cloud over but, after the rain comes, he is clear once again.

"We got us a deer blind, right, Landy?"

I let his energy slide over me, telling myself that it's all right for me to be a child, that it's just fine if I want to race through the forest with my arms open and my head lifted to the sun, screaming magical phrases to the sky. As Stevie does: "Look at me, I can fly!"

I trail after, watching, with my arms half raised to the sky.

Chapter Four

From the front steps of the mansion, I watched the sun going down and wished I had a bowl of popcorn on my lap—even if it were flavored with Stevie's spit, I wouldn't have cared, I was that hungry.

Patchins drove up in a rundown Chevy pickup. In the bed of the truck was a push mower. "You been watering," he called to me. "Yard looks good." He dragged the mower across the parking strip. The rusty blades bent the grass over, but didn't cut it.

Patchins left the mower behind as he pranced up the walk. "As a renter, you'd be responsible for mowing the yard. Course when the other renters come in, you'd all divvy up the job."

"And when are these so-called renters going to be arriving?"

"About the time the college starts up. There'll be so much commotion you'll wish you had the place to yourself again, folks pounding up the stairs asking for a cup of sugar and an ounce of your sweet time."

I stared at the push mower. "The blades need sharpening."

"Got a wet stone in a box there at the end of the hallway."

"It'd take all day just to get the rust off."

"You got anything better to do?" he asked.

"Maybe. Maybe I do."

"Tell you what. I'll bring a file over on Friday. If I play it right, I may even be able to sneak out a bag of pork chops too. See, the wife's got a church meeting that evening." Casting me a sidelong glance, he continued in a raspy voice, as if gravel were stuck in his craw. "We got a helluva lot more food than we can eat, even though the wife tries. Chops galore, beef, eggs, fresh milk. But if it ain't for church charity, the wife won't give a slab of lard away. If I try with one of the renters having some hard times, she says I'm cultivating. Nonsense, huh. I know the difference between dirt and skin, and I never give nothing to dirt."

His wife must not have gone to the church meeting on Friday, because Patchins didn't show at the mansion. I waited until ten p.m. before I ate my last box of macaroni and cheese. I was out of powdered milk and butter, cooked it with water and oil. It had the texture of dirt and tasted as gritty. The weight of it in my stomach made me remember a story of a boy who got lost on Mt. Abercrombie, east of Pike. When the forest ranger found him, the boy was near starved. Too young to know the ways of the berries and bark, he'd eaten crab grass which cut his throat; then, following the confused instincts of his skeletal body, he began to eat dirt.

Leaving the mansion, I walked toward the west end of Willow. The harvest moon lit up a buttermilk sky. It skittered off the backyard gardens smaller than my own in Pike, yet alive with tomatoes and corn. Living off the land. These people didn't really know a thing about it, not like that boy searching for iron in the soil.

My throat ached and my eyes watered as I leaned over a fence, retching into an empty lot. My dinner, grainy and thick as unset cement, washed across the ground. Kneeling on the sidewalk, I concentrated on easing the raggedness of my breath and stopped breathing altogether when the brush rattled behind me. I looked up to see Mike McPherson hoist himself over the fence which enclosed the lot that held the remains of my dinner.

"Here," he said. He pulled a red bandanna from his forehead. "Wipe your lips." Head to the ground, I dabbed the handkerchief to my lips and watched his feet pivot. "That star is Cassiopeia," he suddenly said. I looked up to see him pointing at the sky, but his eyes were focused on me. "Cassiopeia, the queen of Ethiopia."

His earring reflected the moonlight and sent a shaft of light toward me. When a deer is caught in the beams of a spotlight, it freezes, enraptured and terrified, and will remain paralyzed until the light or a bullet sets it free. I felt like a deer in a spotlight as Mike's earring spun in circles; he turned toward a woman who appeared out of nowhere, coming to stand at his side. She was no more than five-feet tall, the top of her head barely reached his shoulders. She wore a red miniskirt made of an elasticized material that clung to her hips, and on her upper body she wore a black top that looked like a brassiere.

"Alex," Mike said, "This is my wife Teresa."

She stared at him with her hands planted on her hips. "You use the term 'wife' loosely."

"Common law," he replied. "Common law by now, Tree-sa." When their gaze connected, I nearly heard sounds—sizzling like the telephone wires overhead. "Alex used to work at the Saddle Inn."

Her voice was flat: "Poor thing."

Mike's jaw tightened, the silver strands streaking through the red of his beard, as he laced his arm through hers and led her away from me. While he spoke to her in a low voice, she flipped her hand through her short blonde hair. Glancing at me, she nodded to whatever it was he was saying.

She pulled the hem of her skirt down as she walked over to me. "Mike tells me you lost your dinner."

Tipping my head, I found Cassiopeia, the queen of Ethiopia, and wondered what tale the rhyme was based upon.

"We have a meal ready at home," Teresa said. "It's not much, but you're welcome to join us."

Mike stood behind her, his hand resting on her shoulder. What kind of man wears a pyramid-shaped earring? What kind of woman wears a black brassiere in the middle of town? As I stared at her, I noticed the patches of pink on her cheeks, the fairness of skin that was not accustomed to being pounded by the light, the fine trail of freckles on the bridge of her nose. Confused, I cocked my head toward her; it was like seeing a porcelain doll clothed in see-through lace.

"Yes or no, no or yes, yes or no," she said.

When I nodded, it was not to feed the hunger in my stomach, but the hunger in my head.

I followed them to a run down house, painted a god-awful pink. Even the door was pink. As Mike pushed it open, it curled back like a tongue. "Have a seat," he said, pulling out a chair for me at the kitchen table. I crossed my hands on my lap as Mike took a pot of soup out of the refrigerator and set it on the table. I waited for them to heat it up, but they didn't. When they filled their bowls, I mimicked them, filling my bowl half-way with the cold red soup.

I took a bite, tasted tomatoes, green peppers, cucumbers, garlic. "You two—you're not from around here, are you?"

Teresa laughed. "I suppose you were expecting meat and potatoes?"

"That's not what I meant. I like the soup—really."

"It's called gazpacho," Mike replied.

Teresa sprinkled pepper into her bowl. "We're from LA. Mike's here to get a Masters in English, and I came along for the ride."

"An M.F.A.," Mike said. "Mother Fucking Artist."

She smiled and raised her arms to the wallpaper cracking on the walls. "Mike and I are experimenting living in poverty."

His eyes met hers. Something sizzled. "My mistress' eyes are nothing like the sun; coral is far more red than her lips' red: if snow be white, why then her breasts are dun; if hairs be wires, black wires grow on her head."

I set my spoon down. "You—you wrote that?"

Teresa laughed. "Billy Shakespeare," she corrected me. "A sonnet. Mike wouldn't dare write one. He has such better poems to write."

Mike gave her a low grin. "You, my muse, doth taunt me."

"Your muse is getting tired of you looking at a blank page." She stood before him, pulled his head to her chest. "Write, Mike, just write." Cradling his head in her hands, she bowed from the waist to kiss his lips.

I stared at my soup for as long as the kiss lasted—a minute or ten minutes. I wondered if the words of others camouflaged his own words. His page was not blank; it was filled with the voices of other poets.

Mike reached out and put a hand on my upper arm. "You done?"

Blankly, I nodded.

He took my bowl and set it in the sink. When Mike and Teresa went to the living room, I followed. Books were everywhere, piled upon the others in the corners, on the sofa, on the chairs. I picked a paperback up, written by some poet I didn't know, and read a poem from top to bottom, and top to bottom again. The poem could have been a paint-by-number selection. You decide which color—you interpret as you go—and I didn't understand it at all. Next to it, I picked up a novel, *Lolita*, written by a guy who'd understand the ingredients of vodka—Nabokov.

"Have you read *Lolita*?" Teresa asked.

When I looked into her sparkling eyes, I found myself lying. "Yes."

Mike sat down on top of a spool used by electric companies to hold wire, now used as a stool, end table, chair. Legs crossed beneath him, he leaned forward and pressed his palms in front of his knees. His eyes were shiny and his hair made a V down his back. He looked like a lion.

"Thank you for the meal," I said.

"De nada," Mike replied.

Teresa walked past him, pausing to tug on the ends of his long hair. "If there's one thing Mikey knows, it's how to cook."

Mikey. He told me, that night at the Saddle, that if I ever made the mistake of calling him 'Mikey' he'd act like someone addressed in the diminutive and piss his pants. But he remained poised on the spool like a lion, meeting Teresa's eyes. King of what jungle?

Putting my hands in the back pockets of my cut-offs, I said: "I'll be going now."

"You're welcome to stay longer," Teresa replied. "We can discuss *Lolita*."

"I didn't...I didn't really read it."

"I know," she replied. "If you'd like, you can borrow it."

"I don't much like to read." Staring at all the books around me, I took a step back. "I guess I'll be going."

Teresa walked me to the door. As I opened it, her hand came to my shoulder. Kneading my skin lightly she said, "Come again."

***

All through my life the closest friend I had was my mother and my brother Stevie. When Dad was out drinking, I let Stevie have Benji over to spend the night. Benji lived a couple of blocks away, and both of his parents were drunks. Not the kind of drunk that doesn't come home like Dad, but a drunk who slouches in the house with a beer and a cigarette, and turns on a blasting television set. They watched trash television. They ate pork rinds and beans. They slept on the sofa and woke with the sun coming up. Everything about them was aged with flat beer.

Least Stevie had me. Benji didn't have anyone.

Stevie kept his door open. Night or day, day or night—it was always wide open. I walked into their room with cups of hot cocoa and found the two of them, pants down, trying to light their farts on fire.

"Now," Benji said, then let out a gaseous fume with a lit match beneath it. The match blazed up until Benji's fingers burned. "Ow! Did you see it? You try. Go ahead, Stevie."

Stevie lit a match and stuck it beneath him. Try as he might, he didn't have a fart left to give. "I don't have any," he said. He grinned at Benji. "I'm fartless."

I set their cups down and left the room, so quietly that neither of them knew I was there, save for the cups of hot cocoa. Backs to me, flaming assholes spurting, I wished I had a friend who wouldn't mind seeing me with my pants down.

When I was in school, I got by on my anonymity: "Oh, that's Landy, she don't care." You could sit in my school chair. You could choose me last during kickball games. You could save my seat for the first one down during spelling bee, even though I could beat the King or Queen Bee. You could try until you were out of breath to get me to talk, and I wouldn't raise my head. I was anonymous and I liked the protection that provided. I was flowers on the wall. Could be roses. Could be thorns.

Thorns were shooting from my fingers when a boy named Jake began to call me a series of names. Jake was a shithead born and bred, and treated me like what he was—a shithead. He called me the whole cascade of curses, a single curse for a single day. Monday I was a bastard, Tuesday a cunt, Wednesday a dogshit, Thursday a god damn hellion, and on Friday I was a motherfucker.

Monday through Thursday I repeated a sentence in my mind: "Sticks and stones can breaks my bones, but names can never harm me." On Friday I went dry. How dare he use my mother to make a god damn curse.

Finally I began to fight back, in my way.

He sat behind me in class. Better, he said, to be able to pull my hair. One day I began to chirp, low and melodious like a meadowlark. My lips nearly met as the song eased from inside me. I remembered what my mother used to say: *It's easy, Landy. Lips nearly closed. That's it, that's right. Do it as if a meadowlark sings inside you. Can you feel it?*

The teacher, Mrs. Bowles, had her arms full returning papers to my class. She looked around the room for the sound of the meadowlark and had no idea that it was coming from me. Whenever she passed by me, she reached out and touched my hair. She always treated me like I was the underdog. An underdog would continue to take Jake's curses; an underdog may as well be Jesus turning his other cheek.

If there was anything wrong in our class, from spitballs to note passing, Mrs. Bowles would always turn to Jake first. About nine times out of ten she was right. Every time she stepped up to him with that ruler glistening in her hands, I would close my eyes, feel her tenderly caress my head as she passed, and then—Woop! Woop! The ruler went down on his hand. I could hear him gulp behind me, could hear a tiny whimper, and then silence. Always, I thought getting his hand beat would cure him. Save for the tiny whimper he would be back same as always. And on Monday, Tuesday, Wednesday, Thursday, Friday— when Mrs. Bowles wasn't looking—he pulled my hair and let out a stream of curses.

Mrs. Bowles zapped onto Jake who was pointing his hand at me. "Landy did it," he said. "I swear to God, Landy did it." I kept my head turned down, looked up to see her glance at the clock—two more hours to go—and gave another birdcall. She stormed past me, gave my down-turned head a caress, and slapped his hand silly.

Every time Jake went for me, I was a meadowlark.

By the end of the year, he no longer pulled my hair or called me motherfucker. He did his homework. He stayed after to help Mrs. Bowles clean the blackboards. Now and then he brought her an apple. And he stayed away from me like wildfire.

A couple of summers ago, he ran into me; his car was all packed and he was leaving Pike to attend college in California. He drove along beside me for two blocks while I kept on walking like he wasn't there—head up, chin out.

"Hey Landy," he said. "Landy?"

I kept walking. Nowhere to go, but you have to keep on going.

"Landy?"

Eyes on the road, I nodded. "Yeah."

"You know…I just wanted you to know that you're the reason I got that scholarship out of here."

I turned, pointing my finger at my chest. "Me."

"If it wasn't for that damn birdcall, I'd probably be a union man at the mill by now. Mrs. Bowles, she gives a mean ruler. Kind of whipped me into shape, I guess."

I stared at him and wondered how he'd ever managed to get so tall; he used to be tow-headed but now his hair was light brown, and he had peach fuzz on his chin. Where had I been while he'd been growing up? Had I been sitting with my head down?

"So, well, thank you, that's all." He tipped his head to me. "See you, Landy."

I waited until his car was out of sight. "Good-bye, Jake."

***

And now, in Willow, I was the same at the core as I'd always been. You could move me all the way to Japan, surround me with kimonos, and I'd still be wearing bluejeans and work boots. I missed the mountain. They say that when a part of your body has been amputated—a leg, an arm—you continue to feel it even after it is gone. That was how I missed my mother and her mountain.

I didn't know how to be comfortable with people outside my blood. Mike and Teresa—I had no idea how to be with them. Be yourself. Fat chance. I didn't have an idea what that self was. Take her mountain, take my soul.

Teresa called what we did 'hanging.' "Let's go to the city park and hang." Every time she said that the shiver would take my spine. But I would come. Hanging with them was preferable to hanging alone in the mansion.

Mike and Teresa had money they'd brought up from LA, but they didn't spend it on food. They spent it on marijuana, *a lot* of marijuana. They'd each smoke a joint for breakfast, a joint for lunch, a joint for dinner, and then another in the evening. But they acted normal, as if they just took a break to smoke a Marlboro, then went on about their business. I waited for them to get the munchies, running down to the IGA for Ding Dongs like the stoners back in Pike would do, but they never did. They smoked dope as if it were cigarettes. Now and then they'd offer me some, but I always refused. I didn't like the idea of smoke—any kind of smoke—going to my lungs.

Teresa inhaled, held it inside her lungs, then blew out smoke. "That's how we stay together," she said, grinning at Mike who was inhaling his own joint. "We share a bathroom, a kitchen, a bed. But we do not share a joint."

Because I had no money to buy food, because they spent their own on dope, we began to meet for weekly raids on the gardens in the rich section of town. After dark, carrying burlap sacks, we climbed the fences surrounding the fancy houses and moved up and down the garden rows, gathering food for dinner. We were selective, taking a little from one garden, a little more from another, so that it wasn't evident that the vegetables were missing. We never took from a house that had peeling paint, poor roofing, or any other signs of poverty. Robin Hoods, we stole from the rich to give to ourselves; I did my best to justify the act, but never tossed the burlap sack over my shoulder without feeling the tug of guilt.

One evening when the heat was unbearable, all I could think about was how it would feel to spread out in a mountain stream and let the water run over my body. "It's hot," I kept saying, too many times.

Mike and Teresa exchanged glances. "Tree," Mike said. "Looks like the young'n needs a swim."

At the city park, we climbed over the locked gate of the public swimming pool. Mike and Teresa weren't interested in going for a swim. They sat on the edge with their feet dangling in the water as I dove off the diving board. I had never gone for a swim in a public pool before and was surprised by the warmth of the water and the stinging in my eyes.

I swam to the pool's floor and thrust upward, springing out of the water like a breaching whale. Bobbing up and down, I swallowed a mouthful of water and came to the surface coughing. Taking a deep breath, I dove under again and cupped my hands over the spigot that sprayed fresh water into the pool. My lungs and eyes burned as I swam to the bottom, chasing after a terry cloth hair tie left by a previous swimmer. Every time I drew near it, the force of my body or a gush of water from one of the spigots swept it away. Air bubbles left my mouth, tickling my nose. My lungs were on fire as I pressed my palms on the floor of the pool, searching for the hair tie. By the time I grasped it and slipped it around my wrist, white spots were spinning behind my eyes. The next instant, the white spots turned to black. Panic gripped my chest as I shoved my feet against the floor of the pool, pushing toward the surface, but deep in the center of the panic was an overwhelming sense of wonder: Is this how it feels to die?

In the darkness of the black spots, I spun and twisted upward; not a beam of light came forward to push the image from my eyes: I saw my mother walking into the roaring river. Water ripped her calves, her waist, her breasts, and then she was gone. I was standing on shore. "Mama?" When I stepped in after her, the water splashed over me. "Mama?" The water overpowered me and took me down. She grabbed my hair and pulled me to the surface, dragged me into shore. Her lips were on mine, then parted. I coughed and coughed.

"Why'd you follow?" she asked.

I stared at her moist head of hair. "Because you were gone."

All of that and more pulled me down in to the Willow city pool, pulling me like a dead weight down.

Mike split the water to my left. His arm encircled my waist as I rose to the surface. I pulled away from him and burst out of the water coughing. Gripping my hips with his hands he hoisted me toward Teresa who pulled me from the pool. She turned me on my side and held my head as I coughed the water's acidic taste from my lungs. The feel of her hands on my head brushed away the roar of the Pend Oreille river that kills one person every six years and nearly killed my mother and me.

"You scared the shit out of us," Mike said as he wrapped a towel around my shoulders. "What were you doing down there?"

I crawled away from him, wringing the water from my t-shirt. "I would've made it up quicker if you hadn't grabbed me."

Arrows of water flew from his hair as he turned to me. "Is that so?"

"Yes."

"So you'd prefer it if we counted stars while you may or may not be drowning on the bottom of the pool?"

I put my hand over the hair tie that encircled my wrist. "I was playing, that's all."

Teresa stood over me. "Tell me, Alex, where did you learn how to play?"

Looking down, I tried to close my eyes, but lies were inside them and I didn't want to see them one more time. *She was going for a swim, Landy, that's all, just a swim.* As I stood, the weight of the water in my cut-offs nearly pulled them off my waist. "I'm sorry. I didn't mean to frighten you."

Teresa rearranged the towel across my back. The pressure of her hand made me wince. "Sunburn," I said. But it was not only the patch of red on my upper shoulders that made me wince; it was being touched.

"Houdini's daughter," Teresa said. "At least you got your swim."

I tossed my head and shook the water from my hair. "You two were smart not to go in. The water stinks from the piss of kids who don't have the good sense to find a tree. And it burns your eyes."

"Chlorine," Mike said.

"Stupid chemicals," I said. "I'd much rather swim in a river."

"So win the lottery and buy a river."

"If I won the lottery I'd buy a whole mountain."

***

We didn't win any lotteries, although now and then we'd put a dollar down and try. No money was coming in. I'd been living on air and stolen vegetables for weeks. I tried to find work, but there were no jobs to be had in Willow.

Mike and Tree and I would eat our stolen vegetables. I'd always think about a thick juicy steak as I bit into a ripe tomato. They didn't think about steaks. They were vegetarians. Teresa said, "Vegans." I suppose maybe I was too, I hadn't had meat for so long. Vegetarian by poverty.

It looked like their money would hold out until September, when Mike began a graduate teaching assistantship. Before, in California time, he had a job as a technical writer, but he didn't have to go into work. He worked at home, on his computer with a modem.

"So you never had to get dressed up?" I asked.

"Shorts. T-shirt." He cocked his head toward his wife. "I made money. Teresa spent it. You know, your basic all American family."

Teresa slipped her sandal off and ran her foot along his calves. "I didn't do anything you didn't want me to, honey."

Mike and Teresa tried to offer me money to pay my electric bill, but I declined. "Who needs electricity anyway? Got nothing to put in my refrigerator. Don't need lights anyway. I don't want to pay them a dime."

"Yes you do," Mike replied. "It costs a lot of money to hook you back up."

I stuck my hands in the back pockets of my cut-offs. "Well," I said. "Fuck them."

"You can work for it." He pulled my right hand free and slapped a fifty in it.

I stared up at him, then beyond him to Teresa—she watching me with a smile. "And what am I supposed to do to earn this?"

"Tsk, tsk," Teresa said. "Don't you trust us, Alex?"

"It's not you I don't trust," I replied. "It's everyone."

"I want you to work on our yard," Mike said. "I want a yard that the president would be happy to visit."

"And his wife," Teresa added.

"And his children."

"And his children's children," Teresa said.

I stared at the money in my hand. "And his children's children's children. Okay."

Teresa rested under the oak in their backyard, while Mike and I went through his garage gathering tools left by his landlord. We found shovels, rakes, a lawn mower, and a pitch fork.

"I guess I can rake her first," I said.

"Her?" he asked. "Rake *her* first? Why can't you rake *him* first?"

I smiled. "I can rake *it*."

Teresa watched us pull our rakes through the grass. She had her knees pulled to her chest and rested her head on top. Slowly, her eyes began to close. I didn't understand the word he used for her, Tree, for she was delicate and would never bear the weight of hoar frost.

As she dozed, Mike pulled his t-shirt over his head. "It must be ninety today," he said.

His upper body, tanned from the sun and polished with sweat, seemed cast in bronze. I'd never noticed the strength in his back before. Surprised, I said: "You have a strong body, Mike."

He wrapped his hands around the end of the rake handle and rested his chin on top. "You're not so shabby yourself, Alex."

I looked down at myself, back at him. "It serves me well enough."

"You know," he began, glancing over at Teresa as she dozed in shade. "Tree and I probably would have been at each other's throats by now if you hadn't come along. It takes a lot of energy to keep her entertained."

"So you're saying that I'm your entertainment?"

"Not exactly." Mike pulled the rake through the grass. "But you do help."

Teresa looked sweet sleeping under the maple tree. Pink-cheeked, content, she showed none of the frustration that carried in her voice some nights when she'd say, "What's on the agenda? Shall we sit and watch the grass grow?" Those nights, the air would become filled with a scent—sex *is* a scent—and I would leave early. Out of boredom rises passion? Probably truer to say that out of boredom comes the quest for entertainment, and they were lucky enough to continue to be entertained by each other's bodies.

When Mike turned to me, his hair tossed upon his back. "Story time," he said. "Give me your life story."

"Raised in Pike, left Pike, came to Willow. To be continued." I looked at him and nodded. "Like a sequel. Like book two."

"You haven't even provided a prologue to book one," he said.

"I was born."

He cupped his hand to his forehead, squinting at me in the bright sun. "You were raised on *Little Women, Red Pony,* and *White Fang.*"

I shook my head, but he did not see.

"Or has the fad of book burning come to your town of Pike?" he continued. "The good citizens burning the classics in a communal fire? Save the children—burn a book."

"No." He didn't know enough of me or my beginnings to know I wasn't speaking the whole truth. Dragging the rake like a lame leg, I walked toward the outside faucet for a drink of water, making sure he couldn't see my eyes. It was important that he didn't see my eyes.

I kneeled before the spigot and grabbed the snaking hose, sprayed water into my face. It streamed into my tank top, down my legs.

"Quitting time," Mike called to me. "I've had it."

He went to the shade of the oak tree where Teresa was dozing. Like Sleeping Beauty, she opened her eyes when he kissed her. Sitting up, she folded his hands in her own, and I knew by the way she set her drowsy eyes on his face that they'd make love as soon as they got inside. Crossing her arms around her knees, she nodded at me where I stood, dripping wet, near the side of the house.

"See you," I called to them.

When Teresa met my eyes, the same look she had given Mike was passed to me. "Come up later if you'd like," she said.

"I think I'll just stay in tonight."

"Sweet, sweet Alex," she said, in a voice that matched her eyes. "Have a good evening."

As I walked down the streets, the sickness churned in my stomach and a metallic taste covered my tongue. *How can it be that making love takes everything away?*

A package was on the steps of the mansion, sealed with masking tape and covered with stamps, from my father. I sat on the steps and carefully pried the box open. Inside were my wool trousers, gold-buttoned cowboy shirt, fatigue jacket with the zip-in liner. My best things. At the bottom of the box was the picture of Dad, Stevie, Hepburn and me taken at the county fair. We looked just like a family in the picture, a family through shit and roses, a family through it all. A letter was attached to the package, addressed in Dad's handwriting. The print mirrored the man he'd become in sobriety, ten years long—arrow-straight, diligently controlled.

Dear Landy. I packed up some things I thought you might like to have. Weather is fine, steady breeze all day. I plan a grouse hunting trip with Steven up to Abercrombie next weekend. So if you had any plans to drop in on us that weekend, call and we'll cancel our trip. Anytime after five I'd be home, call anytime.

On the same sheet of paper, Stevie added a note:

I know you don't want to hear this, but try to anyway. Dad sold the land for us. He wants us to have something for a change and he made a good deal, selling at top dollar. He did what he thought was right. She would have done the same thing if it was him that killed himself there. And she'd have done it a lot quicker than he did. Maybe you think I'm saying this to hurt you, and maybe I am hurting you, but that isn't the point of it. I don't know how you're feeling. All I've ever been able to do is guess at what's inside you. You raised me like a mother, Landy. I may not always understand you, but I do always love you. Dad loves you too, he just doesn't say it well. Write us a letter. Tell us how you are, if you can.

Holding the letter to my chest, I closed my eyes. "Oh I can tell you, Stevie, I can."

Listen Stevie, you don't know, you don't know how she was. But all of it has made me; that thing you hate about me when I won't let you see my eyes—she taught me that. She said that words lied, but eyes didn't. You don't know how sometimes the muteness enfolded her and the only stories she could tell were painted across the canvas of her eyes.

Stevie, one day when her voice was gone she built a fire in our back lot and tossed each volume of the encyclopedia set into it. She loved the encyclopedias, they were a birthday gift from Dad. After they disappeared in the flames, she took the book of nursery rhymes from my hands and tossed it in the fire.

The flames licked her knees, but she didn't seem to feel the heat. I don't know if it came out in words, Stevie, or if it was said in her eyes, but I remember the message, as clear as I remember the pages folding back in the flames: she said that this was what Hell looked like.

I wrapped my arms around her legs, holding her back from the fire. My knuckles blistered two days later from the burns and she covered them with water ferns. They got well, Stevie, they got well.

Her eyes mirrored the flames—red, yellow, gold. I wished I could carry her away, but could only hold her hand and lead her through the empty pastures and muddy ravines until we arrived at the dirt road leading to the mountain where she'd be safe.

She sat in the meadow and pressed her fists into the earth. Standing beside her, I was as tall as the wildflowers which covered the meadow like a purple quilt. I drew back the collar of her white gown and massaged her neck as she would massage our father's, loosening the stiff muscles with my hands.

She patted the ground next to her and I sat down. "I'm sorry I burned your fairy tales, Landy." Easing my head to her lap, she stroked my cheek. "Have you ever seen such a color," she began, pointing to the sky, "As beautiful as that blue?" When she looked at me and smiled, I saw such a color as beautiful as that blue, resting in her eyes.

Stevie, you don't remember. You don't know. All you know is the after. Do you know that sometimes when Dad's long drunk he calls me by her name, calling me 'Lizzy.' Then I become so confused I forget who I am, and don't like who I am, and know I have to go away. I can't be like Dad and let a bottle of whiskey take me away. Only the mountain can do that for me. Shake it roughly. Nothing explodes. No sediment blurs the sky. On the mountain, I am the mountain.

But now in Willow my dreams come differently than they've ever been before. She whistles as she walked the streets, her face is serene and knowing, her body is silken, waist curving into curving hips, long legs, high cheekbones and the deepest eyes. She moves like a shadow to the bed.

I am in the bed, a woman, grown, and she lays beside me and takes me in her arms. And when I awake, I'm crying.

Then she's gone. But I'll find her in my dreams again, or on the mountain, or wherever she appears in whatever form, whatever place and time. I'll know her when she comes; I know her that well. When I find her I'll say: Tell me what your life was like before I was born, tell me, please, how you loved your life.

***

I dropped Stevie's letter to the ground and pulled the picture from the box. Lodged behind the cardboard backing was a snapshot of my mother that I'd hidden there long ago. She was as old—as young—as I am now. In the snapshot, I was standing next to her, five years old.

The edge of the picture blurred, but my mother's eyes didn't. If I held the picture one way, she seemed to be crying. But held another, she seemed to be laughing. I lifted the picture over my head and stared at her. When I began to laugh, tears filled my eyes.

Chapter Five

My job came through in September just as the manager had promised. All the employees at the IGA had nicknames rather than proper names written on their name tags. When the manager asked me what my nickname was, I told him it was Al, though it was Landy, I suppose.

The garden raids ended with my first paycheck. I was relieved that I no longer spent my evenings sneaking around in the dark like a grave robber. I hoped that removing the guilt of stealing things that weren't my own would help me sleep better at night. But it wasn't so. Sleep was elusive; once obtained, it brought no comfort. I would bolt awake in the middle of the night with a scratchy throat and stare at the streetlight outside my bedroom window until I could remember who I was, where I was. Cradling the pillow to my chest, I would tell myself aloud that I was okay, that everything was all right. My voice would be hoarse because I had used it up while I slept, speaking inside my dreams. I hadn't talked in my sleep for years and was frightened that something I had once outgrown after the first years without my mother had come back to grow inside me again. Ages ago, during one of Dad's sober periods, he ran in my room and saw me standing on my bed, flailing at the bedpost with a pillow. He told me that I said, "One, two, three, one, two, three," over and over as I swung the pillow down. I don't remember it at all, only the feeling of my father's arms wrapping around me, telling me to wake up now, to wake out of the bad dream.

In my dreams, I must have talked out all there was to say. I can't swear to it on the Bible, I simply don't remember, but I think I talked to my mother listening from the other side, because she was my first waking thought for two years after her death.

Now, the dreams were back. You'd think I'd outgrow them in the years since her death, like trying to put on a pair of tennis shoes made for a five year old, but they fit as if I'd worn them yesterday. When I felt brave, from the edge of sleep I asked my mind to wake me when a bad dream came, to transport my dreams to waking consciousness so I could look at them with open eyes, but my mind didn't obey me. I would awaken with a sore throat and trembling legs, and in the panic of the blood pounding in my ears, the dream would be gone. If the bed shook beneath my body and the breath caught in my throat, I would take my blanket to the front porch and huddle in the corner against the side of the mansion, shivering in the pre-dawn until the birds began to sing.

My tunnel-like room with its low ceiling made me yearn for a castle with enough space to fit a hundred of me. I was grateful for my job, for it gave me a reason to escape my room. After work, I found other reasons to keep myself away. I visited Mike and Teresa, but all I could think about was leaving. Pacing inside their four walls, I felt suffocated. Mike said I had ants in my pants. Teresa said I needed a couple of skilled hands to take my tension away.

"Come with us," she said. "We're going to a party hosted by the English teaching assistants. For the T.A.s, by the T.A.s, and of the T.A.s. Of course, I'm welcome too—Mike's muse."

"T.A.s." The strands of silver in Mike's beard shimmered. "Tits and asses."

"The letter said to bring your spouse/partner/friend," Teresa said. "So come."

I couldn't imagine myself surrounded by a group of people who read those books that I never would and *discussed* them. You ask them how they're doing and they respond in Shakespeare's tone: "I have of late, wherefore I know not, seem to have lost all my mirth." Just last week, I asked Mike matter-of-factly how he was doing, expecting an answer of fine, and he responded in Shakespeareze: he was mirthless.

I shook my head. "Being around Mike is as close to an English class as I'll get."

"Please," Teresa said. "Please come."

As she and Mike exchanged glances, it occurred to me that if I didn't come, then Mike wasn't going. He didn't like that shit any more than I did. Teresa, on the other hand, loved it; it was something to do.

"Please." Teresa got on her knees in front of me, crossed her hands as if to pray. "Pretty, pretty please."

"All right," I answered, helping her up. "I'll walk in with you both, but if I don't feel like staying I'm free to go."

Crossing her thumb and pinkie together, she gave me the three-fingered Boy Scout salute of honor. "I promise."

Mike stroked his beard. "Welcome to the island of misfit toys."

***

Plenty of misfit toys could fit into the apartment—it was about four of my apartments in one. About twenty people were inside. Mike, Teresa, and I were the only people who came as the Three Musketeers. The rest were in pairs.

Teresa wiggled her way to the icebox sitting on the floor and came back with a beer for Mike and me, but nothing for herself. She leaned toward him, her breasts against his chest. "I'll be back, Mikey," she said. Her head of blonde hair dipped like a mirage out of the kitchen.

Mike and I found a spot near the icebox, near the beer, and settled in. "I'll stay here to keep the wall standing," I said. "You go out and mix."

Mike stood in the corner holding up the wall and surveyed the room with dynamite eyes. "This is fine." He lifted his beer and drank it down, and went into the icebox for another.

"One sec," a man said. "Grab me one, would you?"

Mike tossed the man a beer.

"Thanks." He put out his hand. "Brett Smith."

Mike shifted his beer, freeing his right hand. "Mike McPherson."

"Is this your wife?" Brett asked.

I cocked my head toward Mike as he responded, "One of them."

"One of what?" I asked.

"My wife's here somewhere," Mike said. "This is Alex, a friend of ours."

"You're a student?"

Instantly, I averted my gaze to the far wall. "No."

I stared past him, past Mike, and remembered what I used to know so well: *Do it, Landy, keep your head up, pull your shoulders back, act as if you know where you are going.* But if it weren't for the wall, I would have fallen. Brett asked me a few more questions to which he received a few more blank answers, and then started talking to Mike. Mike—who said I was one of his wives, Mike—who was now on his third beer, Mike—who was listening to Brett talk about his research as if he cared an inch about what he was saying, Mikey, Mikey, Mikey. With each drink, the less his beard shivered—you know, that corner of your jaw that hinges your face together.

I hugged the beer to my front and searched the room for Teresa. I saw her by the clothes she was wearing—black Lycra shorts and a pink t-shirt that she probably purchased from the little girls section. It showed her ribs, it did. Teresa said my problem with her etiquette was that I didn't understand the whole expression: Live and *let live.*

She was talking to another woman, but that woman had her hand over her lips and was shaking her head. But Teresa wasn't taking that shaking head as a symbol of No. She drew her arm up to the woman's shoulder and caressed the skin, the same kind of gesture she had given me the night I had dinner at their house. The woman's eyes shuttered, like a camera. Suddenly they were taking Teresa in, all of her in, from her sandals to the mop of her hair. She lifted Teresa's hand from her shoulder and dropped it like a hot potato.

I watched her walk away, her back to me, and stared at the wisps of her hair tracing her neck. Teresa was blonde—platinum blonde— but this woman was a natural blonde with streaks of light brown hair shooting through her shoulder length hair. She moved as if her legs were used to running, traveling in three-quarter time across the floor as gracefully as an angel. She was about my age, yet when she greet- ed another woman, she seemed a million years older and a million years younger—she was ageless. She smiled at her friend.

Watching with my head against the wall, I felt the numbness in my legs, and I knew that I had to leave. I did not want to *know* her, I wanted to *be* her.

"I'm going," I said to Mike.

He lifted his hand. "Drive safely."

The ridiculousness of that statement made me smile at him. He knew I didn't have a license, he knew I couldn't drive legally, he knew I didn't own a car. "Like a bank robber," I said.

Teresa leaned shoulder-to-shoulder with an ex-fraternity boy. The lettering on his sweatshirt was Greek and it could have said anything, Sigma Whatever, but it may as well be saying: Want to fuck?

"I'm going," I said to Teresa.

"Hey, it's a free country."

I walked out the door and into the street. I walked and walked and walked. In time, the noises of the night became the noise within me—a solid black. No smile—not a hint of a smile from a woman whose name I did not know, whose life I did not know, whose shoe size I did not know—could pierce that black. I walked with my head held high and my chin straight up, aching in the black, basking in the black, forsaking all others into the black. Nothing could hurt me there. Nothing could help me either.

***

From the porch of the mansion, I ate a store-bought watermelon, anticipating the night: in the wildlife refuge I had a favorite tree that rose as high as the sky. My climbing tree, it waited for me like a ladder rising to heaven. The juice from the watermelon made a sloppy red mess across my cheeks and down my shirt, but I didn't care there was no one to notice, until Patchins drove up.

He was driving his second car, a Volkswagen; it inched down the street like a tired gray mare. Sticking his head out the window, he yelled: "Got a renter moving in soon. Get yourself cleaned up or she'll think white trash is living in my home."

I spat a watermelon seed toward him as I approached the street. When Stevie and I were young and shaggy-looking in our worn out clothes, some folks who were trash called us trash, but never to our faces, and never so blatantly as Patchins with such a simpleton's grin.

My hand left a sticky circle on the roof of his car. "Which room is the renter taking?"

"The one across from yours. Second best room in the place. Yours, of course, is best." Patchins lifted a towel off the passenger seat; beneath it was a bag of pork chops. "Snuck these out for you, Girl."

"I'm working now. I can buy my own food."

"What am I supposed to do? Sneak them back?"

"I don't know. Give them to the new renter."

Patchins tossed the package onto the seat. "Like I say, I never give nothing to dirt." Looking at me with steel gray eyes, he wiped the back of his hand across his lips. "Her name's Claire Something. She's studying there at the college. Like she thinks a college education makes her better than me, huh. She's about as friendly as a black widow spider. Wouldn't even stay to pass the time of day when she put the money down on the room. Hate to lay her on you, Girl, but I had no choice. I'm pretty picky about who I rent to, but the wife ain't. She beat me to the phone. She tells me it's high time I rented out some rooms." Patchins hid the bag of pork chops inside the towel. "Yep, that's the story, and you got Claire Something as a neighbor, sorry to say."

Leaning over, I wiped my hands on the moist grass, trying to remove the sticky feeling of the watermelon juice. "Can I ask you how long it's been since you rented out the rooms?"

"I rented to you, didn't I? Had to, or the wife claims she's going to split my head wide open."

"Before me."

"I looked at a lot of people," he said. "They had the wrong character."

"Jesus, Patchins, you rented to me because I had the right character?"

"And because the wife said so."

"She hasn't even met me."

"I know." He shook his head. "She never met that Claire Something either. See how twisted it is being a landlord?"

I stared at the top of his bald head. "Oh yeah," I answered sarcastically. "Twisted."

"New renter's a hermit type," he said. "Don't you be knocking on her door all day. You'd be wise to stay away from her. She gives you grief, just tell me. I know how to handle highbrows." He honked once as he pulled away. A stuffed poodle was perched in his back window; its eyes lit up as he pumped the brakes and rounded the corner.

By the time I got home from work the next day, I had myself a neighbor. As I came up the stairs, I heard furniture scraping against the floor of her room. I stood outside her door trying to decide whether I should knock and introduce myself. Before my knuckles found the wood of her door, I heard the main door open and footsteps pound up the stairs.

"Oh God," a woman's voice said. "It's as bad on the inside as it is on the outside. Why would anybody live here?"

Another woman replied, "There will be no stairmaster today."

Slowly, I turned the knob and entered my room, and did not make a sound as they appeared in the hallway, listening to them speak. There was a childish pleasure that I got from listening and not being seen.

"Hey, open up," she called. "You-who, Claire."

"Open up or I'll huff and I'll puff and I'll knock your door down."

"Blow." The woman laughed. "You'll blow the door down."

The door squealed open. "Hi," Claire answered. "Come on in."

"Anything bite in there?"

"What?" Claire said. "You have something against it?"

Together, both women responded: "Yes."

"You could have stayed with us until an apartment opened," a woman said. "There's always room on the couch."

"I like you both, but I do not like your couch," Claire answered.

"But this...this..."

"This is home, for now," Claire replied. "It's affordable, it's close to the university, and it does not have mice. Now, do I need to move some chairs into the hallway, or are you going to come in?"

Dusky, the color of redwood, her voice seeped into my room like smoke; in timbre, tone, and cadence, it sounded like my mother's. The door squealed shut as I sat on the arm of my couch, listening to a voice that was like my mother's but was not hers. The wall that separated her room from mine was paper thin. It was like listening in a house from bedroom to kitchen. The tone was so similar to my mother's that my throat began to ache.

The two women in the hallway were named April and Sue. I learned that from hearing Claire say, "April, Sue, would you like a drink?"

April or Sue responded, "You can drink the water here?"

"Water?" Claire said. "Fish fuck in it."

I smiled at the door, nodding my head, as laughter traveled in.

"Yes," Claire said. "You can drink the water here." I heard the sound of ice entering a glass, the tiniest tinkle like you get when your brother pees in the toilet for his first time.

"How is your class in speech pathology?" one of the women asked. I imagined she was sitting on the couch, the books beside her, and was thumbing through the pages.

"Yesterday, we had a guest speaker."

"So," the woman said. "So how was it?"

"She's thirty-four years old. She had a stroke a year ago; it left her, at first, paralyzed on her right side and with minimal vocabulary. Her noun retrieval was gone. The neurons transferred information, but the section of her brain that was damaged by the clot of blood—she called it 'the dead part'—wasn't getting the information. When she was in rehab, the speech therapist would point at a picture of a car, and ask its name. She could talk around it, she could tell you that it's driving, that it's carrying passengers to dinner, that it's going fifty-five miles per hour, but she couldn't say that it is a car. She had to make new channels to transmit information, from here to here."

I nodded, and repeated the gesture: from your brain to your mouth.

"We speak without even thinking," Claire said. "We open our mouths and words appear. But it is amazing—the section of the brain that permits speech, and can take it away at random."

The three of them began to speak of noun retrieval, that you can pinpoint the section of the brain where it occurs, but I could not listen anymore. Walking carefully, making no noise, I stared out my window at the breeze hovering in the willow. My mother used to talk about the power of the eye—that it is much greater than the power of speech; one look is more eloquent than a thousand words. To her, a look could make a fir bend.

Sitting on the arm of the couch, I laced my hand against the wall. "Whatever you have to say about this place, go ahead and say it." Claire said. "Be careful, now, because you only get this one opportunity."

I figured out who was April and who was Sue by the sound of the voices matched to the names given by Claire. April had the voice of a hoarse person, like someone who'd been cheering at a game all day. Sue let the end of her sentences trail off, leaving you to interpret the story. April and Sue went through the list of complaints, chief of which was the huge staircase, last of which was the peeling paint.

Claire said, "The landlord, Patchins, says there's one more renter here, and he wouldn't rent to me except that his wife took my call. He wants to keep the place like it is, so that 'his mistress' will be free to come and go as she pleases."

"His mistress?" I whispered, staring at the door. "Me? His mistress?"

"You're kidding," April said.

"I'm pretty sure he's harmless; I can't believe that any women would dare to sleep with him," Claire said. "His wife is the one who puts the ad in paper, not him. He uses the place for drinking, because his wife won't allow it."

"He does?" I whispered.

"He offered me a drink of Jim Beam."

"Did you take…" Sue asked, letting the end of her sentence fade away.

Claire laughed. "He offered me the bottle, after he drank from it. I declined."

"He certainly doesn't put any money into this place," April said. "Which room is she in?"

"Across the hall," Claire answered. "He calls her Girl."

"Girl," I whispered, covering my mouth with a pillow. "Someone should take the son-of-a-bitch out and shoot him."

"Well," April said. "Just keep your eye on him, all right?"

"Ditto," Sue said.

Suddenly, the three voices spoke all at once, as they decided to get wherever they were headed. I managed to hear April refer to a place out by the highway, and listening to Claire and Sue respond, it seemed that they were meeting others down by the highway to clean up the sides of it. I had seen signs up, a section of highway cleaned by the Elks Club, by the Shriners, by a sorority or a fraternity. But they referred to their group as the GPA. I didn't know what the GPA stood for.

The door squealed shut, and footsteps rattled on the staircase. I looked out my window at them on the street below. I could only get a glimpse of April and Sue as they got in their truck, and noticed they were wearing identical clothes in different sizes—same caps, same jeans, same denim shirts. One was taller than the other, and one of them had short brown hair, the other was a redhead. I decided that April had to be the tall woman with muscular arms—the one who had a hoarse voice—and Sue had to be the redhead—the one whose sentences fade away. April was driving.

Claire followed behind. She wore a necklace made from the colors of the rainbow. She stooped down to the ground and picked up a maple leaf, and smiled as she took a breath of its green flesh. It was the smile, aimed at no one but herself, that made my legs begin to tremble: she was the woman at the party who treated Teresa's hand like a hot potato. Claire placed the maple leaf in her hair as if it were a flower.

From my window, I watched them drive away.

***

In the refuge, I didn't have to worry about being surprised by the sound of her voice. It was disquieting to think that I had yearned for someone to move into the mansion, and now that someone had—Claire had—I was terrified to meet her. She was like Christmas morning to me—a gift that has not been opened. Maybe I would like the gift, maybe it would be nothing that I needed, but it was still a gift unopened. With Claire, in time I would open the gift of her; maybe she would become an acquaintance, a friend, or even an enemy. I did not know. But first I had to move my mother's voice out of her body. She was not my mother, and even if I did believe in reincarnation my mother couldn't be Claire because Claire was too young. With all those thoughts running through my head night and day, I couldn't meet Claire, for she could see by looking at the circles under my eyes that I was not right. But, God, her voice—it was like a ghost voice.

My mother believed in ghosts. On the mountain, she saw ghosts in the high grass of the meadow. "Don't be frightened," she would say to me. But I was frightened by the way she waved a greeting to something only she had the power to see. "She has no intention of hurting us, Landy. She's come here to rest."

In the meadow, I saw daisies, dandelions, Indian paintbrush. "It's a girl ghost, Mama? Do you know her?"

My mother's eyes shone as she swept the hem of her gown into her hand, lifted it to her knees, and gave a full curtsy toward the wildflowers in the meadow. "Now I do."

I saw no ghosts as I sat in my tree in the refuge. Beneath my hips, the branch was solid, real; against my back, the trunk was rough, real. Supported so, I didn't need to use my hands to stay balanced in the tree. I took an apple from the pocket of my jacket and rubbed it against my jeans until it was a glossy red. The refuge was so quiet that when I bit into the apple, the sound hung in the air. I placed the core of the apple on the branch across from me, nestled securely against the trunk. A tree squirrel would have a present this night.

Infrequently, the cross country team from Willow High would run the trail. As I heard footsteps below, I assumed it was the group of lanky boys in purple and gray sweats. But it wasn't. It was a woman, running alone. As I brushed a branch aside, she drew near enough for me to give her a name: Claire. My hands began to shake as I stared down at her; I tried to hold myself steady by gripping the branch overhead, but my hands were clubs. I pressed my body into the trunk, locked my legs around it, and melded with the tree like a layer of bark.

My arm knocked against the branch next to me and the apple core fell to the ground. It hit at Claire's feet.

Startled, she trailed her left foot against the path, sending up a stream of dust as she stopped beneath me. When she kneeled, only one knee touched the ground. She lifted the apple by its stem and gazed at my tree. I was certain she couldn't see me where I sat in the crest, surrounded by green.

Cupping her hand to her forehead, she stared up. Through the prickly pine needles I looked into eyes that were like a hot, clear sky. Between the shoulder straps of her tank top, her chest was glazed with beads of sweat which sparkled in the moonlight. Dropping the apple, she backed away and began to run. She moved with long strides down the trail, limber as wind, breaking stride once to glance at the boughs of my tree.

I knew that she hadn't seen me, because she continued to pass through the refuge on her nightly run. The jogging trail was off to the side of my tree, so I was free to watch her without being seen. I learned the cadence of her stride and was never frightened again by her approach. It was like my mother said of ghosts: if you see them enough, they will become known to you, and the known has no fear equal to the unknown. Claire was no ghost, she was as real as the bark beneath my hands, and the more times I saw her running with footsteps that had sound, the less I was afraid. My hands became my own again.

The moon was real. Even though I couldn't touch, smell, or taste it, I knew it was real. My mother used to see women on the moon, different women according to the moon's phase. As with the ghosts, she didn't know who the women were until she saw them, but after she saw them, they were real. Helen. Maureen. Cora. She gave them names. One night her eyes grew cloudy with tears as she stared at the moon. "It isn't her," she said. In the moon and the meadow, she searched for her mother, my grandmother Pearl, who left the world we lived in a year before my birth.

Sitting in the top of my tree in the refuge, if I squinted my eyes and stared at the moon long enough, I saw a woman too, but not many women, just one: my mother. "Hello Mama," I said. I used to offer the same greeting from my mother's mountain, with faith that from such heights my voice would have the power to travel through the silence of the sky. But in the lowlands of Willow, even from the top of the tallest tree, I feared that my words would drop to the ground before a breeze could catch them, and forced my voice to be strong: "Mama? Can you hear me? You always used to tell me how brave I was, do you remember? I wish I could remember how it felt to be brave." I felt braver as I spoke in a voice that I forced to be strong, brave enough and strong enough to force myself to believe that she, that something, heard me.

The woman was full in the moon as I nestled into my tree. When Claire's familiar steps rustled the leaves on the trail, I drew still. She moved in flowing strides; it seemed as though her feet didn't touch the ground. The way she moved...*Whither oh whither oh whither so high? To sweep the cobwebs from the sky, and I'll be with you by and by.*

Directly beneath me, she stopped. Folding her hands behind her back, she stared into the boughs of my tree. "Do you find me an interesting subject?" Smoke was in her voice, fire in her eyes, and steam rose from her body as she pulled her sweatshirt off and tossed it to the ground. Her skin was tan against the stark white of her sleeveless t-shirt. "Take a good look. Is that what you want?"

I prayed that a moonbeam would blind her long enough for me to get away, but her eyes stayed focused on me. When my voice surfaced it frightened me, for it sounded like a child's. "I—I live next to you."

"I know. I've seen you."

"I'm not—" Tapping my forehead against the trunk, I cleared my throat. "I come here and you come here and...you run by."

"And you watch me," she replied. "Every goddamn night. What's it about?"

Anger was a feeling all over my body—hot—anger about the ache of guilt in the pit of my stomach, guilt over something I had not done. "I'm not a Peeping Tom. Put your sweatshirt back on."

"I don't know what you are," she replied. "That's the point. And I'm getting a stiff neck looking up at you."

Sliding from branch to branch, I swung to the ground. "You could always run down a different trail if it bothers you so much."

"This is the only trail that passes through here."

I pointed up at my tree. "But that's the best tree in the whole refuge."

Her eyes were sparkling, as if she were laughing inside her mind. "The best tree?"

"I...I like to climb trees." When she smiled, I kicked a pine cone off the trail. "Why are you smiling?"

"Why aren't you?"

"I was sitting in that tree long before you started jogging out here," I replied. "If you don't like it, don't come here anymore."

"I'm not asking you to give up your tree." Her face was flushed from the run and wisps of hair caught in the trace of sweat on her forehead. "That's not what I'm asking."

I forced my eyes level with hers, made myself look into them, to see that they were blue, not brown, to see that her voice was hers, so like my mother's, but hers. "You better put your sweatshirt back on or you're going to catch a chill." I picked her sweatshirt off the ground and tossed it to her. "Then what are you asking?"

"I'd like you to make yourself present when I come by."

"So if I waved at you or something, you wouldn't feel like I was sitting up there spying. Which I'm not."

Claire smiled. "Exactly."

"I could do that."

"I'd appreciate it."

For a long moment we stood there surveying one another, locked in a game of stare down. "Well," I finally said, backing away from her. "Enjoy your run. Next time you jog by, I'll whistle or wave or something like that."

"Or drop an apple core." She leaned against my tree as I continued to retreat. "It was good to finally meet you, Alexandra."

"You know my name?"

"It's on the mailbox."

"It says Alex on the mailbox."

"For Alexandra, right?"

"That's right," I answered. "It's better than calling me Girl, like Patchins does. And I'm not his mistress either." I met her eyes, looking for signs of disapproval, but they were warm and curious meeting mine.

"So you listened through my walls."

"It's difficult not to, the walls are so thin." She wasn't home much, studying at the library, doing meetings and functions for the GPA. Sometimes her friends came by, April and Sue always together, and other people, but she didn't use the mansion for entertaining. She went out with them. Mostly, she used the mansion to sleep.

She met my eyes. "Sound travels both ways, Alexandra."

I looked down as she pulled her sweatshirt on. "I'm quiet," I said so softly she wouldn't hear.

"Are you walking that way?" she asked, pointing down the trail.

I shook my head.

"Another time, then," she said.

I tried to walk slowly in the opposite direction from her, and turned back once to see her, hands crossed behind her back, watching me. I lifted my hand and waved, and she nodded as she smiled. When she smiled, a large piece of me wanted to go walk with her until daybreak, just walking and seeing that smile. Another part, just as large, told me it was much better to be left alone—*We don't need them, Landy; it's all right to walk where you're headed alone.*

Claire called me Alexandra. No one had called me by that name, ever. It was a nice name. Alexandra.

***

I got off my shift from the IGA at seven p.m. and headed for McDonald's for a quick bite and a chance to rest my dogs. I was munching on a french fry when I looked out the window and saw a group of women heading for a movie at the Micro. The Micro brings in movies cheap, previous to release on video, about a dollar fifty per person. There were April and Sue, wearing identical shorts and t-shirts in different sizes and colors. April was telling some kind of story, listened to by two other women who walked shoulder to shoulder beside her. And there was Claire trapped in the middle of all those faces. When April said something, Claire lifted her head to the sky, laughing and laughing. She didn't see me sitting there smiling as she walked by on the way to the Micro. They went inside.

I ate my dinner slowly, taking each bite of my hamburger, tasting the pickles and the onions and the mustard on my tongue. Somewhere people are starving as they sleep on the streets, somewhere people forget their kids and are letting them starve, somewhere an old person waits for Meals-On-Wheels to find him and they never do, but I did not discuss such starvation in my mind. It came in and I let it go. I ate, it was a Quarter Pounder, and it was good.

Walking off my dinner took me out to Main Street and down by the Christian bookstore, Betty's Jeans and Things, and the Micro. The Micro was an old church converted into a theater. I went up to the front door and studied the poster of the movie they were playing. I thought it would have to be something romantic to get those five women to see it, but the poster had two women together, a long blonde-haired woman and, behind her, a short dark-haired woman. Underneath, it had statements about how these two women come to share their hearts and their souls, searching for sexual awareness.

I studied the picture. The long haired blonde woman had her eyes closed her lips barely open. There was something in her that was very appealing, an earthy sexuality. Behind her was a dark haired woman. She leaned forward and her eyes were also closed. The name of the movie was *Claire of the Moon*. As I stared at the two of them, the dark-haired woman made me begin to smile. I didn't know her name, but she looked a lot like Carol Burnette.

I hoped that inside the church that was now a movie house, Claire was enjoying the show. As for me, seeing a movie about two women revealing their hearts and their souls left nothing to imagine. Take a soul in your left hand, a heart in your right, and what is left, save bones?

***

The next night, from my climbing tree I waited for Claire to jog by. There was no longer a need to hide in the crest; I stayed near the base. When I saw her in the distance, I swung to the lowest tier of branches. I didn't want her to think I hadn't respected what she'd asked of me.

She lifted her hand as she jogged up the trail. When I heard the creaking noise of wood breaking, I knew I'd made a mistake in allowing all of my weight to be supported on the thin lower branch. As Claire approached my tree, I yelled at her to get clear, but the words hadn't left my mouth before the branch splintered. Claire could not escape me as I dropped from the tree like a crow with clipped wings. My elbow struck her across the face.

Our bodies were entwined upon the trail, my arm beneath her hips, her hand upon my waist. Spinning away, I kneeled on all fours and stared at her. She didn't move. Her eyes were closed, blood gushed from her nose, and I knew by the way my heart constricted in cold fear that she was dead.

I crawled up beside her and cradled her head in my hands. Her lips were red with blood. Pale face, alabaster skin. Pictures were painted on her skin: I saw my mother's face as she put the rowboat in the river and said it was a good day for a baptism. *Baked apples she sold and cranberry pies, and she's the woman who never told lies.*

Claire turned toward me. As her face brushed against my front, the cartilage of her nose cracked. Moaning, she gripped my arm and lifted her pelvis in a spasm of pain.

"You're going to be okay," I said. "I promise." The blood continued to pour from her nose, a river of blood. I placed my hand on the nape of her neck and dabbed my handkerchief across her lips and chin. She coughed as the blood ran down her throat. "You're going to be fine," I said, lifting her head higher.

She closed her eyes tightly as if to clear her vision, and focused on me with a questioning look in her eyes. I imagined she saw two of me. "Who are you?" she asked.

"I'm your neighbor—Alexandra."

"No," she said softly. "Who *are* you?"

"You got knocked out. Your nose is probably broken. As soon as the blood stops, we'll go back to the mansion."

"The mansion?"

"Home." Her hair was soft, like silk is soft. "I wish it were me, not you. I'm sorry."

Her eyelids fluttered and closed. "I'll be fine. You promised."

The flow of blood began to lessen—needles of red—then stopped. "Do you think you can walk?" I asked. "I could carry you on my back if you feel too dizzy."

It must have hurt her to smile, for when she did, her grip tightened on my arm. "I'd break your back."

"Oh, I doubt that." Her legs were rubbery; with the first step her knee buckled. I caught her arm before she fell. Leaning into me, she regained her balance. "I'm really sorry, Claire."

She set her hand on the center of my chest and pushed. "I wish you'd stop saying that."

I placed my arm on the small of her back to steady her. "Tell me if you need to rest." She walked with her eyes closed, pacing herself to my slow steps. "It's all right," I said. "All right, Claire." My climbing tree was five miles outside of town; that left five miles for her to walk with a broken nose. Her head was so low she could probably count the ants upon the ground. "Here," I said. "Come here." I leaned her against the side of my body, with her head resting on the top of my shoulder. "I want you to hold onto me." I set my hand along her backside, resting it on her waist, and she did the same to me. "Now, we walk, we're heading out."

"Right, Sarge."

I looked over at her and saw her smile with her eyes closed. "There is an army tune that goes with marching. I don't remember the words, really. My dad taught it to my brother and me."

Eyes closed, she whispered, "Sing."

"Well, it goes something like this. But you have to remember that I can't sing."

"Sing."

"All right, okay." I stared at the tops of the trees as I sang. "Sound off, one two, sound off, three four. Sound off one two, one two three four." I nodded at her. "The rest of the song I can't remember the exact words, so if you know them, please pipe in."

She smiled. "Certainly."

"It goes left-right, left-right, so they can march better." She marched along with the words, left, right, left, right. "Johnny was there when you left, you're right. Johnny was there when you left, you're right. Johnny was there when he left his wife with thirty-eight kids on the brink of starvation with only a johnny-cake left. Left, left, left, right, left. Left, left, left, right, left. Sound off, one two, sound off, three four. Sound off one two, one two three four."

Times when I was younger, trying to get Stevie to find the energy to walk back from the mountain instead of having me carry a ten year old boy home, we'd sing the marching song. It got us off the mountain. And now, it got us out of the refuge.

As we approached the edge of the refuge, her head was low. "It's not much farther." She moved like a sleepwalker down the streets of Willow toward the mansion. "All right, we're home now, we're home." At the foot of the staircase, I tightened my grip on her waist. "Careful up the stairs." She tilted her head toward me; the whites of her eyes were red. "I've got ice," I said. "It'll help the pain."

I brought her into my room. She leaned against my wall as I removed the cushions from the couch and set them on the floor. "The couch springs are broken," I explained, helping her onto the cushions. I emptied the ice tray, wrapped the cubes of ice in a dish towel, and kneeled next to her. "This is going to hurt at first." She gripped my knee as I set the ice across the bridge of her nose, but she didn't make a sound. "How much pain, Claire?"

Somehow, through the pain, she smiled. "Enough to know better than to get in your way again."

"Maybe I should call a doctor."

"There's nothing that can be done for a broken nose." She set her hand on top of mine, holding the ice in place. "I've got it," she said. A leaf was on the carpet near her head. I picked it up and set it on the arm of the couch. "Patchins tells me this is the best room in the house. Which isn't saying much."

"He said the same thing about my room," she replied.

"Is that so?"

"Yes." I followed her gaze as she focused on the windowsill where the picture of my mother and me was balanced against the pane. "Is that you?" she asked.

"And my mother."

I took the picture from the windowsill and offered it to her as I sat on the floor next to her. She rose up on her elbow and looked from the picture to me. "She must have had very strong genes," she said.

"I'm not sure what you mean."

"You look a lot like her."

"If the truth be told, I don't really hold a candle to her." I got up. "Would you like some tea?" I searched my kitchen cabinets looking for the tea, but I could not find it. Did I drink it all? "I don't have tea." My voice verged on breaking, as if not having tea was not having anything at all.

Claire pulled her knees to her front and wrapped her arms around them. "It's not important."

"How's your head?"

"Clear."

My head was not clear. There was an ache far back in my skull, the same kind of ache I would wake with after a bad dream. "You get better and maybe we could take a walk…if you'd like."

After an indecisive moment during which time her eyes never left my own, she nodded. "Teach me how to climb trees."

"You don't know how?"

"I don't know how."

As she walked to my door, her movements had the indifference of one who is totally unconscious of her own grace, and left in me a sense of awe. "If your nose starts bleeding again or if you feel dizzy, just call," I said. "I'll hear you, I'll come."

"I believe you would."

***

In the nights that followed, I watched Claire from my window as she passed beneath the streetlight outside the mansion. Her eyes were black and blue. A pea-sized bump marked the bridge of her nose. I had changed her face. I wanted to touch the bruises around her eyes, to rub the blue away. But I couldn't move from the camouflage of my curtain, couldn't open my door as she knocked, simply could not. And if anyone had held me at the bottom of a river and asked me why, I would have had no reason beyond fear.

I wished for Hank or Mike or someone I hadn't even met to knock on my door. Maybe I would say to them: "I'm ready to know how making love takes everything away." Yet when Claire stopped knocking, I wished for her. Most of all, I wished for the kind of sleep that those who are not ghosts have the fortune to find.

Chapter Six

Nighttime in Willow, I stared at the pieces of peeling paint over my bed, and they became memories. Time may pass, but nothing fades away.

My mother and I pick huckleberries on the north side of the mountain from a patch that borders a small meadow. Following in the wake of her white gown, I carry the berry bucket as she circles the patch. Her fingers move deftly, collecting the dark berries. She offers the biggest berries to me. I open my mouth as she holds them over my head. They are sweet, but become sour as my mother grabs me by the arm and pulls me behind her. Her hand sweeps down to pick a stone from the ground.

In the meadow a black bear mauls a rotten log. Its cub scampers through the brush, batting at a butterfly. When it sees us, the cub makes a sound that is a cross between the laughter of a human and the hiss of a snake. The bear leaps in front of its cub and begins to charge us.

"Landy, stay behind me."

My mother's palms, stained from berries, are dark as a bear's paw. She throws the stone and it gives a dull thud as it hits the bear between the eyes. The bear takes the stone into its mouth and tosses it aside. My mother stamps her feet. Her voice is furious: "Get back, get back." The bear begins to circle us, drawing so close I can smell it. Its fur smells like wet earth and its breath is rotten and fresh: trout, berries, grubs, grass.

Slowly, my mother pivots, keeping the circling bear directly in front of her. Her eyes are wild and taunting. "My, but what large teeth you have," she says.

Grunting, the bear rises onto its hind legs and claps its forepaws together. My mother tosses her head and claps her hands. "If you're going to do it," she screams, "Do it now." She doesn't stop yelling until the bear drops to the ground. "Back up," she whispers. "Slowly, Landy." As the bear sets its eyes on me, I attempt to run. My mother grabs me by the hair and pulls me behind her. "Do you want to die? *Answer me.*"

Staring into her wild eyes, I shake my head.

"Then do what I say. Back up. Slowly. Stay behind me." As we retreat, she lifts her arms over her head and claps her hands. Frustrated, the bear clicks its jaws. "Go away," my mother screams. With a growl, the bear pushes its cub into the forest and disappears.

All the fear I have ever known passes through my eyes as I begin to cry. Kneeling, my mother cups my head to her front. "Don't blame the bear, Landy. I would have done the same thing if I thought someone was coming after you." The tips of her fingers are blue-black from the berries, sweeping the tears from my cheeks. "You're a very brave girl."

She dips her head and hides her face in her hands. Her shoulders shake. I think she is crying. But when she lifts her head, I see that she is laughing. Her laughter is like an underground stream rising to the surface. Her eyes fill with tears the color of stream water as she says: "It's hard to bluff an animal, Landy, much harder than it is to bluff a man. I hope you tell your grandchildren about the day your mother bluffed a black bear."

She tells me we are lucky that the grizzlies have moved to higher ground, for a grizzly would have surely killed us. I try to understand as she explains that the skulls of grizzly bears have not evolved in pace with their brains; the pressure of their brains against their skulls brings on blinding spells of pain. When the spells occur, grizzlies are more dangerous than any creature on earth. My mother sometimes suffers from similar spells of pain. I wonder if her brain is too big for her skull to house.

These are the days that are ours alone, when Stevie is only a plumpness in her stomach and an ache in her breast. On the mountain, the wind tosses her hair across her shoulders like a black shawl. Leaning down to me, she whispers: "I'd be happy to die on this mountain." She braids wild grass into a band and ties it around my forehead; roots cling to the grass and grains of dirt fall into my eyes. My head feels heavy with the weight of the grass band, feels vacant as I watch my mother move among the trees. She does not breathe the air; the air breathes her.

As the sun casts shadows across the peaks, she takes me in her arms and jogs down the dirt road toward Pike. Her feet do not seem to touch the ground. When we reach the cracked sidewalks of Pike, the fluid strides that carry her across the mountain hide inside her legs like memory; she takes careful steps down the sidewalk, as if balancing on a tightrope.

"Your father will be home soon," she says in a voice that is dreamy and tense—split. "Tomorrow we'll go to the mountain again."

At night, my father finds her cooking dinner as if she has been in the kitchen all day, every day. She takes his hands, etched with grains of sawdust, and lays them on her waist. His hands are a decade older than her own, a decade older than she'll become.

Instinctively, her face clouds with the words he says each night with an interrogator's persistence: "Headache?" Holding to her eyes, he searches for signs of pain.

"My head has never been clearer, Daniel." She draws his body to hers. In his arms she seems like a child, as I seem in her own.

He doesn't see me until I scoot from beneath the table and begin to run. When he leans down to me, the scent of pine tar rises from his skin, mixed with the salty smell of sweat.

"Got a hug for your old man, Alex?"

I press into my mother's legs as if there is a magnet inside them and I am metal. "Daniel, I will not have my daughter called by a man's name," she says to him.

He reaches out to me. I feel a tugging sensation as I pull away, but it is not his hands holding me back. It's the pitch attached to his fingers.

"She's like a wild thing," he says as I run away.

At the top of the stairs, I watch her take the butcher knife and cut the fatty edges from the pork chops, toss them in the sink. After she leaves us, I will use that knife to chop off my hair.

He lifts her hair and kisses the nape of her neck. A tremor passes through my body the same instant it passes through hers. When she slides his hand toward her breast, I feel cold and close my eyes. "Lizzy," he whispers. It is the name he calls her.

***

67

In my bed, the gray ceiling was like a flashing picture show. I remembered, through a picture my father burned, my mother and my father at a county fair:

She is dressed in a gauze shirt and a brown skirt which spins about her legs like a funnel cloud. The shirt is open low on her chest and her nipples are revealed through the transparent material, pressing against the gauze. On her hip is a holster. She and Daniel are at the county fair and she will not win the target contest.

Dread is a color in Daniel's eyes, an attentive shade of gray. When her eyes fasten to his, he no longer notices that the men stare at her with something of lust and the women something of envy, drawn to her as one is drawn to foreign things and mysteries.

She is beautiful and he thinks she is his.

***

Above me, the picture show flashed a series of shots. I closed my eyes and still the same pictures played in my mind. It was as if my memories are trying to break out of my head. I let them, I gave them a place on the ceiling of the mansion:

I wear my mother's gauze shirt one Halloween when Dad works swing shift and won't see. When the Widow Kyle opens her door to our call of trick or treat, her mouth falls open like a puppet's. "Your mama used to wear such clothes," she says, sprinkling candy into Stevie's pillowcase, then my own. "I thought the Goodwill came by for her things."

"I hid it," I say. "Don't tell him, please, he'll take it."

Widow Kyle drops an extra candy bar into my pillowcase. "Don't you be wearing that in front of him."

I am in bed, wide awake, when Dad comes home; he looks into the bedroom to see if we are safe and I put my finger to my lips. Stevie's body curls against my own.

Dad speaks in a whisper. "He's old enough to be sleeping in his own bed by now."

"He gets nightmares when he's alone."

"Don't we all." Dad taps the can of beer against the door frame. "I go off swing shift next week. I'll cook you two a spaghetti dinner. G'night now."

I memorize the ingredients of the spaghetti sauce so Stevie and I will have another dish to add to our list. He makes a salad also, with fried bits of bacon. It is always that way. The moment I am at the end of myself trying to trust him, he comes through, sometimes with ten bags of groceries, sometimes a haircut for Stevie, sometimes new shoes for us both. The best of times, he comes through with himself, taking us on afternoon drives down the washed-out roads of Mt. Abercrombie. He tells us stories of his youth as an only child to parents who hunted those roads. They died when a train hit their car as they were crossing the railroad tracks.

He loves us during those good times. You can see it in his hands setting us on his shoulders. A shoulder for me. A shoulder for Stevie. In between the good times, he holds a bottle. Every time he drinks, I know he thinks of my mother and wishes he could reshape the past the way he can shape a piece of hardwood, whittling it with a jackknife, and create a different end to the life of the woman he called Lizzy.

***

She tells me of her father and her mother getting married. Every time her hands relax, so do mine. And every time I feel the shiver take her spine, the anger in her voice, the confusion in her tone, the power of hate, I hold on to her tightly. My hands leave marks on her arms, but she doesn't notice. She has told me ghost stories, but the ghosts are good souls, looking for a place to rest. Now, she is telling me a bad ghost story, bad ghosts with people that she loves and hates dying. I wish the story would end. But it does not end. It continues through her, through me, like bad blood:

Lizzy's father, a rigger with the Redbank logging company, meets the woman who will become Lizzy's mother in a run-down bar on the edge of the Blackfoot Indian reservation near Browning, Montana. He loses a game of stud poker to her, gets drunk with her on Everclear pure grain alcohol and marries her the same night.

She follows him out of the fleabag Pine Cone motel and tips her head on the back of the seat as he begins the drive to Colville, Washington. Her hair is long and black and falls across the sides of her face like the flap of a tent as she drops her head and thinks, My God, what have I done?

As they drive out of Montana, he doesn't speak. Perhaps he wonders too, she thinks, what he's done. She lifts her eyes to his face. "What's our last name?" she asks in a voice as thick as the fog that blankets the highway.

"Gero." His gaze is blurred, as if he were staggering to his feet after a brawl. "Seems if you're my wife, I ought to remember your name. But I don't."

"Pearl." She makes herself sit high in the truck as it takes her away from everything and everyone she has known. Her head is level with his, brushing against the gun rack behind her; she is nearly as tall as he, five feet eleven, as lean as he, her shoulders nearly as wide. Cupping her palms over her eyes, she presses the thought inward, My God, I married a stranger.

He brings her to the outskirts of Colville where his home, a tarpaper shack constructed from scrap lumber, squats at the end of a dirt road. The weathered silver logs of the outhouse mark the west end of his three acres. Isolated, his parcel of land is surrounded by two hundred and fifty acres of forest owned by the city.

In less than a week, before Pearl knows where he keeps the jug of kerosene and the wicks for the lamps, he is leaving on another job. She would have stowed away in the bed of his truck if the job had been in Montana, she would have jumped out at the first stop near Browning and left him behind like a buried bone, but it is not Montana he heads toward. He leaves for a town called Pike, to the north.

Carrying a duffel bag, he pauses on the threshold and stares at Pearl in a demanding way that makes her angry, as if he owns her. He catches her by the arm and presses his mouth against hers. He is her husband and he is a stranger, and she winces as his rough cheek brushes against her own.

The screen door flaps open behind him. The screen is bloated, like the stomach of a pregnant woman; it contracts and expands as the wind sucks it in and blows it out. Pearl will shudder with a similar rhythm nine months later when she goes into labor unattended, thrashing upon the army cot in the corner of the shack. The bluish-colored edges of Lizzy's ears will redden as her mother's cries force her from the womb.

As she watches the dust rise behind his truck, Pearl wonders again what she did on that drunken night in Browning, and says aloud, "I married him," as if that is an answer she will learn to understand.

He leaves her for months at a time as he hitches on with logging crews that travel throughout northeastern Washington, northern Idaho, Montana. He returns to the shack for two and three-day visits which satisfy his needs. Pearl thinks of his sperm as slow swimmers, drowning before they find her eggs. But the thrusting that places them inside her is not slow. Quick he rolls atop her. The moistness he leaves is not mixed with the salty-sweet juice of her own arousal. She is thankful for the one child he fathers and is relieved that no more come.

Lizzy does not think of him as a father, for he is a father by blood only, white blood, and by the checks he sometimes sends from places with colorful names: Gypsy Ridge, China Falls, Jade Creek. He is her father, and he is a stranger, and she winces when she hears the sound of his truck coming up the dirt road.

Near Lizzy's seventeenth birthday, he returns from a job in Diamondback Valley. On her cot, Lizzy pulls the covers over her head as he says to Pearl, "You're my wife, that's why."

When he pins Pearl against the kitchen table and presses his body into hers, she scrapes her fingernails down his face. She hunches over as he strikes her in the stomach, but straightens when he steps toward her. She reaches behind her for the kerosene lamp and splinters it against his skull. From the floor, he kicks her legs and knocks her to the ground, and she continues to fight him with the understanding that she will kill him rather than bear the pain of him shoving inside her like a knife. For every blow he gives she gives one in return, until both of them are lying on their backs, covered with sweat, side by side on the plywood floor.

"Find a knothole," she says, crawling away. "It's all the same to you." She swings back the sheet, nailed to the ceiling, which separates Lizzy's cot from her own. The cot moans as Lizzy makes room for Pearl.

"Sleep with your daughter, will you?" he yells. "But not your husband?"

"Cover your ears," Pearl says.

Lizzy cups her hands over her ears. "He's too loud."

"Half-breed bitch," he screams. "I bring you here, I give you a home—this is what I get?"

"Shh," Pearl whispers, as Lizzy's body curves into her. "I used to sing you songs. Do you remember?"

"Oh, God," Lizzy answers. She rests her head on her mother's breasts as he paces in the outer room. "You won't let him in, right Mama?"

"Never." Pearl sings in a guttural voice: "Hush little baby, don't say a word. Mama's going to buy you a mockingbird, and if that mockingbird don't sing, Mama's going to buy you a diamond ring."

The form of his body appears behind the sheet, passes.

Pearl places her hands on the nape of Lizzy's neck. "And if that diamond ring don't shine, it's gonna surely break this heart of mine."

He has been gone a month when he returns from a job in Redrock Hills. Lizzy huddles in the corner as he throws Pearl against the wall. Hate is not a strong enough word to describe what she feels for him— bigger than hate, broader than hate, wider than hate. The hate is so strong she kneels under the table and wishes the ceiling would crash down on him. She would take her mother and run over the top of him as they vanished.

Her father does not believe Pearl when she tells him the check he mailed a week earlier hadn't arrived. He cups her throat in his hand. "Spent it, did you?" Pearl inches her head to the left and spits the taste of his whiskey-breath from her mouth. "Where's the check, bitch?"

"It's not," Pearl begins, "*Here*," and thrusts her knee into his groin, throwing him off her.

Groaning, he repeats: "Where's the check?"

Pearl lifts the lid from the wood stove and tosses it at his feet. "Get me some firewood and you'll get your check."

"You blackmailing me?"

"I am." She keeps her eyes fastened to his as he edges by her out of the shack. Casting her a piercing glance, he tosses the chain saw into the truckbed.

Pearl pulls Lizzy to her feet. "He'll be gone in a few days," she says. "We can live through it."

Lizzy watches him drive away. In the back of her mind, Lizzy wishes she was a fly swooping around his face as he take his firewood from the acres owned by the city, as he has for a decade. She knows that he hates flies, and if she were a fly she could drive him mad.

His parcel of land holds stumps and chokecherry bushes, ditches and dirt, and no trees worth cutting even to burn. He parks the truck at the side of a logging road a mile from the shack and carries the chain saw into the forest. A slick of sweat covers his forehead. He wipes his hands across his face and rubs them on his jeans, trying to free the oily sweat from his palms. Coming upon a fallen pine, he rips the cord and sets the blade spinning. "Rotten," he says, and plunges the nose of the chain saw into the tree. "Rotten bitch."

The saw hisses like a wild animal in his hands and springs

upward. He tries to tighten his grip, but his palms are coated with a sheet of oil. His left hand falls free as the saw strikes at a branch and recoils. "I'll beat you one-handed, bitch." He stumbles as the blade whips into the trunk and careens upward. Holding the saw over his head, he begins to fall. The blade spins toward his face, but he will not toss the saw clear even as he hits the ground, for he cannot believe that he will lose. Only when the saw slices across his cheekbone does he release the trigger. In the split second before the saw silences, the blade bites into his neck.

The school bus drops Lizzy where the dirt road meets the paved street, at the edge of the acreage owned by the city. As she runs through the forest, grains of dust give her hair a grayish tint. When she sees him, she cups her hands over her mouth and flees, falls to the ground retching outside the shack. The horror of seeing him is so great she cannot feel what lies beneath it: she is happy he is gone. She is so happy that each time she retches it feels like a spasm of delight. "His head, Mama, his head," Lizzy says, over and over, as she leads Pearl into the forest.

The first thing Pearl feels when she sees him is relief, and for a long while no greater feeling replaces it. "I tried to tell you," she says, staring down at him, "That I never got the goddamn check." He is sprawled across the ground. His head is nearly severed from his body and his lips are drawn back in a hideous smile. Pearl twists the head and tears it free, drops it into a water bucket and carries it to the shack. She buries it in the compost pile under four feet of earth, oak leaves, rabbit shit, eggshells, chicken feathers and ash.

Returning to his decapitated body, she picks up the chain saw and carries it toward the shack. As she walks down the leafy path, she traces the footsteps of her years with him, trying to find some sense in a senseless pair of lives. She searches for a feeling other than relief— grief? horror?—but feels nothing less than a pure sense of freedom.

As she wipes a handful of dirt against the blade of the chain saw, she has no fear that her heart is breaking. The fear is that her mind is breaking. The questions turn sideways, upon herself: How could she have lived with his name for eighteen years and only know enough of him to hate him, without having loved him? For eighteen years she hadn't returned to Browning, held back by a stubborn pride that she now hated more than she hated him.

She waits for him to emerge from the shadows, swinging his smiling head by the hair, and searches for him under the army cot she uses for a bed, under the wobbly kitchen table, under the floorboards where the pack rats hide spoons, quarters and bottle caps. Under the fragile layers of her mind, Pearl waits for him to appear.

She fears to sleep alone and draws Lizzy into the cot with her. One night she wakes screaming, wraps her legs around Lizzy and shivers until the sun breaks through the curtains she'd sewn from the shreds of a tablecloth, illuminating the patterns of red apples and yellow pears.

"It's daylight, open your eyes, Mama." Lizzy kisses Pearl's leathered cheek. She hopes that the dreams will stay at night, be a part of nightmares—a dream for her, another for her mother—and have no interference in the day. But they are different now, Lizzy and Pearl. Lizzy is certain that her father died simply because she asked for it; she wanted him dead and he died. She is careful of what she wishes for now. Good things. Maybe a mountain where no one can bother them. They did not need a house, a tree fort would be fine. Only a mountain, that's enough. She and her mother could live there, forever after.

"It's over," she said, running her hand across her mother's cheeks. "It's over."

"It's not over. We never buried his body." Pearl pulls his coveralls over her nightshirt and goes to the shed. Grabbing two shovels, she races down the dirt road. The nightshirt slides up from her waist and gathers in a ball between the coverall straps. Lizzy hesitates, her flannel nightgown flying in the wind, and follows Pearl into the woods a mile east of the shack where his body is partially hidden in a huckleberry patch.

"Dig," Pearl says, handing Lizzy a shovel. Together they dig a shallow grave. Sick from the stench, Lizzy retches into his grave. "We'll move him with the shovels," Pearl says. "Don't touch him, Liz. And don't look at him if you can help it." Lizzy turns away, her nostrils burning, and pushes the shovel into the small of his back. A tube-like object falls from his neck. Dropping the shovel, she jumps away. "It's his windpipe," Pearl says gently. "What'd you think it was?"

"I *thought* it was his windpipe."

Pearl stares down at him. "He was always an ugly sonofabitch."

His thighs are slashed from the teeth of coyotes, the beaks of magpies and crows. Thousands of maggots squirm across his flesh, hiding from the light. "They'll probably get food poisoning from eating you," Pearl says. Turning toward Lizzy, she begins to laugh. "Food poisoning."

Lizzy falls to all fours and holds her hair from the sides of her face as she retches. But there is nothing left inside her. She crawls away. "Just finish it, Ma." She watches from fifty yards away, a hundred, two hundred, as Pearl drops the shovels into his grave and tosses dirt into the place where his face had once been.

Again, Pearl begins to sleep alone. Each morning, she waves good-bye as Lizzy runs to the bus stop. As she has done since the day she found his body, Lizzy stays on the dirt road that leads from the shack to the paved street. She takes no diversions through the forest. She runs.

Pearl watches until Lizzy is out of sight. Only then does she stop waving. The moment she grows still, sharp pains sweep from her chest down her left arm. Pacing, sweeping, singing to herself, she stocks the wood stove in the June morning with no intention of baking. She spreads a mixture of mud and grass around the frame of the single window, closing the open space so that neither light, wind, nor mice can pass through, swings the hoe like an ax between the newly planted garden rows, and fastens her gaze on the sky as she tosses the kitchen scraps into the compost pile. The sweat forms in pools across her stomach and her chest aches, her heart pounds weakly. Wiping the sweat from her upper lip, she allows herself to rest. Sitting cross-legged on the ground outside the rabbit hutch, she offers lettuce to the rabbits, dropping the leaves between the mesh of chicken wire that encloses the circle of land.

She wraps her fingers around the wire and shakes the fence. The rabbits bound to the corner of the caged area; their ears fold back in fear. As they scurry from her, she thinks, I'm driving the rabbits mad. But she cannot keep from pummeling her fists into the chicken wire.

The nose of a rabbit with white hair twitches, and its eyes blink rapidly. Pearl tips her head to the side; her graying hair touches the ground. "What do you smell?" she asks. "Sweat? Not so pretty, is it?" In a single lunge, she thrusts her fingers through the mesh. Sniffing the air, the rabbit jumps away. Pearl stares into its pink eyes. "Gero?" The wire bites into the soft flesh between her fingers as she shakes the fence, screaming the only name she had ever called him, his last:

"Gero! Gero!"

She crooks her index finger through the wire and beckons the rabbit: "Come on, then, Gero, come on." She grabs the spade and opens the door of the hutch, corners the rabbit, takes its head in her hands and thrusts the spade into its neck. The moment its head rolls free, the pain rises from her heart and settles like a time bomb in her chest. Without Gero to hate and be hated by, her life has become an endless charade of washing dishes, cooking meals, cleaning up. She needs more, she *needs* the hate. She squints as she closes her eyes. The time bomb explodes.

As Lizzy approaches the lot, she hears the rabbits flinging themselves against the chicken wire. Inside the hutch, Pearl's back is pressed against the corner post, her head is cocked to the side and in her hands is the head of the white rabbit. Her face is splattered with blood and she wears the same smile her husband had worn in death, hideous and fierce, yet her eyes are open, staring at the head in her hands.

Lizzy doesn't know that Pearl is dead until she reaches out to her. As Pearl topples, the rabbits pat their hind legs against the earth, but their legs take them nowhere.

Lizzy dips the hem of her dress into the water bucket and washes the blood from Pearl's face, pries the head of the rabbit free and tosses it over the fence. She brushes her lips across Pearl's thick brows and smoothes them into a calm line, places her fingertips on the eyelids. For hours, she cannot find the power within herself to draw the eyelids closed. Pearl's eyes turn amber as shafts of sunlight pierce through them.

"You should have taken me with you," Lizzy whispers. The tears run down her cheeks and drop into Pearl's open eyes. Lizzy cannot bear to see her mother cry, so she closes her eyes, draws her fingers down and closes her mother's.

***

"Sometimes I think I see her," my mother says to me. "In the meadow. In the moon." A chill runs through my body as I look into my mother's dark eyes. "I keep looking. But it's never her."

***

Over my bed, in the dullness of gray paint, I saw a face, and it was Pearl's, then it became my mother's, then it became me.

Chapter Seven

Claire must have got a telephone, because it rang one evening. I was sitting on the arm of my couch, reading a back issue of *Cosmopolitan*. Now that the new issues were out, my manager at the IGA, Tiny, told me to tear off the covers and leave the old issues in the back room. I asked if I could take the magazine home, and he insisted it was a racy piece of reading, but if I had the yearning for it, go ahead and tear the cover off, put it in a bag, and take it home to read in the privacy of my four walls.

Through the thin plaster, Claire's telephone rang a second time. Claire called, "Can you get the phone?"

"You bet," April called back. I recognized the hoarseness of her voice, as if she'd been cheering at a game. And if April was there, that meant Sue was there. The dynamic duo, never apart. I wondered how two women could get along so well.

I leaned my head against the wall, thumbing through the magazine that Tiny thought was racy. One article caught my attention: how to ensure your husband is sexually satisfied to be certain he won't have an affair on you. The article said that to please him, pretend you just met him at a fancy restaurant—you don't even know his name—and in a titillating fashion ask him to return home with you. I questioned why you would want to treat a life-long lover, with ages of history between you, like a stranger. Teresa would know the answer to that: "For the fun of it." I read my *Cosmopolitan*, page after page, as if it was reading material for a course, like lifeguarding or CPR or the Heimlich maneuver, something that bores me now but would help me in the end.

Through the wall, I heard April talking on the phone. She called out to Claire, "It's long distance from Seattle. Your mom."

"Tell her I'll call her back in a moment."

April spoke into the phone, then called out to Claire, "She'll wait till you get out of the shower."

Claire was in the shower? She took a shower when her friends were there?

While Claire got dressed, April stood as a go-between, sending messages back and forth. In the past, it seemed she had conversations with the mother, for she referred to her as Mamaso, which is the expression Claire used with her.

"Mamaso is ready to kill your sister Kim," April called. Then she lowered her voice and spoke into the telephone: "Well, that's what you said. You said that you were ready to kill Kim." The hoarseness of April's laughter traveled to my room. "She's not ready to kill her," she called to Claire. "She's ready to take her over her knee and spank her."

"Tell her that'll be the day."

Sue's voice broke in, with the end of her sentences trailing off. "Is Kim your oldest…"

"No, the youngest," Claire responded. "Seventeen."

I turned my head to the wall and listened to Claire who had just gotten out of the shower. Probably, her hair was still damp and she wore a towel around her neck to catch its dew. Probably, she walked barefoot to the telephone.

"Mamaso," she said. "Uh-huh. Yeah." I heard a chair pull out, then Claire sat within it. "She did that?" Laughing, Claire tapped the wall. "What'd you say back? Oh Jesus."

I tried to listen, but April's and Sue's voices came into my room, talking about—of all the things in the world—NFL football. They loved the Seattle Seahawks and talked like this was the year they'd move out of the doldrums. "Blades is back," Sue said. She said it like a song. Blades is back, get back jack, as a matter of fact, get out of my sack, Blades is back.

I wanted them to lower their voices. I wanted to be able to hear Claire speak to that woman on the phone, her mother. To see how other people lived, how other children spoke to their mothers. To see, maybe, how it was done. But all that was delivered was, "Blades is back."

I was reading an article on cellulite in my *Cosmo*, and I'd stopped paying attention to the conversation in Claire's room. I heard the three of them start to motor, footsteps preparing to leave, and the magazine dropped from my hands. I didn't have to think about it, for if I thought I wouldn't be able to open my door and meet them in the hallway. Do not think, just act.

Her door and my door opened at the same time. I hadn't seen her since I broke her nose. Three times she had knocked; three times I could not answer my door. The blackness was gone from around her eyes, and her eyes were the brightest blue as she looked at me.

"Hi," I said.

"Hello, Alexandra." Behind her, April and Sue came out of her room, holding hands. "This is Alexandra," Claire said. "April, Sue." I backed into my door as they lifted their two hands that were one toward me.

April smiled. "So you're the mistress."

Before I knew what was happening, I had moved so close to her our chests almost met. She was almost as tall as I was. "I am not a fucking mistress," I said, pointing my finger at her face. "Have you got it?"

"It was a joke." April dropped Sue's hand and put her own up in surrender. "I'm sorry."

Sue had moved toward the stairs. She was smaller than April, and she looked at me with eyes that burn. "April, let's go," she said. "Come on."

"I am not his mistress," I said. "Everyone says I am, but I'm not."

Claire had taken a step and was now in between April and me. "All right."

"But you don't understand, none of you can understand."

Claire turned to her friends. "I'll meet you at the truck." She watched them walk down the stairs, then faced me. "Alexandra—"

"Your god damn voice, god damn it." I covered my ears and huddled on the floor against my door.

"What about my voice?"

My head went left and right along my door. "You don't know me."

"What about my voice."

I screamed, "It's not yours, it's hers, it's my mother's." There was a tightness in my chest, like you feel when you can't breathe. "Your voice is like hers. Sometimes…it frightens me."

"Why? Because I frighten you?"

"No. She…she does." I stared at the ocean of blue on the ceiling and watched it become a mountain. And then the mountain became

Claire, for she had moved my face to look at her own. Her finger was on my chin, and her hair was still damp from the shower, curling on her neck.

"My name is Claire Thomas," she said.

"I know that."

"No, you don't. Not in here." She placed her hand on my heart.

"Your name is Claire Thomas," I repeated. "Sometimes you sound like my mother, but you are not my mother."

"No," she replied. "I am not your mother."

"I'm so sorry, to act like this. I'm sorry, to have yelled so. I just wasn't thinking." When I began to rise up, Claire held her hands upon my knees.

"The three of us are headed to a barbecue," she said. "Why don't you come along."

"Me?"

For the first time, she smiled. "Yes," she said, ruffling my hair. "You."

"I can't."

"I thought you'd say that," she replied. "Why?"

"Because...because..." I took a deep honest breath and continued. "I will be ready someday, but today I'm not. If you ask me in, say, a couple of weeks from now, then I'll be ready. But I'm not today."

"You said before, that I don't know you."

"And I don't know you."

"Exactly," she replied. "And this is the way—very simple, very easy, a barbecue—that we can break that barrier."

"I'm really going to have to say no."

She helped me to my feet. "You know, this doesn't happen to me much anymore."

"What?"

"Getting turned down." She smiled. "See you, Stranger."

With her back to me, going down the stairs, she waved good-bye. In my room, I watched the three of them get into April's truck and drive away. April and Sue, they were probably lesbians. No wonder they were always together. And Claire...Claire was Claire, she was a woman, she had deep blue eyes and hair that was curly after she'd just gotten out of the shower, and she may as well be sleeping with dogs for all I cared. Claire was Claire, and until I learned otherwise that was as far as I took it. It became buried in that part of my brain that speaks when I am asleep.

***

I was nearing the end of my eight-to-five shift at the IGA when the bell above the door chimed and Hank, the bartender from the Saddle Inn, walked into the store. He didn't see me at first, not until I was at his side.

"You're looking good," I said, but it was a lie. He looked absolutely worn out, dog tired.

He reached into his pocket for a dollar bill. "I ran out of change," he said. "Quarters will be fine."

Putting the dollar in my till, I said softly: "For the laundromat?" When he nodded, that was all I needed to know that he had separated from his wife. People with homes and families, as he once had, don't spend their Friday nights at the laundromat. "There's spare rooms in my building, if you need a place to live."

"I found an apartment," he replied. "Up on sixth."

"It's not the black building, is it?" There was an apartment building, kitty-corner from Mike and Tree's house, that was painted all black, from the window frames to the walls to the door.

"That's the one."

I felt sorry that Hank had to live in such a place, though the mansion wouldn't have been much better. "If you ever feel like the walls are closing in on you or anything, you could get in your car and come visit me. I always have a spare cup of coffee." I dropped the money, a coin at a time, into his palm, as he leaned back on the heels of his feet, his eyes roving across my face. "Hot coffee. Anytime, Hank."

I cleaned my checkstand, readying it for the relief checker who came on at five o'clock. I wasn't in any hurry to go back to the mansion, would just as soon have stayed on until the store closed at nine. Most evenings I'd walk around town, sometimes dropping in on Mike and Teresa, and come back to the mansion after Claire's lights were out. It wasn't time to see her yet, it just wasn't the time. You see, I had this number in my head and that number was two weeks. In two weeks I would be ready to see her, but not today, because the two weeks hadn't passed yet. Maybe, in two weeks, we could go for a walk. Maybe I could teach her how to climb a tree. Maybe we could stay in that tree and have a conversation. But not now, because it wasn't two weeks yet. Somehow, I hoped that I would grow up in that two week period.

And, maybe, this night I would stay in, not that Claire would knock on my door, but in case Hank happened to knock on my door. I would take his hand and lead him to my bed. I would tell him: "I'll make you feel better, Hank." I would do that, if he let me, I would. Then I would know certain things, be a certain way, be a woman.

I began to fill the cigarette rack, putting the packs in neat rows; when I looked up, Teresa was standing in my checkstand. Her silent presence made me drop a pack of cigarettes.

"Come up for dinner after work," she said. "It's my birthday."

"You didn't tell me."

"I just did." Teresa set her hand on the small of my back as she leaned toward me: "And you know what good girls get on their birthdays."

As her eyes toyed with mine, my cheeks grew hot. "No."

"The birthday ball, Alex."

Her sweater-dress molded to her body like a second skin. There was no doubt she would know what to do if Hank ever knocked on her door. I could learn from her, just by watching. But I couldn't force myself to watch for longer than an instant as she flipped her hand through her hair and winked at me as she walked away. Her body, in that sweater dress—it was like watching the shadow of a woman moving behind a paper screen.

After work, as I headed up the hill toward Sixth, I stopped at a florist and bought Teresa a red rose and a yellow one, for a birthday present.

She met me at the door. She was dressed in a bathrobe and her hair was wet. "I'm early?" I asked.

"You're perfect."

"For you." I gave her the roses.

She brushed the petals of the red rose against her cheek; her cheek was the same color as the rose. Mike stepped out of the bathroom, zipping up his jeans and pulling a shirt over his head. He flipped the water from his hair as he went to the stove. Stiff backed, he said in a tense voice: "I hope you like spaghetti, Alex." Teresa shadowed him as he stirred the sauce, pressing her body into the back of his. When she whispered something into his ear, his jaw tightened and he tossed the spoon into the sink.

Teresa handed me a glass of wine and sat down for the meal, still dressed in her terry cloth bathrobe. It was open at her neck, revealing a patch of freckles on her chest. The belt was tied loosely. Any sudden movement would set it free.

"We aren't in such a hurry to eat that Teresa doesn't have time to get dressed, are we?" I asked Mike as he dropped the roll of French bread on the table.

He focused on Teresa with a distant gaze as she crossed her legs and placed her hand atop her bare knee. "I'm comfortable," she said. "Does my attire bother you, Alex?"

Taking a long drink of wine, I shook my head. "It's your birthday."

Throughout dinner, Mike was silent. It seemed to me, on his wife's birthday, he could have tried to be in a better mood.

"Did you see the roses Alex brought me?" she asked him.

Mike's eyes were neither warm nor cold, neither gentle nor harsh, meeting my own. "That was considerate of you."

Teresa kissed the skin above the line of his beard. "Mike has a gift too, don't you, Mike?"

When he tipped his chair back, crossing his arms to his front, I set my fork down and said to him: "Did you have a bad day?"

He took the bottle of wine and went to the living room, dropped onto the couch. He took a long swig of wine, then rolled himself a joint. Teresa sat in the easy chair across from him, and rolled her own joint. I didn't particularly want to sit next to Mike when he was in such a mood, so I sat on the floor at the end of the couch, my back to the wall. "Mike needs to unwind," she said. "He's been working on a poem. It's called, 'Marriage Sucks'."

Mike blew a cloud of smoke to the ceiling. " 'The Entrails' is what it's called."

"You know the poem," she began. "'Roses are red, violets are blue, sugar is sweet, and so are you'?"

"Yes."

"Well, it isn't like that. But that's all right, at least Mike is working."

"Of course we all know what John Dos Passos says: 'If there is a special hell for writers, it would be the forced contemplation of their own works.' " Mike dashed the cigarette butt into the ash tray. "That is, if I even considered myself a writer."

"A writer is what a writer does," Teresa said. "Today, yesterday, the day before, the day before that, you sit down and you write. Maybe it's doggerel and maybe it's not, but bullshit if you say you aren't writing." She looked at him and broke into a smile. "You just did it, didn't you? Changed the conversation, didn't you, Mikey?"

He gave a false, nauseous smile, like a used-car salesman. "We can talk about the price of tea in China."

"End of conversation." Teresa raised her glass. "Now, can we talk about something cheery, the fact that today is my birthday. Eat, drink, and be merry. I'm thirty years old today."

Mike slammed the bottle of wine down and began to pace the room in forceful strides as if he were trying to break the floor open. Leaning toward Teresa, I whispered: "What's the matter with him?"

"Ask him."

Mike wheeled around. "I'm a prince."

"Don't I know it, Mikey," she replied.

I stared at the two of them, not understanding anything of what was going on. Setting my drink on the floor, I said: "Maybe I should go."

Teresa had secrets in her eyes, I saw them there, but didn't know what they were. Flashing, bold, taunting. "What are you afraid of, Alex?"

For the first time, it occurred to me that I was afraid of her, and that I always had been. I was frightened of the way she wore her sexuality on her sleeve, frightened of the way she liked to wave that sleeve at me.

Pointing my finger at her, I said: "*You.*"

"And why do you think that is?"

"You have all the answers. You tell me."

"That's right. I do have some answers."

Mike stepped in front of her. "Lay off her, Tree."

She sidled past him, to me. "Are you comfortable sitting on the floor?"

"Yes."

"Floors are for dogs."

Inching away from her outstretched hand, I sat down on the couch. "I know things," I said to her. "I may not walk around showing it, but I know some things."

"I have no doubt about that, Alex."

As I stared at her red-painted toenails, part of me wanted to leave and part of me wanted to stay, so I could ask her about some of the things I didn't know, things maybe she would know. 'Endless light'—I wanted to know what was so mysterious and wonderful about those words. My mother said she sometimes felt 'endless light' with my father.

I felt endless darkness as Teresa smoothed the bathrobe at her neck and said: "There are rituals to sexual passage." Mike was no longer pacing. He leaned against the far wall. His head was tipped to the ceiling and his eyes were nearly closed. "But most aren't practiced anymore," Teresa said. "That's unfortunate, don't you think?" My wine glass turned red as she refilled it. "One ritual involves an older, experienced man. And of course the mandatory virgin."

I took deep breaths, staring at the floor, as she continued: "Egg whites are massaged across the girl's vulva. He eases her open with his fingers. Gently, no hurry. His role is to ensure only pleasure when she accepts him. No pain." Teresa went to the kitchen and came back with an egg in her hand. "If you were treated that gently, there'd be no need for fear. So the question remains—what are you afraid of?"

From the shadows, Mike met my eyes. "Is this your idea?" I asked him. His earring shifted like a triangle with sides that never settle as he shook his head. I emptied my wine glass, looking from one of them to the other. "Do you two do this all the time, or is this a one-shot deal?"

"It's actually a birthday present," Teresa replied. "From Mike to me. From us to you."

"You *want* this?"

"The thought certainly intrigues me."

"But he's your husband."

"So?"

"You wouldn't be able to do it," I said to Mike.

"I'm sorry," he replied. "But you're wrong."

I felt cold all over as I began to laugh. "You two deserve each other."

Teresa smiled. "We all deserve each other. That's the point."

"You will not touch me," I said to her. "You will stay right where you are."

"No insult intended, Alex, but I'm not interested in touching you. Mike. Mike only."

I took the egg from Teresa and tossed it in the garbage pail. "Happy birthday." Walking to their bedroom, I called, "So show me how it's done, Mikey."

He leaned against the threshold as I took off my clothing and threw it to the floor. When he reached for the light switch, I took his hand. "Leave the light on," I said. "But close the door."

The sheets were cold. Mike did not join me within them. He sat on the edge of the bed with his hands on his knees. "Do you know what you're doing?" he asked.

"I was hoping that you did."

"We can leave this room," he replied. "We can try to act like this didn't happen."

"Whatever does or doesn't happen now, it's already happened, Mike." He tipped his head to the ceiling as I slipped his shirt off. Unbuttoning his jeans, I pulled the zipper down. "Get in." His body was hot. I felt its heat as I ran my hand across his thighs. "Come on now, Mikey, you can do it."

When I slid my body on top of his, he placed his hands on the sides of my waist and turned me, so that we were side by side. "Slow down," he said.

I held to his shoulders as I rolled onto my back, pulling his body to mine. "Fuck you, Mike, fuck you." Digging my fingers into his thighs, I pulled him inside me. When he tried to move away, I grabbed a handful of his hair and whipped his face to mine. "You like it, don't you, Mikey, you like how I can do." Closing my eyes, I pressed my face into his neck. My words came like memory—a memory I could not grasp. "Hit me, Mikey, you know I like it when you hit me." Confused and frightened, I hid my face in his neck. "You know I like it."

"Well I don't," he replied.

When I struck him in the face, he grabbed my arms and pinned them behind my head. "Fuck you," I said. His mouth swallowed my words, but my voice came back, louder, urgent, out of control: "Come on, Mikey, show me how it's done." I bit his shoulder and he released my arms. His back tensed as I scraped my fingernails down the line of his spine. "Hit me, you bastard, hit me."

"In your dreams, Alex."

I wrapped my legs around his and dug my toes into his flesh. "Motherfucker, motherfucker." As he lunged deeper inside me, I bit his lip and tasted his blood. "Yes you do," I said. "You like how I can do."

I looked past his back as the door opened. Teresa slid her hand into her bathrobe as Mike's hips rocked in rhythm to mine. Digging my fingers into his spine, I stared at the ceiling and felt his body tremble, felt his breath rush against my neck. There was no endless light. Everything was dark. In that darkness, I threw Mike's body off me. Turning my back to Teresa, I pulled on my shirt and jeans.

"I always knew you had it in you," she said. "I see I wasn't wrong." She looked at Mike who lay on his back, his forearm covering his eyes. "You had yourself a handful, didn't you, Mikey?"

Pushing past her, I stumbled as I left the room. "Leave me alone," I said. "You got what you wanted."

"You're forgetting something," she replied. "You also got what you wanted."

I ran down the streets to the mansion. Dark outside, everything dark. In my room, I filled the bathtub with boiling hot water. The water burned my skin red, leaving a dividing line in the center of body. I dried my legs, wiped the droplets of water from my face, and pulled the sleeping shirt over my body. When I looked in the mirror, I threw up.

In the living room, I sat on the floor and stared at the picture of my mother resting on the windowsill. I tried to think of good things, but everything that had once been good was now an ache in my head. I tried to say a prayer, but every prayer became a nursery story that did not rhyme. As I stared at my mother's picture, I thought of the mountain and began to shiver. The memories filtered out of her eyes and into mine.

Like this:

Kneeling next to the stream, she cups water to her mouth and swallows the pill that never has the power to take the pain out of her head. When she rises, she grips my hand and leads me to the meadow where our blanket is spread. Her eyes are glassy. I know what they mean.

"Come here, Landy."

She lifts her hands over her head and I pull the gown off, set it at the foot of the blanket. When she opens her arms, I fold against her body. Her breasts are like pillows. For a moment, I feel safe. But I am afraid as she lifts my face in the palm of her hand.

"Hit me," she says.

I close my eyes. "No, Mama."

She takes my hands and places them on top of her skull. Her voice is pleading. "When you hit me, the pain goes away."

Into my hand she places a long sinewy branch; she has removed the bark and the needles. It is like a whip in my hand.

"Please, Landy," she says, as she lays on her stomach. Her back is unmarked. No welts remain from the last time the pain was this bad. "Make it go away," she says.

My legs shake when I stand. Her fingers dig into the earth as I bring the branch down as hard as I can, over and over. "One, two, three," she whispers. "One, two, three." I collapse on the blanket next to her, hide my face in the small of her back.

Her voice is weak. "Thank you, baby."

As she draws me to her front, her voice changes; it is the color of redwood. "How was I so fortunate as to receive you?" Looking into my eyes, she lowers my head to her breast. My mouth finds her nipple. "You know I love you, Landy, you know I do."

She guides my fingers inside her; they are small fingers, three, four and five years old. They disappear inside her. She directs my lips to the moist fold of skin between her legs. "You're so good, baby, so good." She places the branch in my hand and presses my head to her thighs as I bring the branch down across her chest. "So good," she says. "So good."

I drop the branch as she trembles beneath me. "Yes, like that." In the dark afternoons, the bright mornings, the humid days of summer, she cradles my head, saying: "Like that."

She trembles as if in pain, yet she tells me this is not pain, this stops the pain, this is like God. Holding my shoulders, she makes sounds as if in pain, yet this is not pain. *She told me this was not pain.* Her hips lift off the blanket. "You know I like it, baby," she says. "I like how you do."

Her voice becomes the sound of breath only and her hands fall from my head. The sun looks down at us. It offers no forgiveness, for we ask for none.

"It's a narrow-minded world that would condemn us. They'll never understand." She tips her head and stares at the sky. "Endless light. A few times I've even felt it with Daniel." Smiling, she winks at me. "More times, I simply pretend. You'll understand someday." She traces her finger across my shoulders. "You're getting sunburned. Here, let's put your dress back on." I stand as she pulls my dress over my head. She licks her fingers and smoothes my hair. "Don't let anyone tell you this is wrong."

***

I was in the corner of my room, huddled on the floor, when I saw Claire kneeling in front me. Her hands were on the sides of my face and she was calling me by a name that was not my own. Her eyes were misty—blue—fastened on my own.

"I don't know what to do," I said. "Tell me what to do."

Above us, the shadow of my mother appeared on the ceiling. Her hips slid down the walls. But she wasn't in the ceiling and she wasn't in the walls. She was sitting on the windowsill, staring at me. Reaching up, I turned her picture over so that I would not have to see her dark eyes.

Pressing my face into Claire's hands, I said, "She died. I was five. My father sold her mountain. Sold her grave. June, last June. No one forgets. She died." My voice was hoarse, scratchy. I began to cough. When Claire offered me a glass of water, I spilled it down my front. "Oh look, look at what I've done."

Claire cupped her hands to my knees. Her hands were shaking. "You're not to blame."

"You—you were lonely? You came to visit me?"

"You were screaming, Alexandra."

"I don't do that."

"Yes," she replied. "You do."

Outside my window, the sun was rising like heartache, shedding a gray light on the trees. I stared at it for a long while, folding my hand across my throat, before I could find the power to turn back to Claire. "Mary Magdalene washed Jesus' feet and he blessed her, that is true?"

As she cocked her head, I hoped she would tell me, Yes, He will make me pure because He was given to this world for sins such as my mother's and mine.

"Do you believe in Him, Claire?"

Tapping her hands against my knees, she stared at me, but did not answer.

"There is yes. There is no. There is black. There is white. Please don't tell me it is gray."

Once again, Claire's hands came to the sides of my face. "There are people who can help you," she said. "But I don't know how,

89

Alexandra. I don't know how."

Pulling away from her, I backed into the window, reached behind for the picture of my mother, and braced it against the pane. "You don't know? You don't, huh? They don't teach you that in speech pathology school?"

She was standing near the window, and her body shadowed my mother's picture. "Not this, no."

I set my hands on my hips and stared at her. "You didn't hear a thing," I said. "Not a fucking thing. My real life is this—this is my real life. I don't even live near a mountain anymore, for Christ's sake."

"You speak in your dreams," she whispered. "That's what I heard."

"Lots of people talk in their sleep."

"You said, 'One, two, three, one, two, three.' You remember, Alexandra, I know you do. You've got to talk about it to someone."

"Shut up!"

She held to my shoulders. "You were hitting the arm of the sofa."

"I told you to shut up."

"And you were crying, and begging your mother to please stop making you hit her. You looked at me with the eyes of five year old child, begging me to make it stop. And I am, Alexandra. You don't have to talk to me, but you need to deal with this."

I stared beneath her, at the picture of my mother. "Deal with it?"

"Yes." Then, slowly, she said, "Incest."

"She never once touched me in her life, not once." I shrugged her hands off my shoulders. "You don't know." She searched my face as if looking for that five year old child who answered to Landy. "It hasn't been two weeks yet," I whispered. "Not even two weeks."

"Two weeks?"

"In two weeks I was going to be a new kind of woman. But I don't feel new. Everything is ragged inside." The eyes of my mother caught my own and wouldn't let go. "It was a spell, that's all. I'm fine now."

Claire tipped her head and stared at the ceiling. "I have no idea how to help you."

"Help? I never asked for help from anyone." I pushed her away from me and kept my eyes focused on the shaggy carpet. Claire's eyes, my mother's eyes—I wanted them all to go away. "I don't need you, I don't want your help. You're going to get nothing from me, nothing. It's my life and I control it. *I* control it. And I am asking you to leave my room."

When I looked up, I saw fear in her eyes. "It was a five year old child who was huddled in this corner. It was no spell."

"I'm not five anymore. And I'm telling you it's over."

Claire paused, one foot in my room, the other out, indecisive in her pose. "It's not."

As she left my room, I kneeled before the windowsill. My mother looked down at me. "It isn't so," I whispered. "It isn't so."

Chapter Eight

Kneeling by the window, I look above the picture of my mother and into the world. Clouds scatter the sky, dousing the stars. I put my arms on the sill and rest my head on top, and stare at the sky. My mother says a rhyme: *Roses are red, violets are blue; because you love me, I will love you. Let the birds sing and the lambs play; we shall be safe, out of harm's way.* The clouds in the newly breaking day become memories of that time when we were not safe, in harm's way:

Stevie is with us only at night, when Dad is home. During the day, my mother leaves him with the Ramsteads who live in a shack near Mill Creek Road, while we go to the mountain. She pays Mrs. Ramstead for the care and the secret with pieces of clothing, and sometimes with Ben Franklin half-dollars taken from Dad's coin collection, as I will take them after she is gone. She returns for Stevie each night before Dad's shift ends. When he cries for food, she gives him a bottle and not her breast.

Stevie sleeps in a crib in the room next to mine. I hear no sounds from him as I lie in my bed. I cannot sleep. I take my blanket and huddle at the top of the stairs, look down at the two of them. I do this every night after she tucks me in, watch them until my eyes grow tired. Dad sits on the couch. He is reading the evening paper. Beside him, my mother studies a magazine that has pictures of beautiful homes, beautiful gardens. She has been careless this night; her collar is open low on her chest. His eyes make a path to the welts that crease across her upper chest.

"What happened?" he asks.

"I was working in the yard," she says coolly, smoothing the collar of her shirt. "You know that root you keep promising to dig up? It caught my foot. The rake was waiting."

"I'll dig it up," he says. "This weekend." He holds the newspaper in one hand; his other hand is draped across my mother's shoulder. He lowers his head and reads. She stares up the staircase, sees me hidden behind the railing. I have never seen such a look in her eyes before—more than grief, more than sorrow. Her hand shakes as she fastens the top button of her collar. The shame of looking at me is so great that she closes her eyes.

The next morning when I wake up, the Widow Kyle is in our kitchen. Her back to me, she is on her knees, scrubbing at dark pools that stain the hardwood kitchen floor. Behind her is the wastebasket. A dish towel sits atop an empty milk carton. White, it is stained with dried blood. The Widow's hair is the color of a mouse and it falls over her eyes as she scrapes the steel wool against the dark circles on the floor. She does not see me as I pick the towel up. Beneath it is the butcher knife. Its wooden handle is brown with blood. *Red blood, she was a red woman.*

The Widow lurches as the knife falls from my hand and drops to the floor. She turns to me, wiping her hands on her apron. Her voice is quivering. "Your mother, she never does keep a clean kitchen floor." I nearly trip over Stevie as I run into the living room. He is playing with toys Dad carved from cedar; building blocks with the letters of the alphabet whittled into them, a six-inch canoe, a car with wooden wheels that don't move. The Widow grabs me when I try to run past her up the stairs. Her hands hold me down as I fight to get away. "Your mama is sick," she says. "Your daddy took her to the hospital. He'll be home soon."

Stevie crawls across the floor. His diapers hang low on his hips and his stomach is a pink melon. He pushes his head into my feet and sucks on the end of my shoelace. When the Widow reaches for him, I run to the kitchen and hide beneath the table. The Widow can do nothing to make me come out and finally leaves me there with a blanket and a pillow, until Dad returns.

He kneels on the floor and reaches for me. I curl into a ball.

"She tripped on the root," I whisper. "She fell on the rake."

"She's going to be all right," he tells me.

When he pulls me to him, I bury my head in his chest. "She's coming home?"

"When she's well," he says. "She's coming home." We sway forward and back, like a rocking chair will do long after a body has risen. "She's going to be fine," he tells me, over and over again.

He leaves Stevie and me with the Widow Kyle while he is at the mill or visiting my mother in Spokane, two hundred miles south of Pike, in a place called Pleasant View. Every night, I watch as he spoons the baby food into Stevie's mouth and places him in his crib. He covers Stevie with the blanket the Widow made for him. It is blue with strips of green satin on the border. At my bedtime, he kisses the top of my head and covers me with the blanket the Widow made me. It is pink with red satin strips on the border. When he closes my door, I kick until the blanket falls to the floor.

Forehead pressed against the Widow's picture window, I search for my mother, but she doesn't appear on any horizon beyond my mind for an eternity, half a year. She comes back to us on New Year's day of my fifth year. I run outside as Dad's truck pulls into the driveway. Before she can step down, I throw her door open and wrap my arms around her legs. But she does not embrace me, she does not move or say my name. Dad comes to me; gently, he pries my hands from her legs. As he helps her out of the truck, the hot ash of tears starts up in my eyes. Her skin is the color of old newspaper. Her lips are white, dry and cracked. Her fingernails are bitten away. Jagged scars criss-cross both of her wrists.

Dad brushes the Christmas tree with his shoulder as he leads her to the living room. An ornament falls. My mother jumps away from it and wraps her arms around herself. She stares at her feet as Dad leads her up the staircase to their room. Not once does she look at me.

Outside their closed door, I listen to the sound of his voice saying words I cannot hear and awake in my own bed where one of them placed me deep in the night.

He stays home for a week to care for her. She spends the days sitting in the easy chair in front of the picture window. Even when I stand in front of her, she will not look at me. Dad places me on his lap and reads me stories about horses and lions. He tells me that she needs to rest, that she will be fine in time. When Stevie crawls up to her she stares at my father and he takes Stevie into his arms. He tells me we need to be patient, that all we have is time.

But he runs out of time. His sick leave from the mill is used up. They will permit him to remain with us for as long as he needs, but they cannot pay him for it. As he leaves for work, the Widow Kyle meets him on the walk and takes Stevie from him. He gives her a bag filled with everything that Stevie needs: bottle, baby food, stuffed animal, blue blanket. In that bag are also the things he thinks I need: books, crayons, drawing paper.

He leans down and sets his hands on top of my feet. The snow that is caught in the cuffs of my pants melts with his touch. "Do what Mona tells you," he says.

The Widow pulls her coat over Stevie to protect him from the winter air. "I can check in on Lizzy while you're to the mill if you like." I look up at her and remember how the lines would furrow into her forehead when she used to watch my mother from her picture window. I can tell, by the slow way Dad places his hands in the hip pockets of his trousers, that he remembers it too. "I'm not saying I'll pull up a chair and drink the morning coffee with her," the Widow says. "But I'll look in if it'll help you rest easier."

"I'd be grateful."

The Widow gazes at our house. Her jawbone tightens beneath the folds of her skin as she turns away. "They send some medicine back with her?"

"Drugs to keep her calm and drugs to regulate her chemistry," Dad replies in a voice that floats far over my head. "They gave me two choices: allow them to give her more electric shock, or bring her home and see if memory will do its healing." As if she hears him, my mother opens the curtain and stands framed in the window in a stark white gown.

"They give you any reasons why this happened in the first place?"

"Yes," he says. "When she first came to, she talked to them. But she hasn't been talking much since."

My insides shake as I stare up at him, but my voice doesn't leave my head. *She fell on the rake.*

"They say it's things from before she came here," he says.

"What might you be talking about—things?"

He stares at my mother as she stands in the picture window. "Seeing as how she never felt comfortable telling me, and everything I know comes from the men in white jackets, I don't think she'd be too happy if I told you."

"You've always been a loyal man," the Widow replies. She shifts Stevie from one hip to the other. Oblivious, he begins to laugh. "Some would say it's your best trait. I'm not sure I'm one of them."

"Every one of you in this town looked for a reason to hide her," he says. "Now you've got it."

A flurry of snow encircles the Widow's boots as she steps toward him. "Don't you think it's strange she's never bothered to share a word with a one of us? Not even to answer a simple howdy-do? For months after you first brought her here we tried to get her to come to one house or another for a cup of coffee. No doing. Not even a thank you for asking. Any hiding was done by her, not us." When the Widow shakes her head, her hair frames her face like gray strings. "You don't need fancy doctors to figure out how she got in this condition. Common sense will tell you it's her way of living that did it. If I lived in the isolation she's created for herself, I'd be sleeping with my chickens and thinking they could tell me goodnight."

Dad's voice is soft. "You don't know a thing about it, Mona."

"I do know one thing. Women are social creatures. God knows I loved my own children but I certainly would've been in a crazy house if I hadn't been able to send them off with some other kids now and then and share a cup of coffee with my neighbors. Didn't you ever wonder about that? Don't you ever worry about your daughter not ever having the chance to spend time with kids her own age? It's not natural. Not for the mother and not for the child."

Dad puts his hand on top of my head. "She'll be in school soon. There'll be plenty of opportunity to play with kids."

Lines of age cross down the Widow's upper lip and to the lower, like the teeth of a zipper, as she gazes at my house. "I can't say I've ever understood your wife. Fact is, she makes me nervous. Always has. But I'll look in on her while you're to the mill." She throws her door open and the heat from her wood stove blasts out. "You better get yourself to work before Hogan fires you." Dad takes long steps down the sidewalk he'd shoveled for her the day before, now covered from the night's snowfall. He'd shovel it again that night, and the next, throughout the winter, as he'd done every winter since Mr. Kyle packed a single suitcase and left.

The Widow Kyle guides me inside. Her house smells of calamine ointment, bacon, coffee, lavender bath powder. "Settle in, Landy." She pulls a chair from the kitchen table and sets me in it, shifts Stevie to her front and begins to wash her morning dishes one-handed, scraping the bacon grease from the frying pan and slopping it into an empty coffee can. A poinsettia is potted in a butter churn on the kitchen counter. She tosses an eggshell into its soil and crushes it with her fingers. She doesn't notice I am going until I am already gone.

Every morning Dad leaves us with the Widow and every morning I run away. Placing Stevie in the playpen Dad built from scrap lumber, the Widow follows my footprints in the snow to the door of our house. She searches for me under the beds, in the kitchen cabinets, the root cellar. I hide beneath the couch. She can't find me because she won't go near my mother who sits in the center of the couch, her hands folded atop her knees.

"I know she's here somewhere," the Widow says. "And if you're worried about your son, you'll tell me where she is, 'cause I'm not leaving here until I find her. Stevie's in my house, all alone. God knows what he's into. So where is Landy? I'm not leaving without her."

Silent, my mother rests her eyes on the Widow's face.

"I'm not leaving."

My mother lifts her right eyebrow.

The Widow slaps her hands against her hips. "Send her over, do you understand?"

When the Widow leaves, my mother does not send me away. She opens the book of nursery rhymes that she bought me after my book was burned in the fire in our back lot. She flips the pages, stopping in the center of the book. I cannot read the words to the nursery rhyme, but I know them by heart from the drawings which surround them, from the days when my mother used to recite them for me. She traces the drawings on the page—blue ribbons, blue bows. I hear the words inside my mind: *If you love me, love me true; send me a ribbon, and let it be blue. If you hate me, let it be seen; send me a ribbon, a ribbon of green.*

I find her sewing basket in the hall closet—red, yellow, blue and green ribbons inside. I throw the green ribbon aside and lift the blue one toward her. It dangles like a thin strip of sky. She turns the page.

Widow Kyle catches me by sneaking in through the back door and snatches me from the couch. Every day it is the same. After a month, her ankles are swollen from chasing after me and her cheeks are a constant red flame. "I can't control her, Daniel."

Dad begins to take me to the mill with him. He brings a red kickball, crayons, coloring books, a box of raisins, a carton of juice, and seats me at the table in the lunchroom. On his morning break, he checks in on me and I am gone. He finds me at home with my mother, the two of us silent as winter.

He carries me back to the mill and sets me at the table in the lunchroom, places the box of crayons in my hand. "I'll have to spank you if I come out here and you're home again. Don't make me do it, Landy."

When he finds me at home, I follow him without argument to the woodshed. He sits on the chopping block and I drape across his knees. As he taps my backside with his open hand, there is no pain for me, but it seems he will cry from it. "I hope you've learned your lesson," he says.

At the mill, he sets me on the tailgate of his truck and lifts my head. I have nowhere to look but at his gray eyes; they are moist, like raindrops on granite. "I can't be letting you stay with her, not yet. She's in no shape to care for a child. When she's better, it'll be different. But for now you have to do what I ask." Unmoving, I stare up at him. "I'm not trying to punish you by keeping you here," he says. "How can I make you understand?"

How could I make him understand? My mother needed me to turn the pages of her book, to fill her glass with water, to pass my hand across her eyes. She needed me to remind herself that she was not dead. "If I go," she once said, "You're going with me." I needed to be there in case she decided to go away.

The moment he leaves me in the lunchroom, I run down the streets past the mill and into our house, sit on the couch next to her. A fly walks across her wrist. I shoo it away and stare at the jagged pink scars. Dad finds me at break time. "If this is a contest of wills, you ought to know right now that you're going to lose." He sets me on the kitchen table and places his hands on my knees. "I want you to listen to me—" My mother grabs his hands and lifts them over her head. Sounds surface from her throat, but no words come.

"Lizzy?" He pulls her arms down to her sides. When he touches her shoulders, it is as if her spine is breaking, the vertebrae shattering into the pockets of her lungs. She stares at his chest as he pulls a greasy strand of hair from the corner of her mouth. He picks up the phone and calls the mill. He doesn't go back to work for a week.

I hide behind the woodshed as the Widow brings him a cup of tea while he shovels our walk, then starts on hers. "Maybe I was wrong bringing her back here," he says to the Widow. "She's not getting any better."

"Have you talked to the doctors?"

"They say maybe…maybe she won't get any better."

"You got a hard choice ahead of you, Daniel."

His hands encircle the cup. Steam rises into his eyes. "She's off somewhere in her head and when she gets her fill of it there, she'll come back to us. She just needs to be given the time."

My mother is calm when he takes me with him and leaves for the mill. She sits on the couch and turns the pages of the magazine he bought for her, with pictures inside of beautiful houses, beautiful gardens. At the door, I watch as she curves her lips around my name. He sets me on his shoulders as he walks across the lot to the mill. "Suppose you wonder why she won't talk?" he asks. When I don't answer, he continues in a voice stronger than the one he uses with her, as if I am less of a child than she. "Could be many reasons. Could be she doesn't want to. Can you tell me why it is for you?" Staring at the mountain of sawdust ahead of us, I shake my head. "We got time, Landy, plenty of time."

He sets me at the table in the lunchroom and places the box of toys in front of me. "I thought I'd stop by the inn on the way home and bring your mom a treat. Cheeseburgers. Fries. Chocolate shakes. Think she'd like that?"

"Strawberry," I say softly. "She likes strawberry shakes."

Dad smiles. "When you hear the noon whistle, you be ready to run on over to the inn with me, all right?"

By the time the noon whistle sounds, I am with my mother. He does not stop at the inn when he comes to fetch me. Months pass like this, with neither of us backing down. Then Hogan tells Dad that chasing after me week in, week out, is leaving him short-handed too many times a day. Dad begins to leave me again, with Stevie, at Widow Kyle's where nothing changes. One evening the Widow meets him on the walk and hands me over like a lost cause. "I'll keep trying if you want," she says, "But it seems nothing short of a chain is going to keep her away from her mother." Sawdust clings to Dad's neck, grainy as dirt, as he stares down at me. I expect him to look angry, but he doesn't. He looks tired, gray circles under gray eyes. "Landy's already spending more time over there than she does with me," the Widow says. Stevie's head pokes out of the top of the Widow's coat. He makes gurgling noises as she cups his head in her hands. "Course I'd keep Stevie as long you need me to. And I'd look in on Landy and her mother."

When Dad leans down to me, I place my index finger on his neck and make a path in the sawdust as my mother used to do. She had great power when she touched him that way. "What do you do all day?" he asks.

"We read."

"Read?"

"Nursery rhymes."

He takes my hand from his neck, holds it in his own. "If anything frightens you, go straight to Mona's. Anything at all. A tree slapping the window. Anything. You go straight to Mona's. All right?"

"Yes," I say, but it is a lie. Nothing could be so frightening as to make me run away from her. Just that morning, she had taken a graying snapshot from her cedar chest. The woman in the snapshot had features like my mother's, but harsher; cheekbones like cliffs, hooded eyes, thick lips. My mother lit the picture on fire and didn't release it until the flames burned her fingertips. I had been afraid of the way she keened as the picture burned, but I wouldn't tell Dad that, because he'd send her back to the place that took her language away. He called it the asylum. The asylum equals 'A Sky Limb,' a sky limb burning inside Hell. No one had to tell me. A Sky Limb took her language away. My father sent her there once and he had the power to send her there again. I would go with her even there, to A Sky Limb inside Hell.

"Promise me," Dad says.

"Yes."

With that promise, he does not take me away from her again. Each morning, she takes pills the color of a rainbow. Throughout the day, based on a schedule Dad writes in a tablet, she takes the tranquilizers. Dad takes one of her tranquilizers once, to understand their effect on her. All day he walks around the house in a daze and speaks to her as she stares at him like a mirror: "No wonder you don't talk. Christ."

One day we are drawing pictures at the kitchen table and she doesn't take the mid-morning dosage. When afternoon comes, she doesn't rise from the sheets of drawing paper to take her pill. By evening she is staring out the window with her eyes focused on her mountain. She does not swallow a single pill again. In the morning, she takes the pills from Dad's hand and presses them under her tongue. When he turns away, she spits them into a napkin. Throughout the day she leaves check marks next to the dosage schedule, removes the pills from the bottle and washes them down the drain. Her pictures, drawn with every color in the crayon box, begin to multiply and change. She draws roses, houses with picket fences, children who smile, the mountain. Her way with Dad begins to change. She greets him on the walk in the evenings and laces her arm through his. Her voice returns, strong enough to whisper words in his ear as she takes his hand and leads him up the stairs to their room. In the mornings before he leaves for work, he tells her that he loves her. And she says it back.

I watch them from the top of the stairs as she tells him that she wants Stevie to continue staying with the Widow during the days. "I just need a little more time, Dan."

"All we've got is time." He says it differently now; he says it with hope.

Her voice is the color of redwood, telling me nursery rhymes, as we walk to the mountain. Her voice can make brown leaves green. I have missed the sound of her voice, I have missed her. She holds my hand as we walk across the meadow. "There's no reason to be jealous of your father. I love him differently than I love you. No one can please him more than I. There is strength in that, Landy."

I follow her to the edge of the canyon. She kicks a stone and it drops down the sheer walls. Holding to her gown, I say: "I can't fly, Mama."

"I won't leave you again."

Above us, a crow stretches its wings and draws circles in the sky. In its shadow, she removes her gown and asks me to take her pain away. She is my mother and I will do anything to ease her pain, to make her stay.

***

After her death, Dad sets her pill bottles in a row in front of him; his voice is the sound of a beehive: "I didn't see it coming," he says, "How could I not have seen it coming?" He throws the door open and goes to the shed. The tears explode from his eyes as he swings the ax into a chunk of pine. The wood gives no answers as it splits beneath his hands, nor does the bottle ledged atop a rafter. He raises it to his lips and drinks. The Widow tries to remind him of who he is, but he does not want to remember. All the time he thought he had has been taken from him and what is left is disbelief. He cannot believe she is gone.

An avalanche forms behind my back and does not leave for years;

always I look behind, but the avalanche never falls.

The Widow realizes there is nothing she can do to help Dad, but she continues to watch out for Stevie and me. She tells Dad that the least he can do is get a dog for us. "It just might make your kids feel a bit safer at night," she tells him. "When you're passed out on the couch." He agrees to the idea, but he doesn't get us a dog. I give up on him, look behind me for the avalanche that never falls.

He is off drunk somewhere when the Widow brings over a Labrador puppy draped in a red bow. "I gave her a name," the Widow says. "Hepburn."

One night, after she has guarded our house for five years, Hepburn jumps out of sleep growling and stands at my side with her hackles raised as I open the door. Dad is draped across Parson's shoulders. In the bitter cold of night, sweat glazes his face and the scent of whiskey bleeds from his pores. As Parson drops him onto the couch, I stare down at him and feel nothing. No love, no hate, no hope. Everything is dry inside and has been for a long time.

Parson strikes a wooden match against the heel of his boot and lights a cigarette. He throws the match into the wood stove. "What you burning in here? Newspapers?"

Stevie's body has not caught up to his age. At seven years old, he is shorter and frailer than I was at five. But his voice is more fierce than mine ever was. "Got no wood," he says. "Got no oil for the furnace. Burning garbage. Cowpies. Anything we can dig up."

"I got some black pine to spare," Parson replies. "Me and the boys'll bring it over tomorrow."

"We'll do some work for you to pay it back," I say.

"Don't need to pay it back."

"We'll pay it back."

"Dad's been going to get wood for two weeks," Stevie says. "Comes home drunk, no wood, stinking drunk."

Parson blows a cloud of smoke toward the ceiling. For a moment, the odor of tobacco overtakes the smell of burning trash. "Have your fun with hating him now, 'cause someday pure hate won't make sense to you anymore." Parson tosses his cigarette into the wood stove. "I ain't defending him for what he is now, cause it can't be defended. I'm just saying you walk around in his shoes a single day and then hate him if you like. Hate yourself silly, Steve." Leaning into the wall, he looks at me for a time that seems interminable. "Wouldn't take Steve to the mountain anymore if I was you. He ain't you, to be holding onto what he never had."

Stevie grabs Hepburn by the collar and keeps her from attacking Parson as I charge him, throwing my fist toward his stomach. He catches my wrist. "One day you're going to hurt someone," he says, and leaves.

Stevie releases Hepburn and scratches her ear, watching me from the corner of his eye. He'd witnessed such outbursts often when the rough boys who lived in shacks near Mill Creek road saw me coming off the mountain and taunted me: "Landy Dandy talks to the dead, Landy Dandy thinks a grave is a bed, Landy Dandy ain't right in the head." Those boys would pull themselves off the ground with marks from my walking stick across their backs.

Stevie strokes Hepburn's head as he stares at me. "Dad said once, he said how you never hung around other kids when you were little. He says that's why you don't know how to be around folks now, 'cause you never learned how to. He says I was more lucky 'cause I played with kids and things like that."

"He's right," I say. "You did."

After my mother went away, the Widow Kyle continued to keep Stevie. She'd take him with her when she visited Mrs. Brown down the road who had a boy Stevie's age. She wanted to keep me too, after I'd come home from school, but she couldn't. Some things never do change.

"He wasn't lying, then?" Stevie asks. "You didn't play with other kids?"

"Didn't want to," I say, as I tear up one of the Widow Kyle's precious egg cartons and toss the pieces into the stove. "Still don't want to."

The next morning Stevie wakes up sick. He is burning with fever and his glands are swollen as plums. Dad isn't on the couch or in his bed. He is gone. The house is freezing. Our breath snakes over our heads. "Boxes hidden in the root cellar," Stevie says in a hoarse voice. "Burn her clothes for firewood."

"No. We'll go to the Widow's."

The falling snow clings to Stevie's sweat-dampened hair as he follows me across the yard. Widow Kyle eases him to her couch, turns to me where I stand at her door.

"I'm going after firewood," I tell her.

"You ought not go out in this storm."

"Got no choice."

She drags me fighting into her house. "I'll be damned if I'm going to let you go up to that mountain in this cold. Where's your pa?"

"Drunk," Stevie murmurs.

Dad's truck backfires as it pulls into our drive. In the truck-bed is a load of wood. Widow Kyle marches out of the house and grabs Dad by the collar as he steps down. "You got a sick boy in there, Daniel. You plan to stay around until he gets well or is this just some miracle we can expect to end by nightfall?"

Stevie follows me to the street. Glancing at us, Dad says to the Widow: "Thank you for taking them in, Mona."

"When it comes to your children, it seems I've never had a choice."

Stevie's voice is wild and reckless. "Fucking drunk."

"Not such a drunk that I don't know a fever when I see it," Dad replies. In our house, he puts Stevie on the couch with juice beside him and blankets atop him, and makes a fire in the wood stove. "Parson had some feed he needed moved," he says. "Traded my back for the wood. Quite a trade, I'd say."

Stevie's hair falls across his forehead, like black arrows drawn on white paper. "Why don't you stop drinking."

"It's got me good," Dad answers. "I try, son."

"Try harder," Stevie replies.

I follow Dad to the shed, crawl onto the truck bed and toss the wood to the ground. He picks it up and piles it. He doesn't touch a drink until all the wood is stacked, braced with a two-by-four to keep it from swaying in the roughest wind. Then he opens his bottle of whiskey. With the first drink, his eyes turn old. I kick the woodpile until it topples around me. "For someone who doesn't talk much, you have a way of getting a point across, Landy." He sets the bottle down and begins to rebuild the woodpile. At his side, I hand him chunks of pine.

That night, I crawl into bed next to Stevie, Hepburn nestled between us, and read a book by flashlight so Stevie won't wake up. Dad stumbles up the staircase and falls into his bed. The noise wakes Stevie.

"Dad drunk again?"

"Sounds like it."

"Parson's right. Love ain't so easy as hate." He grows quiet for a long while, finally nudges my shoulder. "Why do you think Parson says I shouldn't go to the mountain with you anymore?"

"Everyone thinks it's better not to remember."

"But I don't remember," Stevie replies. "I don't remember anything about her." The heat of his fever spreads under the blankets to me. "She'd never have let us run out firewood, huh, Landy?"

"That's right."

"And she'd never stand for him to be drinking all the time, would she?"

"Nope." Sleeping on the bedspread between us, Hepburn yelps softly, kicking her legs. I put my hand on her head and she grows calm. "Dad says you're getting too old for us to be sleeping together. He say that to you?"

"I'll be quiet."

"It's not a matter of being quiet," I say. "It's not...It's not natural."

"Over at the Brady's, Bill and Jim sleep together."

"They're both boys."

"So?" Stevie grins at me. "You could whip both of them with one hand tied behind your back."

"After tonight I want you to start sleeping in your own room."

"You could whip them with both hands tied behind your back."

"Stevie."

He shakes his head. "I don't want to."

"You can have Hepburn. She can sleep with you."

"Aren't you going to be scared?"

"What's to be scared of?"

Stevie stares at the ceiling. "The dark," he finally says.

"Dark is just dark," I say. "Now go to sleep."

When the months passed and summer came, we spent a lot of time up on the mountain. Tree frogs clasp their sticky three-fingered feet to our hands, and horned toads—big as softballs—stare at us with slippery eyes. When we catch them, they leave a pond of urine in our hands. So we catch polliwogs from the creek instead. They do not piss on us. They squirm inside the water bucket as we bring them into town and fill a ten gallon galvanized tub for them to live in. The next morning they spread across the surface of the water like an oil spill. We decide heartbreak killed them and never bring another creature down from the mountain to live inside the walls of town. As we carry the polliwogs to the creek and slide them into the water, we hope that somehow the water will have the magic power to bring them back to life. With the same sense of hope, I bring Mason jars filled with creek water home for Stevie when he suffers bouts of tonsillitis. Dad thinks I'm crazy to believe that water from the mountain has curative powers. But it must have—Stevie always got well.

Stevie believes in the magic of the creek water, but he stops believing in our father. On the day he turns eight, he says to Dad: "I hate your guts."

Hands trembling from a ten-day drunk, Dad stumbles to the couch as I present Stevie a red matchbox car and a tin sheriff's badge, paid for with money stolen from Dad's wallet. Stevie's birthday card has a cartoon-like drawing of a mouse sitting on top of a birthday cake, eating a square of cheese. Inside, it reads: Happy Birthday to the Big Cheese. I signed my name with my right hand, and Dad's with my left, so that it would not seem obvious that I had forged Dad's name. But Stevie is not fooled.

Dad trips as he walks up the staircase and loses his balance again as he comes down. A backpack swings in his hands. "I want the two of you to make a list of every reason you got for hating me. I'll look at it when I get back." Beneath the ragged edge of his voice, a tone of gentleness surfaces. "If there's anything left you can believe from me, believe that when I come back I won't be a drunk no longer." He takes out his wallet and drops a handful of bills onto the table. When he passes Stevie on the way to the door, he brushes his hand over Stevie's shoulder.

"Where are you going?" Stevie asks.

"Some place where there ain't no liquor."

I step far out of his path as he heads for the door, watch as he throws the backpack into his truck and drives away. Stevie and I are accustomed to Dad's disappearances, but he'd never left this way before—with clothing and a good-bye. I don't think he'll come back. But when Stevie asks me, I say that he will. Stevie believes me, because he wants to believe. Every evening, the whole third week that Dad is gone, Stevie makes rounds at the picture window, looking out. When Dad's Chevy finally appears, it cuts the center of the street in a straight line. Dad's jeans hang low on his waist like the clothing on a scarecrow, his face is clean-shaven, and the whites of his eyes are polished-looking.

He settles into the easy chair, drifts his eyes about the room, and steadies them on my face. "Think I ran out on you?" he asks.

"Yes."

He smiles. "Sure didn't raise you for a fool, did I?"

"You didn't raise me at all."

Stevie echoes me, but his voice isn't as certain as mine. "Me too," he says.

Looking at Stevie, Dad nods. "You write things down like I asked?"

Stevie slides the wrinkled sheet from his back pocket where he'd kept it close at hand, adding to it whenever a new hate came to him. He stares at the sheet, but doesn't have to read it to know what it says. "You don't take me hunting or fishing like other kids' fathers. Sometimes you don't come home and we don't know where you are. You say you're getting firewood and then you don't get it. You tell me you're going to take me to your barber for a haircut and then you don't do it. You tell us you're going to buy us a dog, but you don't and the Widow has to do it for you." His voice falls; with an effort he brings it back: "You forgot my birthday and you're a goddamn drunk." He crumples the paper and throws it on the floor.

"That's a pretty good-sized list," Dad says.

"So?" Stevie asks.

"So I'm saying I've got a hell of a lot to make up for. You got a list, Landy?"

I unfold my sheet of paper and hand it to him. It holds a single sentence. "You never got a headstone for my mother's grave."

Dad stares at me for a long while. "Landy," he says. His voice breaks and then he is silent all over again, rubbing his forehead. "I suppose I should have," he says. "I can go on over to Harley's and pick one out. If you'd like, you can come along. Help me pick out the words to write on it."

"It's too late now," I say. "It doesn't matter now."

"It mattered enough to write it down."

For the first time in my life, I lift my voice to my father, so loud that I'm screaming. "I used to know just exactly what I'd say on it, but I've forgotten all the words, I can't remember them anymore."

He pushes himself out of the easy chair and comes to the couch where Stevie and I sit; he settles in between us like he belongs there.

"We can come up with some words," he says.

Sliding away from him, I stand against the wall and realize the mistake I have made; I don't want him to carry a headstone to the mountain, I don't want him to go near the meadow, the lilac tree, the grave. It is none of his and we need nothing from him. "There's better ways to spend that money," I say. "You want to do us a favor, buy Stevie a bicycle. Every boy should have a bicycle. He doesn't even have a fucking bicycle."

Dad nods. "Done," he says. "What about you?"

"Me?"

"Must be something you're needing."

I tap the side of my head against wall. "I don't know."

"There must be something."

I try, but I can't think of anything I need that money can buy. I can think of a whole list of things that Stevie needs, new shoes, new jeans, new haircut, but I can't think of anything I need.

"Maybe you'd like a dress?" he asks.

I begin to laugh, a hard kind of laugh that makes my throat hurt. "I don't wear dresses," I say.

"Well maybe you'd like to?"

I shake my head.

"I'm not saying I'm made of money, but might be a few things I can get for you kids," he says.

Stevie stares at him like he's a gift sent to us out of the sky. His voice is hesitant. "I would like a bicycle."

Dad's hand wanders in the air and comes down on top of Stevie's head. "And a fishing partner, huh?"

"My own fishing pole."

"Fish should be biting with these clouds overhead," Dad says. He looks toward me. "If you two are willing, we could set some lines in Lake Sullivan."

"Right now?" Stevie asks.

"No better time." He ruffles Stevie's hair and goes toward the door.

Stevie begins to follow him and stops. Caught in the frame of Dad on one side of the room, me on the other, he says: "Let's go, Landy."

"I don't think I'll be coming."

Dad turns to me, his hands in the front pockets of his jeans. "Might be fun to learn how to catch a fish," he says.

When I reply, it is a taunt and a lie. "I know how to catch a fish. Mama taught me."

"She never did, Landy." Inside the pocket of his jeans, he draws his hands into fists. "We went fishing one time, before you were born. Every fish we caught, she threw back. She didn't much like fishing." As he meets my eyes, my head hurts, far in the back of my skull. "You can hate me for her dying," he says softly. "There might be nothing I can do to stop you from that. God knows, I spent enough years hating myself for it. I don't claim to know what made your mother live or what made her die. I don't want to use up any more of years trying to figure out something I'll probably never understand."

In the back of my head things are moving, dark images that don't become clear even as I close my eyes. Stevie taps my leg. "Tell him," he says. He looks up at me, his eyebrows arching. "Tell him, Landy." When I don't speak, Stevie turns to Dad. "Landy says she went away to be with her mother. That's why she died."

I rest my hand on Stevie's head and feel the thickness of his hair. "That's right," I say.

Dad has the same gentle tone he used to take with my mother during the time when she had lost her voice. "Fish are waiting, Landy."

"You two go. I thought I'd go to the mountain and pick some berries."

"The berries will always be there tomorrow," Dad says.

I lean down for Stevie's crumpled hate list, toss it in the wood stove. "I thought I'd make us a huckleberry cobbler," I say. "If you've got the time, after you're done fishing you might want to pick me up a baking pan from the IGA. The long square kind. I could use one of those."

Dad hesitates at the door. "I suppose I could just throw you over my shoulder and put you in the truck," he says.

As I stare at his polished eyes, I remember how my mother said it was so easy to bluff a man, especially this man. "And a cube of butter," I say. "If you've got the time." My shoulders relax as he picks up the tackle box and leaves the house. Stevie follows, but he walks backwards, watching the door until he's in the truck. They drive away, my father and his son.

I tell myself that Stevie needs a father, always has, and that it will be good for him to spend this time with him. Even though I don't ask for it, Dad buys me a radio. I think that a good daughter would kiss his cheek or hug him for such a wonderful present, but I just shake his hand. In my room, I listen to the only station the radio picks up, a country station from Colville. Dad buys Stevie a bicycle and a fishing pole. When Stevie is old enough, Dad buys him a shotgun and takes him hunting. Whenever he gives Stevie a present, he always thinks he needs to be equal by getting something for me. This time, he brings me a wool coat with pearlized buttons and real fake fur on the collar, bought in the women's department of the Sears in Colville.

One day after bird hunting at Mt. Abercrombie, Stevie cleans the grouse and joins me in the kitchen where I am preparing dinner. His hands are sticky with blood. Grouse feathers cling to his fingers. "Thought you should know that Dad's thinking of selling the mountain." He dips his hands under the faucet. "He doesn't think it's so good for you to be spending all your free time up there." His voice cracks, in limbo between man and boy. "You could go hunting with us at Abercrombie. You don't even need to carry a rifle. Just walk along."

I lean into the counter. "I don't want to. Is that such a sin?"

Stevie slaps the dish towel against the counter. "Goddamn it, what is it with you?"

"Listen, it's not my fault if you let yourself get embarrassed because I don't get named Miss Popularity in the school yearbook."

Red lines streak across his cheeks. "I'm not embarrassed by you."

"The hell you're not."

"Well," he says softly. "You could try a little harder to get people to like you, you know, instead of walking around town like everyone you meet on the street is invisible. Folks think you're stuck up, that's all."

I grab three plates from the shelf and set them on the table. "Tell Dad dinner'll be ready soon, would you, Stevie?"

"The name's Steven," he says. "Rhymes with Even." He has a real haircut these days. His ears show—pink and clean. The back of his neck is shaved. I hate his haircut.

Stevie gets a job at the mill as janitor, then as apprentice to lead man on green chain, and he and Dad eat at the Pioneer Diner each morning, sometimes stop there for dinner at night. After graduation, on my free days, I go to the mountain. Hepburn is with me as I walk down the railroad tracks. We part from them at the foothills on the edge of town. As we reach the dirt road leading to the mountain,

Hepburn bounds ahead of me. Her tail waves like a black flag. There is nothing new in walking the road, not in the huckleberry bushes stripped by bear or the furry places under the bows of a cedar where a deer has nested, but as it is every time I set foot on it, I am filled with anticipation of the silence I'll find at the mountain top.

As I approach the meadow, the roar of chain saws and the guttural tone of men's voices drifts from the forest. Hepburn bounds ahead as a logger appears. His silver hard hat bears the emblem of a Colville logging operation. Hepburn begins to circle him. I don't call her back, because I cannot speak.

"I'd appreciate it if you and your dog would stay clear," he says. Trees are dropping all around us. When I try to walk past the logger, heading for the lilac tree, he grabs my arm. "You can't go over there," he says. Wheeling out of his grip, I throw my fist at his face. He blocks my arm and takes ahold of my wrist. Hepburn pushes between us, baring her teeth. He squeezes my wrist. "Call off your dog."

I look down at her. "Back." She stands behind me, her eyes focused on his neck.

"I'm going to let go of you and I want you to head out of here the same way you came. All right?" I nod. But the moment he releases my wrist, I strike him on the jaw. It's like hitting stone. He grabs my leg as I kick him and flips me to the ground. Hepburn crouches, ready to spring at his neck; I hold her collar and pull her back. His steel-tipped boot could crush her skull. "Get out of here, the both of you," he says. "This ain't no place for a crazy girl and a wild dog."

From the ground, I say: "I own this mountain." The roar of the chain saws overpowers my voice. The bulldozer presses into the deer blind Stevie and I made, scattering the rocks and logs into a heap. Even with my fingers over my eyes, I can see the shadow of the bulldozer's blade approaching my mother's lilac tree. Its corner slits across the base, but the tree keeps standing, marking her grave.

Hepburn nudges my leg as I walk off the mountain. I pass Dad's truck parked in the lot of the mill. Stevie's 1968 Willy's jeep is parked beside it. He washes and waxes the jeep before each date with Shannon, his new girl, his only girl, his first girl and probably his last. It shines. I get into his jeep and fumble through the glove compartment, looking for a pencil. Pressing my forehead into the palm of my hand, I put the pencil to the paper: "I'll drop you a line when I get wherever it is I'm going. And by the way—it was a chickenshit thing to do, not telling me the mountain was sold, the both of you, a chickenshit thing to do." I get out of the jeep and let the tailgate down. "Get in, Hep." She jumps up, sits next to Stevie's toolbox. "I'm going now," I say to her, patting her on the head. "I'll be going now." I turn around and race to my house. In my room, I open my drawers and fill a duffel bag with clothing. When I come down the stairs, I fill Hepburn's bowl with dog food, and then I leave.

As I walk toward the highway, I cannot blame the wind for the tears that burn my eyes, for the air is still. Once I start to cry, I can't stop. After being without them from the age of five, the tears find their way to my eyes. On the highway leading south, I stretch my arm out and point my thumb at the sky. An echoing roar filters from the mountain top. As I travel down the state toward Willow, the sounds don't lessen. They could drive a deaf man mad.

Chapter Nine

When I got off my half-day shift, I saw Claire walking ahead of me up the sidewalk toward the mansion. I had not spoken to her since the night she found me huddled in the corner of my room, weeks before. I remembered looking at her shoes on my carpet—they came forward, then backed away—and more than anything I wanted to make her mad at me, that's what I wanted, to make her mad. But I couldn't do it, and I was forced to watch her shoes moving forward and back.

Back home, I tried to have that power with Stevie, to make him so angry he would hit me. One Saturday morning, we were playing in the school grounds. No one else was around. He got on a swing set and I got on the swing next to him. We didn't swing together, we went in the opposite direction, so that we were an X in the sky. He looked so young and helpless, holding on to the ropes for dear life, and yet his legs were pumping him into the sky.

"I can go even higher, Landy." He took his hand off to wave. "No hands!" A moment later, his hand was back on the rope.

As I swung my legs and drew near Stevie, I waited until his face was a foot from my own, and spat on him. He jerked his head. "What'd you do that for?" he said. The spittle marked his forehead. Again, I swung my legs and spat on his cheek. "Come on, Stevie, get me back." He didn't get me back. Ten times I passed, ten times covering his face with my spit, until finally he stuck his hands over his face and stopped pumping his legs.

"Landy...why? Why did you spit at me?"

I jumped to the ground. "You were supposed to fight back, Stevie."

"Landy?" He looked awful, sitting on that swing covered with my saliva. "We aren't going to do it again, are we?"

I lifted him off the swing and brushed his face with the end of my shirt. "No."

"That's good." He smiled up at me. "I nearly drowned up there."

Stevie's reaction was similar to the one I got from Claire—neither of them would fight back. I wondered if there would be anyone in my life who would love me enough to strike me.

Now, Claire strolled toward the mansion, and as I watched her easy strides a feeling of delight rose inside me, so overpowering I put my hands on top of my head and smiled. My feet tapped against the pavement as I ran toward her. Stopping beside her, I pulled my hair from the sides of my face, so that she could see my whole face and know: I am a woman, old and grown; despite what you saw of me huddled in the corner of my room weeks before, saying *one two three, one two three*, I am old and grown.

"Once you said you wanted to learn how to climb trees," I said. "I could teach you. We could go to the refuge."

I must have surprised her by running at her so quickly; she took a step back from me. "You frighten me, Alexandra."

"I didn't mean to scare you."

She stood away from me, her hand cupped to the side of her face. "It happened again. You don't remember, do you?" The panic came out of the sky and dropped behind my eyes, a white light. "Last night…you wouldn't calm down," she said. "Do you remember any of it?"

Looking at her was dangerous, like staring at the noontime sun. I prayed for it to stop before the white became black, I prayed to remember that anything is possible if you do not fold, as my mother had taught me. She said it is much more difficult to bluff a wild animal than it is to bluff a man, yet still she faced down a black bear and won. If it is so much easier to bluff a man, could it be so easy, then, to bluff a woman?

I stared at the circle of white spinning above Claire's head. "I remember. I don't like to be seen that way. I'd rather forget it."

When I met her eyes, there were no white lights in them. Blue, dark, and narrowing; she had not believed me, I saw it in her eyes.

"I didn't ask for this role," she said. "I didn't ask for this."

"Then stop doing it."

She gave a harsh laugh. "I was wearing earplugs, but the noise you were making travels right through them."

I sat down on the steps of the mansion and stared at the yellowed lawn. "In the daylight, I'm fine, well…fine enough." On the lawn, an ant walked upon the grass. I remembered a song my mother used to sing: *Just what makes that little old ant think he can move a rubber tree plant, everyone knows an ant can't move a rubber tree plant.* With my index fingers, I covered my ears for a moment, then set my hands upon the steps of the mansion. "I'm very sorry I woke you."

She sat down next to me, put her chin in her hand and stared out. "You don't remember last night, do you?"

"No. I don't. Please don't tell me about it. Later, you can tell me, but not now."

"When? In two weeks time?"

I looked at her and smiled. "Maybe." The tops of the maples billowed in the breeze. "My mother, she was put in an asylum. You see, she tried to slit her wrists. But she didn't die in the asylum. She came home to die." Claire had turned and was facing me. Her eyes were moist, as mine were becoming. "I called the asylum, A-Sky-Limb, the place that took her voice away."

"She didn't speak?"

"Now that's up your ally, isn't it, Miss Speech Path?" I smiled. "She didn't speak for a long time. Her speech wasn't gone, it just wasn't ready."

"Kind of like you," Claire said.

As I met her eyes, I nodded. "So, do you feel like climbing a tree?" For a long while, she was silent, staring at me with her chin resting in her hand. "I like you, Alexandra. God help me, but I do." Claire touched the tip of her index finger to the bridge of her nose. Flecks of gold flashed in her eyes. "I'm not going to come home with anything broken, am I?"

The heat crossed my cheeks and the words came out of my mouth before my lips could close: "I'm no heartbreaker."

We jogged to the refuge and I found the perfect tree for her, rising like a spear in the sky. As I looked at it, I remembered a game Stevie and Dad played after the drunken days ended: Dad would lift his hand over his head and drop it to his knees, like falling lumber. "Timber," he would say. Loving the ritual, Stevie would thrust his hand through the air in two quick karate blows: "Chop chop." That is how they said hello and good-bye.

Standing at the foot of the tree, I turned to Claire. "All you need to do is hoist yourself up by one of the branches. It's simple, really."

The lowest branch was far above her head. "And if I can't reach it?"

"I can make a foothold with my hands and lift you."

"How will you get up?"

"Oh, don't worry about me."

She placed her foot inside my hands and shimmied into the tree. When she was safe on one of the lower branches, I climbed up, grabbed to a sturdy branch and pulled myself above her. "Make sure you've always got one hand wrapped around the trunk, in case your foot slips." I moved to a higher branch and held my hand out to her. When she reached for me, I wrapped my hand around her wrist and her hand encircled mine. In that way, a branch at a time, a wrist at a time, we climbed until we were fifty yards into the sky.

"This is good enough, I think," I said.

She sat down on a branch and held to the trunk with both hands. After a few minutes, she became more comfortable and eased up on the trunk, freeing her hands. I sat on the branch below her.

The silence of late fall fell like a blanket around us. In the silence, without words, I pointed out a red-winged blackbird that was perched at the top of our tree. The branch rustled as Claire looked up; the blackbird opened its wings and took flight. I was not saddened that it left us, for only in flight can you see its full beauty: the patches of scarlet like shields on its outspread wings.

As Claire looked down at me, in her face I saw such beauty, but it was a beauty of approach, not retreat. "They call it a red-winged blackbird," I said. "That's why. It stays here through the winter."

Once again, we grew silent, looking at the world below. I touched her leg and pointed toward the pond to the east of us. On its edge was a blue heron. It stretched its lanky legs and began to trot across the pond's edge; as it took flight, my breath went with it. Blue wings merged with the sky.

From the ground, you can see only those things that want to be seen. From a tree, you see what a tree sees. I pointed out the white-tail deer drinking from the pond, the squirrel scampering in the tree next to us, the rabbit scurrying through the underbrush, the shiny-feathered pheasant feeding on the edge of the trail. We stayed until dusk began to fall, then we lowered ourselves, a branch at a time, out of the tree.

We walked side by side down the trail. The trail was so narrow our shoulders touched.

"On our mountain, you won't hear a single city sound," I said. "Just animals. Wind. Birds. My mother took me to the mountain nearly everyday. Then, after, I kept going back. You can imagine you're touching heaven when you're in the top of those pines. I'd be a happy person spending my lifetime teaching people how to climb trees. Wouldn't make much of a living, I suppose, but I'd be happy."

Flecks of gold sparkled in Claire's blue eyes. This day, I had seen the look enough to know that it meant she was smiling inside her mind. "And your student needs to pee."

"Have you ever pissed in the woods before?"

The smile came as I knew it would. "I've never had that honor."

"You've led a very sheltered life, Claire."

Lifting her eyebrows to me, she stepped behind the privacy of an Oregon grape bush. I waited with my back to her in the tent-like shelter of a cedar tree. When she reappeared we rejoined the highway, jogging on the center white line. I plodded and I endured, but I did not dance down the blacktop as Claire did. Even with my longer legs, I couldn't keep pace with the way she moved. Ahead of us, fine bits of frost laced the road.

"You grew up in Seattle?"

"Yes."

"Then you must know about the ocean, same as I know about the woods?"

"I don't think I know anything as well as you know the woods."

"Big family, yours?"

"I have a mother and two sisters who still live there."

"I heard you talking on the phone," I said. "To your mother about Kim."

Facing me, she smiled on one side of her face; the left edge of her lip raised into a broad smile, and the dimple showed below her cheek. "You put a glass up to the wall and listen?"

"Sound just travels, that's all."

"I know," she replied. "The same with you." She blew on her hands as she ran beside me. "You're lucky there's only me sleeping in my room, Alexandra. What would you do if I had a lover over?"

I came to a dead stop. "Do you have a lover?"

"Not for a while," she said. She raised her head, and it was seeming she meant to say more, but I didn't let her. Claire was Claire, period. The end. I couldn't handle anymore than that. I wasn't ready for anymore—not from her, but from myself. Start looking inside and everything is jangled in a mess.

"Well, if I ever hear a lover, I'll start wearing your earplugs," I said. "Now, back to your mother. You called her Mamaso. Why?"

"My mother?"

I nodded. "Why'd you call her Mamaso?"

"We started when we were babies. Most mothers teach their kids to say Mom or Mama, but she taught us how to say Mamaso. It's been Mamaso ever since."

"But why that word—Mamaso?"

She shrugged. "Why not?"

"You have a good relationship with her?"

"It's becoming good, yes. But it wasn't always. You see, Mamaso went to night school to get her B.A. There were a lot of years when she worked all day and went to college in the evenings. I mean, we always lived in a decent house in a good neighborhood, went to good schools, but Mamaso wasn't around much. She put in an eight-hour shift at the teller line, went to her college classes, and came home to us. And when she was there, she had three of us girls all over her trying to get her attention."

"She did that alone?"

"Are you asking if she had a husband?" Claire said.

"I'm asking if you had a father."

"We did," she replied flatly. "And then he left for Alaska."

"No child support payments, nothing?"

"Nothing. Mamaso decided that welfare wasn't for her. Now, she's got her degree, she has a job as a loan officer, and Kim is driving her crazy."

"Kim lives there with her?"

"Um-huh." When she looked at me, her breath fogged about her face. "You have a lot of questions, don't you?"

"Yes."

"Can I ask why?"

"Because....maybe I can learn from your family....like I learn from you."

Her hands were wrapped in a circle at her mouth. Foggy breath warmed them. "What have you learned from me?"

"That it's all right not to run. That's what I've learned." Taking a step down the highway, I said: "Your sister?"

"Kim," she said, smiling. "She's a cheerleader, on the honor roll, class president, in drama club, part of the debate team, and she plays varsity tennis. She is a type A personality all the way."

"How come your mom wants to kill her?"

"Her Visa card was taken from her wallet," Claire replied. "Kim came home with a new outfit—that's why she wants to kill her."

I smiled. "Oh., I can see how that'd make you into an axe murderer."

She ran her hands across her forehead, pushing back the locks. "Kim's been on the honor roll since seventh grade."

"Your mother doesn't tell her that she has to stay on it, does she?"

"Christ no. My mother went through Jeannie and me getting anything except straight A's. She was happy, even if we got a C, as long as we gave it our best shot."

"And did you?"

"Jeannie did. I didn't." She pulled the sleeves of her sweatshirt down over her hands. "I'm sure there are a lot of reasons why Kim joins every club she can. You don't grow up in my family without carrying some baggage with you. All of us have it." On the flat pavement, she ran backwards ahead of me, her arms moving like pistons. She slowed down and joined my pace, brushing her arm against mine. I wouldn't have minded if it had stayed there, brushing against my own, even as she asked: "How did your mother die?"

"She killed herself. On the mountain." I turned my whole face to her, meeting her eyes. "You said I scare you. Sometimes I scare me too. I know I'm not doing a very good job of living right now. But I'm going to fix it. I just need some time." Ahead of us, the sign marked the border of the refuge. I came to a stop. "You wouldn't mind going back to the mansion alone? I'd like to stay out here a while longer."

Claire walked back to me and laced her arm through mine. "You made this date," she said. "The honorable thing to do is see me to the door."

And so I did. At the door of the mansion, I waved at her as she went inside. I jogged to the refuge, climbed into the boughs of my tree and stared at the moon. I saw no face on its silver skin.

***

A foot of snow fell upon Willow within the week. Such a storm in

November, people said, implied a rough winter ahead. I didn't think it could be anything near the winters we'd have back home. I looked out my window and thought, baby snow, just baby snow. But still, before I left for the IGA in the morning, I dressed in all of my winter gear. As I walked down the streets, my footprints dotted the pavement. They would be gone soon with the new snow falling, but they were there now, perfect and mine.

The store was still locked when I arrived ten minutes early for my eight to five shift. Tiny let me in. "Good morning, Al."

"Morning, Tiny."

He poured me a cup of coffee from his thermos. "Take the sleep out of your voice."

I sipped the coffee as I walked to the back room, discarding a piece of clothing at a time—fatigue jacket, muffler, cap, mittens—and managed to kick out of my boots and slide my feet into my tennis shoes just as Tiny opened the store for business.

As it was every Monday morning since I'd worked at the IGA, Mrs. Snipes was outside, waiting to do her weekly shopping. "Winter's on the way," she said to me as she shook the snow out of her hair. She wrestled a cart out the grasp of another and pushed it down the aisle. She was a big woman; a whole ham fit in her hands.

After she was through shopping, I rang up her goods and loaded them into the back of her four-by-four. When I came back in, Tiny brought the monthly checkers' calendar over to me. "I was looking ahead at the Thanksgiving schedule," he said. "I could work in some time off for you if you'd like to spend Thanksgiving with your folks in Pike. I don't have any problem with that."

I sat on a crate against the wall. For once, Tiny was taller than me. "I was thinking I'd just stay here."

"You might consider going home. Thanksgiving, you know."

Staring down, I wove my fingers inside my palms, a game my mother and I used to play. My thumbs made a church steeple and my fingers represented the congregation. *Here is the church and here is the steeple. Look inside and see all the people.* How she would laugh at my tiny squirming fingers.

"So how do you want me to schedule it?" he asked.

"Schedule me here." I stood, safe in my great height. "I'll be stocking if you need me."

"If something's too heavy for you to lift, I want you to call me. I mean it, Al." He went to his office where a snapshot of his wife and kids were taped to the safe, all of them taller than he was.

The dolly was stacked past my head with crates of beans, creamed corn, peas. I didn't call Tiny for help I didn't need and he couldn't really give as I lifted the crates down. The older canned goods came forward, expiration dates checked, and the newer ones were relegated to the back of the shelf. Postdated and dented cans went to the garbage bin where poor folks liberated them and Tiny pretended not to know.

I looked up and saw Hank enter the store. He looked good, he did, with no lines of sleep under his eyes. I was leaning on my dolly when he approached.

"Hey, Alex."

"You look good, Hank, you really do."

He lifted a packet of bologna. "Must be the food I've been eating." He followed me to the register. I believe I felt his eyes roving my backside. I wouldn't have sworn it, but it felt like his brown eyes were sheltering my legs and buttocks with their glance.

At the register, I rung up his things and packed them into a bag. "Here you go," I said, handing him his bag.

He sat unmoving in the main aisle, and his bag swung left and right across his side. "See you, Alex."

I smiled. "You have a very good day, Hank."

I went back to my dolly and was setting out rows of beans. Dear, dear Hank—how a man must feel when his wife chooses not to be with him. He lost the partner of his life. The closest thing I had to compare with it was losing my mother. Except she isn't coming back.

When I looked up Mike and Teresa were standing on either side of me. I backed away, freeing myself from their containment. Teresa lifted a postdated can of corn from the throwaway box. "This would go well with dinner tonight," she said.

I took the can out of her hand and tossed it in the box.

"All right," she replied. "No corn then. But you, we need. Pot roast. Six o'clock."

Mike leaned into the shelf, his arms crossed to his chest. "We'd like you to come, Alex."

When I shook my head, Teresa dabbed her lips on the back of her hand. "We've missed you," she said. "We'd like a second chance with you and we hope you'll give it to us."

"No."

Mike pushed away from the shelf. "Come around when you're ready," he said. "We'll be there."

I walked away from them to the back room, shoving my shoulder into the sign on the swinging metal doors, Employees Only. I hoped they wouldn't follow me, that it was one rule they wouldn't break, for if they had, I was not sure I could keep myself from breaking a rule I'd made years ago after I nearly broke the arm of one of the boys from Mill Creek road: to hold my hands to my sides and walk away, no matter what is said, to walk away.

***

When my shift ended at five, I headed toward the mansion at a dead run. I'd just gotten out of my IGA uniform and into a wool sweater and jeans when Patchins' rhythmical knock was upon my door.

"I'm not your mistress," I said, leaning over to throw the door open. "I am not your mistress, Patchins."

His coat was wet with snow. He ran his hand up his front, undoing the buttons, then he buttoned them again. Alcohol was on his breath. "Well, this is my house, and I'm the master of it, and you're the mistress. I don't see what's wrong with that."

"You know what I'm talking about," I said. "Mistress not of this mansion, but of you."

"Oh, no, Girl. If I want a mistress, I certainly won't take her in my own back forty. Nope, I certainly won't do that." He stuck his hands into the pockets of his jacket. "God almighty, it's freezing in here."

"The radiator's broken."

"I can see that."

"Well what do you plan to do about it?"

"One thing about me, I always take care of my renters."

"You bet, Patchins." I slapped my mittens against the arm of the couch. Droplets of water sprung free and fell like sleet. "Until you fix the radiator, we need one space heater apiece or we won't pay next month's rent."

"We?"

"Claire and me. We won't pay for a house that's freezing."

"This blackmail her idea?"

"It's mine."

"You and her becoming allies, huh? Miss Pure won't let me in her door like she's such a good woman when we both know she ain't."

I sat on the arm of the couch, rested my feet on the ragged cushions. "What do you want, Patchins?"

"She doesn't like men, that's the truth of it. I been telling you to watch out for her. Before you know it, she'll have you in her snare."

"You make up a lot of stories," I replied. "Some people might even call you a liar."

Patchins pulled his red-checked wool cap low on his brow. "And you know what your problem is? You'd like Lucifer if he smiled at you, an absolute babe in the woods. I'm telling you—"

Cupping my hand to my ear, I broke him off. "I think I hear the wife calling you, Patchins."

He pointed his finger at my face. I wanted to bite it off. "That Claire-Thing pretends to be operating out of the goodness of her heart, but it's all a sham. Miss Pure Heaven Sent running to your room when a bad dream wakes you in the night."

"What?"

"Heard you. Was rambling the town while the wife was keeping time at a church dance marathon, and I thought I'd bring some chops over for you. Was late and all, but what the hell, you're young right? I come up the stairs and I hear you screaming bloody murder in your room."

Staring at the floor, I asked, "When was this?"

"Didn't mark it on my calendar. Last week sometime."

"I don't want to hear about it," I whispered. Claire had told me it had happened, yes, but she didn't tell me all the things I couldn't remember. I covered my ears as Patchins spoke, but his voice was so rough it broke through my hands.

"You will hear about it, because then you'll know what she's got in store for you, Girl. I run up the stairs and there she is pounding on your door, but you ain't answering. You're yelling out whole sentences, tossing in your bed like someone is raping you. I says to her, go back to bed, I'll handle this. Her legs is showing under the nightgown and she don't even try to cover them. Then I think, okay woman, just go on teasing me like this and someday I'll take you up on it, and won't neither of us be a bit surprised. Then you scream again and she yanks the key chain off my belt and opens your door. There you are under the kitchen table stark naked."

I closed my eyes. My mother's voice said: *You'll be the same,*

Landy, the same.

"She wraps the blanket around you and you're crying like a baby, and I think to myself, the girl's on drugs, sure as my name is Patchins, the girl's on drugs. So I tell her to just leave you alone to fight it out with yourself, ain't nothing we can do. I says to her, I got a bottle in the Volkswagen, how about a drink to pass the time. I can see she's got a temper, that's sure. She tells me to get out. But I stay for a minute while she puts you to bed, talking softly like she ought to have been talking to me. Knowing all this, you can still sit there and tell me she ain't a butch in lamb's clothing, laying there on your bed, holding you in her very own arms?"

"Get out of my house."

"What you say?"

"Get out of my house."

"My house, Girl, my house."

***

Not long after Patchins slammed my door, I pulled on my fatigue jacket and left the mansion. Claire's room was dark as I passed beneath it, crossing through the front yard—she had not been there to hear Patchins' rough voice and I was thankful for that, that she had not heard how he had spoken of her.

I walked along the railroad tracks, taking long strides so that my feet came down on the solidness of the ties. Near the tracks at the edge of town was a bar that catered to folks who shook so bad they held their drinks with both hands and still spilled half. No one—no customers from the IGA, no folks from the Saddle, no Mike, no Teresa, no Hank—would see me there. No one I knew by name or face would have the bad sense to come into such a place, which meant it was the place I wanted to be.

I took a table in the back and stared out the window, drinking beer after beer. An old man wearing shoes with newspaper soles came up to ask me for a dollar. I gave him a five.

"I don't want to be handing out any more of my money," I said to him. "You tell any of these other folks I gave that to you, I'm going to find you and take it back. "

He had no teeth, poor fool, and he believed me, so much that he took his five dollars and stumbled out the door.

No one bothered me as I sat at my table in the corner. No one caught my eye. No one asked me for the time of day. I couldn't have given it if they had.

When the lights dimmed for closing, I left the bar and began walking around town. I could tell it was cold outside from the frost on the parked cars, but I didn't feel cold. I wandered up the hill toward sixth, walking in the center of the street. No cars passed. Dead town.

I stared ahead at Mike and Teresa's house. Their lights were out. Kitty-corner from it a black apartment spread before me as I walked back and forth. I found the mailboxes and searched for Hank's name. His apartment was number ten.

I stood outside his apartment. Dark inside. He would be in there, asleep. He had nowhere else to be. I tried his door. It was open. Careless small-town boy who thinks it is safe to leave a door unlocked.

I closed the door softly behind me and leaned against the wall. As my eyes adjusted to the darkness, I saw the bed in the corner of the studio apartment. Hank was sleeping on his side, his right leg sprawled across the top of his bedspread. Good strong leg, good small-town boy.

I made no sound as I pulled off my boots and began to undress. He didn't awaken as I crawled under the covers next to him, he didn't awaken as I caressed him, even as his body met my own. He moved like a dreamer as I opened my legs and pulled him to me. I stroked the back of his thighs and smiled as his eyes opened, as he awoke.

"Hey, Hank."

He became dead weight atop me, staring down at my face. When he began to pull away, I wrapped my legs around his. "Don't be afraid Hank. It's only me."

He locked his elbows as he lifted his upper body away from mine. "What are you doing here?"

"I'd say that's a pretty stupid question."

His voice was foggy with sleep. "I don't think so."

"We may as well finish what we started, Hank." When he did not lower himself to me, I wrapped my arms around his shoulders and pulled my body up to his. Suspended in air, I whispered in his ear: "It'll be fun. Trust me." The strength drained from my arms and I dropped onto the bed. "Go back to sleep. You were more fun when you were asleep."

A crease from the pillow was on his cheek. He turned his head away as I touched it. "You don't give a man half a chance to make up his mind, do you Alex?"

"I can make up both of our minds."

"What if I don't want you to make up my mind?"

"Oh, but you will, Hank, you will. Just give it a chance."

His body relaxed as he lowered himself down to me. "Tell me this is not your first time," he said in a soft voice.

"This is not my first time."

I closed my eyes. It felt too good, too good, as his tongue made circles across my breasts. *Oh God, Mama, this is how it felt?* His hands cupped me to him and it felt so good I couldn't bear it. *Mama, this is how it felt?*

"Please, Hank, hit me please." His body grew still as he stared down at me. I couldn't look at his eyes. "It would be a favor to me if you would, Hank."

When he pulled away, I didn't try to stop him. He sat up and pressed his back into the headboard.

The instant the tears rose in my eyes, the anger came to cover me, to save me. "Of course you wouldn't lower yourself to such a thing, right Hank? An All American Boy such as yourself."

"Not this way," he said.

My hair fell over the sides of my face as I stared at him. "You're full of shit, all of you are full of shit. It's in your head, don't tell me it's never been in your head. Fucking chickenshits, all of you."

Hank folded the pillow behind his back. "And afterwards I'd ask you to leave and I'd never see you again. Is it worth it to you? Because it's not to me."

"Stuff your conscience up your asshole, Hank." Throwing the covers off me, I got out of bed.

"Where are you going?"

When I turned to him, once again the tears burned my eyes. This time no anger came to stop them. "You don't expect me to stay?"

"I'd like you to."

"And if I stayed, it'd be your way?"

"It'd be a different way," he replied.

"I can imagine you're really sweet and all, Hank. But I don't want it a different way."

I turned my back on him as I dressed. Hopping on one foot, he pulled his jeans on and followed me to the door. "It's freezing out there," he said. "Let me drive you home."

I lifted his hand and kissed his wrists. "Always the gentleman. I can walk, I'd rather walk."

He stood in the threshold as I stepped down the sidewalk. "Alex?" he called. "If it has to be like this, I'd prefer it if you didn't come back here anymore."

"I don't expect I'll be coming back, Hank."

It took me an hour to get to the mansion. I walked slowly, in the opposite direction, before I could find the power to turn around. I tried to walk quietly up the mansion stairs, but my boots were heavy and knocked against the wood. Behind me, the door opened, and I turned to see Claire coming up the staircase. I sat down on the top of the stairs and nodded.

"Long so," I said.

"What?"

"Long so. Your mother says her name's Mamaso, and I say *long so* means hello. It's Blackfoot, I think. My mother would say it. Long so. It means how do you do. Or maybe it's good-bye, I don't remember. Maybe it's not even *long so* after all." Claire stopped at the top of the stairs. I hated to have her look at me from above. "Sit down."

She settled in next to me. "Smells like a still around here."

"Patchins came by. That's what stinks."

She brushed my shoulders with her own. "I mean you."

"I don't smell like a still. I smell like beer. Patchins, he reeks to high heaven. He told me about coming to my room the other night. Thank you, for all you did for me. I wish there was something I could do to show my appreciation, but all I've got is thank you." I reached for my head and pretended to take off my hat, lowering it to my chest. "Thank you, Claire."

She smiled. "You're welcome."

"Were you out wandering around the town?"

"I went to a party."

"It was fun?"

"Um-huh, it was." She pulled her knees to her chest and wrapped her arms around them. "Patchins came—"

"I told you I don't want to talk about it! Nothing, not a word out of your mouth. I said it, and I mean it, and if you don't like it, you can just go to hell!"

Claire got up. "You know, I'd rather talk to a blank wall than to you."

I stood up and blocked her way to the door. "Oh, come on now, Claire. You think you know so fucking much. Tell me this, tell me who you've slept with. Come on, I said tell me. Slept with a fucking lot of men, huh?"

She nodded. "Yes, a fucking lot."

"Men, huh. Were they trying to get their rocks off, or were you?" She tried to get me to move, but I did not. I blocked her way. "Tell me, are these men of the Seattle variety, or can we look at the penises and see some of your cum on the men in Willow?" It must have happened in a split second, but it seemed to take forever—her body trying to push me back, her hand rising and slapping me across the cheek. I sat there, stunned, trying to understand the meaning beneath the stinging cheek, to understand that getting hit is a way to take all of the pain away, as my mother insisted, to take it all away. But there was no one beneath me, no one inside me, no voices, no words, no Mama.

Claire stood there looking blankly at her open palm. "Did you like it, Alexandra? Did you like it as much as your mother did?"

"No," I whispered. I touched my cheek. "No." The tears came to my eyes. "No, I didn't like it, no, no." I sat down on the stairs and the tears stung my stricken cheek. Claire lowered herself to my back, holding me, her legs spread out around me, her arms at my front, rocking with me. I wondered how I had found her, someone in my life who could love me enough not to strike me, but to hold me.

Chapter Ten

I had just gotten home from work when Claire knocked on my door and asked me to a spaghetti feed. It was a fundraiser put on by Willow's Search and Rescue Crew. She knew some people who were organizing it. "It's tonight," she said.

Outside my window, the snow was falling in tiny flakes that did not stick to the ground. "Two weeks has long since passed," I said, smiling at her. "Back then, you asked me to a barbecue."

She lifted her shoulders and dropped them in an obvious shrug. "Oh well, see you later."

As she was going down the stairs, I watched her with my head against the wall. "That was a yes, Claire." She leaned against the railing, the left side of her mouth drawing into a broad smile, while the right was raised only slightly. "Yes," I said. "I would love to go to a spaghetti feed with you."

"April will pick us up at about seven."

"I need to apologize to April anyway, you know, for yelling at her that time she called me Patchins' mistress. What about Sue, isn't she coming?"

"She has to work tonight."

"She works?"

"Sue is a nurse, and April is a P.E. teacher."

"That's why April's always hoarse."

"April was born hoarse," Claire said.

Come seven o'clock, April's horn sounded. I met Claire in the hallway. "You changed," she said.

I had changed out of my green t-shirt and a pair of faded green dungarees, and into Levis and a sweater. "The marines are looking for a few good men," I replied, but she didn't know I was talking about my army clothes until I explained it to her.

She smiled. "The proud, the few, the women."

Once we were outside, April continued to honk her horn. Claire strolled to her truck and made a gesture as if she were waiting for some man to pick her up—she pushed one side of her leather coat back and pulled up on her jeans until her shins showed. "Going my way?" she asked.

She got in first, nearest to April, and I followed. "Hey," April said, waving her hand to me. "How've you been?"

"Fine, thank you," I responded. "And you?"

"I've been fine." To Claire, she asked, "And you?"

"Fucking miserable." Looking at me, she broke into a smile. "So how've you been, really, Alexandra?"

I couldn't help but smile back. "Fucking miserable."

"The street is fucking miserable," April said. "Too many god damn potholes."

As April pulled up near the Willow Community Center where the spaghetti feed would be, she mentioned a GPA rally. It was scheduled for next Spring, months away. April said they've lined up a band to play in the park. "Rock and roll," April said. I wondered what G.P.A. stood for. Probably, the G stood for Gay, it had to be, with a rally coming up; I had read about such a thing in my *Time* magazine. Twenty-five years ago at Stonewall in New York, there began a revolution, and it is celebrated today with a gay pride rally. All of these thoughts spun in my head, but none of them were mentioned, because Claire was part of April who was part of Sue, who were a part of homosexuality—and all that I did not want to think about. Someday, yes, but not yet…two weeks time.

April parked her truck and got out, and did some shoulder stretches. Watching her as she shifted to a hip rotation, swinging her pelvis in and out, I held the door for Claire, then slammed it shut. "I wanted to apologize for getting mad at you," I said to April. "It was my fault and I'm sorry."

She brought her hips in and out. "Past is past," she said. "Now is now…and I'm starved."

Snow dotted the road, not enough to leave our tracks. I walked with my hands in the pocket of my jacket, and April did the same. Claire strolled with her hands in front of her face, catching bits of falling snow. Inside the community center, we had to pay a women who looked like a well dressed hiker—top of the line boots, L.L. Bean matching maroon sweatshirt and turtleneck, and pants that were so tight she could crawl into caves and out of them. To Claire, as we walked away, I said, "I don't think she knows how to climb a tree."

The room was arranged with oblong tables. In the front of the room the food was spread. "All right," April said. "Make sure you eat five dollars worth." As I followed April to the food, Claire saw a woman and stopped for a few words with her. I looked up to see Claire mouth my name—Alexandra—and the woman with auburn hair lifted her hand to me. My hands were full with my plate of spaghetti, French bread, and grape juice, but I managed to greet her back: "Hello." I followed April to an empty table near the entrance. In a moment, Claire was sitting down with her own plate of food.

"What's her name?" I asked.

"Jill—she helped to organize it."

April lifted a bite full of spaghetti. "The first bite is for Search and Rescue, but the rest is for me," April said. "And since Sue's not here, for her too." I didn't know how to eat spaghetti without slurping the ends of it into my mouth. I had my fork full and glanced at April; she was slurping to beat the band. "Good, good food," she said. Claire had her head down over her plate and nodded. Finally, I took a bite and tasted loads of tomato sauce.

There were all sorts of people around us, young, old, and in between. A lot of the men and women were dressed kind of strangely—peasant skirts, medicine bags, and jewelry made of beads. A man walked by, and he wore moccasins that touched his knees.

"Moccasins?" I asked.

April replied: "Are you talking about the granolas?"

"Granolas?"

"Yeah." April sipped her juice. "Granolas."

"Great," Claire said. "Another sub-division in our American culture. We have the Blacks, the Hispanics, the Asians, the Whites, and the Granolas."

"Could that be—Granolas—the same kind you eat for breakfast?"

"That's why they're Granolas," April said.

"Oh." I lay my hand on the table, palm up. "There are so many things I don't know."

I met Claire's eyes as she brushed a napkin over her lips. "And there are so many things that you do." The color of her lips was not one color, but many—pink, red, the color of a nipple. Slowly, I turned my eyes away.

There, at a table in the very far end of the room, were Mike and Teresa. What in the world were they doing at a fund-raiser for Search and Rescue? It was probably Teresa's idea; she could search and rescue some poor fool, and take him home. Mike must have been watching me, because as I stared at him he lifted his Styrofoam cup in a toast to me, then drank it down. Teresa didn't know I was there, or she would have come to me instantly, telling Claire and April just what a good friend they have in me. She was sitting next to Mike, but was talking to a man at her right. She set her hand on the middle of his chest and said all sorts of things that guys like to hear. Poor man, didn't know what he was getting into, or maybe he did know but didn't care.

Mike held my eyes. Slowly, I shook my head. He was the first one to look away.

"I used to hang out with them," I said to Claire. She followed my eyes to Mike and Teresa. "Not anymore."

April pushed back from the table with her plate in hand. "I'm going for seconds," she said. "Anyone else?"

Claire handed her empty cup to April. "I could use some more juice."

"You?" she said to me.

I looked down at my full plate of food. "No thanks."

April set her head next to mine and spoke into my ear. "You know, if you wait too long to eat, your spaghetti becomes rubber."

When she walked away, I said to Claire, "You have good friends. I like her."

"Me too." She pushed her plate away, leaned back from the table stretching her arms out to her sides.

"Well, we've done it."

She stretched her arms over her head. "Done what?"

"Eaten together."

"Eaten together?"

"That's right. You ate, I ate, we ate."

She lowered her arms to the tabletop. "You don't normally eat with other people?"

"Not normally, no."

"Well…" She smiled. "How was it?"

I was about to respond when I felt a hand on my shoulder. "Alex, you've made a friend?" I looked up and saw Teresa's mop of platinum blonde hair. "I know you," she said to Claire. I remembered the time they met; at a party Claire dropped Teresa's hand from her shoulder. I could see in her eyes that she remembered it too. "Yes," Teresa said. "We have met."

Claire's voice was ice cold. "I'm afraid not."

Teresa moved her hand up and down my shoulder. "Since Alex is playing the poor hostess, I guess I'll have to introduce us. My name is Teresa. I don't believe I've gotten your name, have I?"

"That's right."

She massaged the back of my neck. With each stroke of her hand I felt myself grow tenser, the muscles in my back becoming concrete. "Alex, you forgot to introduce me to your friend."

Claire stood. "Let's go, Alexandra."

Teresa pressed both hands on my shoulders, pinning me to the chair. "Alexandra? She calls you Alexan—"

I thrust out of my chair and grabbed Teresa's wrist. So fragile the bones, I could have broken them with a snap across my knee.

Claire spoke gently: "I said let's go."

Teresa's wrist fell from my hands. "Okay," I said. "All right, okay."

"My, my," Teresa said. "She calls you Alexandra?"

I met Claire's eyes. "Let's go," she said again. Claire and I walked away. We went toward the front of the room where the spaghetti was spread, searching for April. She was kneeling with her empty plate in her hand, talking to two women. "I don't much like Teresa," I said to Claire.

"Neither do I."

April saw Claire standing with her arms crossed to her front. "What's up?"

"McDonald's," Claire replied. "I buy."

As the three of us walked out, I saw Mike sitting in his chair with Teresa in his lap. When she moved his collar back and caressed his neck, flashing me a smile, I flipped them off. "Fuckers," I said. Claire glanced at me. She couldn't know Teresa had watched me have sex with Mike, she couldn't know, and I didn't want to tell her. April walked beside us. She was nearly as tall as me, yet muscular. Her brown hair was cut short, showing her ears which were clean and shiny. "Does your school have a basketball team?" I asked her, to lead the conversation off of me.

"We sure do," she replied. "The best."

We got in April's truck and went to McDonalds. I couldn't bear to think of anything in my stomach, but April ordered a burger, and Claire had a cup of coffee. April began to talk about her job, and I prodded her for more. Claire drank her coffee and watched me, smiling a little, not smiling a lot.

"I've got to pick Sue up at the hospital," April said. "You've got to go to the library, right?"

"Yes," Claire said.

"I'll drop you off. And you, Alexandra, do you want to be dropped at home?"

"I'll walk," I said.

"You're sure? It's cold outside."

"I'll be fine."

Shaking her head, Claire ran her fingers through her hair, glancing at me from the corner of her eyes. "Later."

"Good-bye, Claire."

She walked with April out the door. Without turning back to me, she waved good-bye. Some old man who was walking in thought the wave was for him, and gave her a big molarless smile.

***

One evening after work, heavy boots plodded up the stairs, followed by Patchins' rhythmical knock on my door. "Anyone here?" he called.

I opened the door and blocked the entrance so Patchins wouldn't waltz in and make himself at home like he'd usually do. Since the last time he'd come by, telling me how he'd seen Claire hold me as I fought my way out of a dream, I'd had a change of heart about him. He wasn't good, and he didn't have good intentions.

He had a space heater under each arm. "Told you I'd get you some heat," he said. He pointed his chin toward Claire's room. "She home?"

"No." She wasn't there—I hadn't heard her come up the stairs.

Patchins gave me one of the space heaters, but kept the other locked under his arm. I tossed the space heater onto my couch where it instantly sunk into the springs. "I'll bring it on over for her later," he said. When he smiled, his lips were thin, like taught rubber bands.

"Leave it with me," I said. "I'll give it to her."

"She's a hot one, that's sure."

Before he saw my hand coming, I snatched the space heater from him and dropped it on my couch. "I'll give it to her," I said.

Patchins inched toward me. He smelled like he'd bathed in vodka. Bits of grime were caught in the crevices on his forehead; they didn't dislodge as he smacked his hand into his forehead and backed away from the border of my room. "Here I bring over the heaters just like you asked, and this is what I get? The cold shoulder?"

"Yep."

"You let that Claire-Thing in your door, but you won't let old Patchins inside, huh?"

"Her name is Claire Thomas," I said. "I don't want you to call her names in front of me."

"Yeah? You going to call up the Name-Police and report me?" Patchins stepped toward me, stopping at arm's length from my door. "She's one of them Femme-Lezzies, that's what she is. I saw a group of them on the Donahue show. Wearing their nice dresses and their pretty faces, legs crossed and all. She'd fit right in with them. If you'd watched that show, you wouldn't be fooled by her."

When I started to close my door, Patchins blocked it with his foot. "Move it," I said in a flat voice.

He did not. He pressed his face in the crack of my door. It would have been so easy to slam the door and smash his head like a rotten egg. "The way I see it, if they got to be homos, it's their own misery. But the least thing they can do is look like homos instead of like real women so folks can know the difference. That Claire, she ain't playing fair dressing like a real woman. If she dressed more like you, flannel shirts and such, it wouldn't be like she was teasing—"

Swinging the door open, I grabbed his shirt. "Her name is Claire Thomas."

Patchins grinned as he lifted his arms over his head. "I surrender."

"I'm going to make you a deal," I said, as I backed into the wall opposite him and crossed my hands behind me. "You don't come around here anymore. You don't bring me pork chops. You don't knock on my door. If anything goes wrong with the place, like a broken window, I'll fix it myself and deduct it from the rent. See, Patchins, the deal is that you become invisible."

"I don't go in for one-sided deals."

"But there's more. If you choose not to become invisible, you know what I'm going to do?"

Patchins lowered his head like a bull will do before it charges. "This is my house. I could kick you out this very day."

Shrugging, I replied, "I'm going to call up your wife. I don't exactly know what I'm going to tell her, but I've got a real active imagination. I'm sure I can come up with something."

"The wife would think you were a crazy renter, that's all."

"If you're so sure of that, you just keep on coming around here and bugging me, and we'll find out, won't we?"

Patchins got wall-eyed as he stared at me. "I never done nothing illegal with you or that Claire...Claire Thomas."

"But you'd like to, wouldn't you? You said it yourself. You said if Claire keeps teasing you—which she never once did—you'd show her." I tapped my finger to the center of my forehead. "It's all in here. Every rotten thing that's ever come out of your mouth. Right in here."

Patchins wiped his hands on the front of his overalls. "I get the picture, Girl. You're on top and she's on bottom, I get it."

Looking at him was like looking into the face of Dirk Ramstead all over again. The anger in my stomach was the same, and the readiness to strike was the same. One good push and Patchins would topple down the stairs. Stevie once said I used my fists to settle things because I hadn't learned to be around people when I was young, that I didn't know how to settle things in other ways. It was true back then, but I could make it different now. It wasn't true with Teresa, and it wasn't true with Patchins. Whatever Patchins was, he didn't deserve a broken neck.

I stepped away from him so I wouldn't be tempted. "I don't like you, Patchins."

He leaned into the railing at the top of the stairs. "You got me wrong, Girl. I don't wear a black hat."

"You sure don't wear a white one."

"Never said I did." He walked down the stairs sideways, holding the railing hand-over-hand to keep himself steady. "Make sure you send me the rent on time or I'll have you and your girlfriend out of here."

***

He was long gone by the time Claire came home. I had been waiting for her. We had gotten onto a schedule a couple of times a week, jogging together in the evenings. We didn't go to the refuge, for the snow was too deep. We ran in town, down the plowed streets.

When I heard her come up the stairs, I opened my door and waved her into my room. "Patchins dropped some space heaters off for us." She sat on one arm of my couch and I sat on the other. "He won't be coming around anymore. I blackmailed him." I explained the whole thing, leaving out the parts about what he'd said of her and me. "I think he'll take me seriously. His wife has him fairly well buffaloed."

"You have him fairly well buffaloed."

A pot of tea was waiting in the kitchen. I brought it into the living room and filled our cups. "Maybe I should have blackmailed him into getting me a new couch while I was at it, seeing as how he rents this place as furnished."

"I've got a couch you can actually sit on," Claire said. "Join me?"

"Sure." It was the first time I had accepted an invitation to her room. Three times before she had asked me, offering to feed me dinner after a run, but I had refused. Both times it had been more embarrassment than fear that made me say no; I didn't want her to notice the acrid scent of my body after a hard run, and she would have within the closed space of her room.

I waited in the hall as she tossed some books off the couch, clearing a place for us to sit. She didn't have a full-sized couch, but one that was made for two people to sit on. The springs were firm. I balanced my cup on my knee as Claire sat next to me.

"This is a nice couch," I said. "I'm surprised Patchins let it stay here."

"He didn't," she replied. "I cleared out all his furniture when I moved in."

"Everything here is yours?"

She nodded. She had real things, like a person who has lived on her own for a long time. She had a rocking chair, with wicker on the seat and back. In front of the couch was an end table with glass on the top. Sitting atop it was a mahogany statue in the shape of a woman. A lamp with a soft green light was in the corner of the room. Hanging on the wall was a painting in a glass frame of a solitary woman sitting at a table in a cafe. Overhead, all around her room, were hanging plants: a huge fern, a fragile-looking plant with furry purple leaves, and a vine-like plant with green leaves that were striped with lines of white.

"Your place," I began, "it looks like a real home."

Claire went to her compact disk player and thumbed through the disks. Often I had heard her play music, seeping into my room, of women I did not know. She chose between two artists—Melissa Etheridge and k.d. lang—choosing the second. I didn't have any idea of either of them, except they were women who sang in beautiful voices. Claire kicked her loafers off and pulled her knees to her chest as she turned sideways on the couch facing me. She wore a spruce-colored blouse and tan slacks—femme, Patchins had called her, and she looked so, much more than I. I wore an old pair of Levis that had a tear in the knee, a boxy sweater, tennis shoes. I turned from Claire to focus on the statue of the woman on the end table. Its eyes were marked with topaz stones. I knew that stones couldn't look back, but it felt as if they were. "I've never seen a statue like that," I said.

"It was a gift from my sister."

"Kim?"

"No. Jeannie. My oldest sister. I've got some pictures, if you'd like to see them."

I followed her to her bedroom. In the corner a bulletin board hung on the wall. Photographs covered every free inch of the cork. She took one of the photos down and handed it to me. "That's my family," she said.

Four women were in the photograph, crammed onto a couch that wasn't much bigger than the one in Claire's room. "That's...that's your mother?" Claire nodded. She was dressed in a purple blouse and gray slacks. Her hair was the color of pewter, settling in loose curls upon her shoulders. Her eyes were brown. All the daughters were blue. "You don't have a picture of your father," I said. "He must have had blue eyes."

"When I was in grade school, he had just started a job as a substitute teacher." She looked at me with steel blue eyes. "Mamaso had just gotten her job at the bank. Kim was a toddler. Jeannie was eight years old, and I was seven. He always took it out on Jeannie. Never me, never Kim." She pointed at her bedroom door. "He'd set her there," she said. "On top of the door. He'd tell me to watch her, because I was next."

I looked up at the door, whispered, "There's no room."

"She'd brace her stomach across it, holding on with her arms and legs. Her head would be over the end of it, staring down. I'd bring a chair over and give her books to read. Sometimes I'd bring her a doll, sometimes a matchbox car. We'd play cards, anything to pass the time.

She'd tell me to go outside and play, but she was my sister—I stayed."

"How..." I cleared my voice. "How long?"

"The least was an hour. The most was four. He'd tell us exactly how long she was to be there. If she called for him early, it meant she would stay for another hour. He wouldn't let her down to go to the bathroom. If I had to go, I wouldn't. I'd wait till she came down. She would go first and then I would go. He'd stand at the door laughing at the two of us. *Good hearted laughter.* He'd ruffle our hair and tell us to behave or Jeannie would end up there again. Kim would be playing at his feet. He'd lean down to tickle her, and then he'd go back to his television. The only memory she has of him is his hands tickling her stomach."

"Your mother—she didn't know?"

"No. We thought it was as normal as getting up in the morning, just another part of our day. I remember when Mamaso found out. She came home sick from work. We had just gotten home from school. Jeannie walked in front on his TV set, and he immediately set her up on the door. She didn't fight, didn't scream. She never did. She just held onto the door. It was always the door leading into the kitchen, the back door. Jeannie was hanging onto it when the screen door opened. We heard Mamaso cough, and when she looked up the breath caught in her throat. Jeannie's head was leaning over the door, and her eyes were half closed. When Mamaso took her down, she wet her pants. He was standing against the wall, watching. She held Jeannie to her front, me and Kim at her sides, and she told him to get out. We were still holding onto her when he packed a suitcase and came down the stairs. He said good-bye to us. He kissed us—" She reached up and put her hand on her cheek. "And when he tried to kiss Mamaso, she moved her head aside. Her hands were shaking as he told her that we were all going to be whores, if she didn't punish us. He walked out and it's the last I've seen of him."

She took in a ragged sigh as she ran her fingers across the picture. "Jeannie and I managed to get through it, more or less, together. Kim—" She ran her finger over Kim's face. "She would watch him lift Jeannie to the top of the door. She would giggle, pointing her finger up. Jeannie spent the entire year on the top of the door, Kim believed it was a game, and I was the watcher." She massaged her eyes. "He writes us Christmas cards—to his daughters. Kim keeps them in her room, every single one of them. Kim knows. She doesn't acknowledge it, but she knows. It doesn't fit within the picture of him tickling her sides."

I looked at the three sisters; all of them had Claire's sandy colored hair. Kim's was darker, like wet sand; Jeannie's was lighter, like dry sand, but all were the shades of sand. Jeannie smiled, not in her lips but in her eyes, the kind of smile worn by people who think the world is one big crazy joke. Kim sat in the center of the couch. Her left hand was on Mamaso's shoulder, her right on Claire's. She had the look of a beauty queen—her hair neatly combed, her eyes a vivid blue inside lashes that shone from mascara, her skin shaded beige, her lips painted pink. Underneath all the covers was a babe in swaddling clothes.

Claire pointed up to the corner of the bulletin board at a picture of a baby. "That's Jeannie's girl, Ruby."

In the picture, a baby girl was in the bathtub, waist deep in bubble-coated water. Her hair was dark and dripping wet, and her eyes were luminous, focused at a point off to the side of the camera's lens. In her hands, she held a plastic shovel. So tiny, her fingers—no more than three years old.

"Do you think you would want one—a baby of your own someday?"

"Yes," Claire replied. "Someday."

When she looked at me, I focused on her eyes until my own stopped hurting—something about that picture, about all of this, was making me want to cry. "Would you want a boy or a girl?"

"Whatever comes," she replied.

"Jeannie's how old?"

"She's twenty-four, a year older than me."

"Is Jeannie married?"

"Divorced. She got married right out of high school. They made it work for about three years. Which is a lot more than I did. During high school, I had tons of boyfriends."

"That's okay, lots of people have boyfriends."

"I *slept* with one every couple of months." She laced her hands in the pockets of her jeans. "I kept trying to find the right man, but he doesn't exist, not for me anyway. I gave up on it in college. Mamaso knows about it now, but she didn't back then. She always wants to be perfect, the perfect mom, but things keep getting in her way."

"What things?"

Claire smiled. "Her personality."

I followed Claire out of the room and settled into her couch. She crossed her legs under her as she sat down next to me. In the background, k.d. lang was singing about love that washed her clean. "Tell me—would you have tried to break Teresa's wrist?"

"I don't think so, but the thought certainly crossed my mind." I crossed my left leg over my right, a man's way of crossing his legs, but I did not feel like a man. "I slept with Mike. Teresa watched. It wasn't enjoyable." Claire nodded and acted as if she knew this; she didn't once take a breath in surprise. I folded my hand upon my right ankle and shook the foot back and forth. "Have you made plans for Thanksgiving?"

"Yes," she replied. "You?"

"I told Tiny to schedule me to work."

"Is it too late to change the schedule?"

"Why?"

"I'm going home for Thanksgiving. You'd be more than welcome to join me."

I picked my tea cup off the table, but was shaking so badly I spilled tea on my leg, but the tea was cold by now and didn't burn me. "I don't have anything to wear."

Claire set her elbows on her knees and cupped her chin in her hand. "That's the best excuse you can come up with?"

"We'd fly over?"

"We'd drive."

"I don't have a car."

She put her hand on her chest. "I have a car."

"You have snow tires, of course?"

"Of course," she replied. "Have you ever been to Seattle?"

"Nope."

"Have you ever been anywhere?"

I shrugged. "You can bring a horse to water, but you can't make him drink."

"What is that supposed to mean?"

I didn't have the foggiest idea—the words just came out of my mouth. "Nothing."

"Would you like to see Seattle?"

"Yes."

"Is that an answer?"

I smiled as I stared at her. "Your family, they won't mind?"

"What are you going to do, steal the turkey and run?"

I put my hand on the back of my neck and rubbed the tight muscles. "I would like to see Seattle. I'll check with Tiny tomorrow. If he can find someone to fill in for me, I'd like to go with you."

"I didn't think you'd do it, Alexandra, I didn't think you would."

"Maybe you don't know me so well." Reaching for her hand, I said, "I want to teach you something my Dad and my brother Stevie used to do. It's kind of a...a logger's greeting." Folding my fingers through hers, I lifted my hand and brought it down, sideways, between the two of us. "Dad would do that and say, 'Timber!'." Gripping her hand in mine, I made two quick karate motions, striking to the side. "And then Stevie would say, 'Chop, chop.' That's how they said hello and good-bye."

When I got up to leave, Claire lifted her hand and let it fall. In reply, my hand sliced the air. In the whole town of Willow, there was probably not a person outside of us who would have known what our hands said.

***

Tiny was so happy I wasn't going to be spending my Thanksgiving alone that he offered me a week off. But I told him I just needed three days. We were leaving on Wednesday, as soon as Claire was done with school, Thanksgiving was Thursday, and we were coming back on Friday. Claire had three tests coming up.

When Claire came up the stairs, I beckoned her into my room. "Let me show you the dress I planned on wearing."

She grinned. "Oh my god, she's wearing a dress."

She waited in the living room while I went into my bedroom to change. Hanging in my closet was a white gown made of cotton gauze-like material. Red lace lined the collar and the bottom of the sleeves. The front was cut so low that the top of my bra showed, so I took it off.

Claire stood as I entered the room. She looked from me to the picture sitting on my windowsill. In the picture, my mother was wearing this gown.

"My mother...these are the kind of clothes she liked to wear on the mountain. At home, she dressed more plain, like other folks. But on the mountain, she liked gowns. White gowns, mostly."

Claire stared at the picture on the windowsill. Her voice was the middle line between hard and soft. "Why white?"

I fingered the red lace on the bottom of the sleeves. "I don't know. She just did."

Claire's gaze shifted, from the top of my head to the top of my bare feet. "If I had a body like yours, I'd give it my own clothing."

Nodding, I said: "You would."

"Think about it," she replied. "Take a good look and tell me why you shouldn't."

She set her hand on my back and pulled the zipper down. The dress fell to the floor. Stunned, I felt like a robot with buttons embedded on the curve my spine as Claire placed her hand on the small of my back and turned me to face the full-length mirror attached to my bedroom door. Never in my life had I looked at myself so directly, at my own naked body, as I did then. Always, I would cover my body with a towel when facing a mirror and my own eyes.

I stared into the mirror, cocking my head. A tiny black mole dotted my skin, low on my right breast. I had never seen it before. When I caught Claire's eye in the mirror, my cheeks burned and turned red. She had seen me before without clothing, Patchins had said so, she'd seen me stark naked under the kitchen table. But unlike then, I now had the eyes to see myself at the same time.

She sat on my bed while I placed my hands on my hips and stared into the mirror. I told myself I'd keep looking until I counted to a hundred, but I could only make it to forty-one. I pulled my bathrobe off the hook and wrapped myself in it, sat down next to Claire on the bed. For a long time I simply stared at her, noticing the fine slivers of gold in her blue eyes. "Your eyes are beautiful," I whispered. "They're blue and gold... What does the GPA stand for, Claire?"

She held my eyes. "The Gay Pride Association."

As I looked at her, I nodded. "I thought so."

"Then why did you ask?"

"To *know* so." The circle of gold lessened until her eyes were a luminous blue. "They change, your eyes. The gold is gone now, all blue...so you're a lesbian."

She cocked her head toward me. "Certainly, you're not surprised."

"Boys didn't fit the bill, huh?"

"No. It was not an easy time, always looking for Mr. Wonderful. I suppose he does exist for certain women, but not for me."

"And were the women... Miss Wonderful?"

She smiled. "Well, the sex was good."

"How come—April has Sue, Sue has April—how come... "

"How come *what*, Alexandra?"

I spoke softly. "You don't have anyone."

"I'm not looking for anyone." She shook her head. "I feel like I'm having a lesbian oriented mother-daughter talk with you."

"Did you have a lover, before you moved in here?"

"I was living in an expensive apartment, and my money was running out. I looked for a cheap place to rent, close to campus, and found this. But the thing is, I've got a next door neighbor who likes to talk in her sleep."

"If she talks too much, you could always move."

"I tried," she replied. "All the apartments are extremely expensive."

"Well, it looks like you're going to keep your nightmare neighbor, I guess."

She smiled in the way that was hers alone—the left side of her lips raised in a broad smile, the right stayed the same. "Looks like it."

"So you didn't have a lover."

"I had a lover, but now she's engaged to a man."

"To a man?" I said. "Then what we're you two doing together?"

"A little bit more than playing house. She wants to marry him and start it going again with me. Her illicit lesbian affair."

"And you said?"

She lifted her hand and waved it in the air. "Bye bye." When she faced me, the gold shimmered in her eyes. "You're going to go for a run in that?"

I rose and turned my back on her, let the robe fall to the ground. As I began to put on my running clothes, I said, "I'll beat you with my eyes closed."

Out in the streets of Willow, we ran our five mile route down the plowed streets until our bodies melted from the strain. We ran down to our mile marker near the edge of town. She beat me by three blocks, but that was okay, I knew she would. It was in the endurance end of things where I shone. She ran quickly, but five or six miles was her limit. I could plod on, taking my time, forever.

After we got back to the mansion, she said she had some spare food if I'd like a bite. I set my sweaty body down at her table and ate a plateful of steamed vegetables and rice. When I apologized for the salty smell of my body, she said it was an odor that she didn't find offensive.

***

I decided I would buy myself new clothes to take with me for Thanksgiving. With all the money I'd managed to save since I'd been working at the IGA, I could afford to buy myself some nice things.

I took a handful of my money to a shop in downtown Willow that sold women's wear. On the racks, I found a pair of crisp-looking wool pants, not the kind of wool pants you wear when you're in the woods to keep yourself dry, but a kind of wool that was soft, not scratchy, and carried a crease. If I hadn't read the label, I wouldn't have known it was wool. Black, the pants had cuffs at the bottom sewn right into them. I took them to the dressing room and put them on. They fit so well I got myself a tan pair of the same type. To wear with them, I bought two blouses that felt soft against my skin. The tags said they were rayon.

I didn't want to show up in Seattle toting my new clothes in a duffel bag, so I bought a suitcase. The last place I put money down was at the record store. I wanted to buy a tape to play on the ride to Seattle, just in case Claire and I ran out of things to talk about. I didn't know many of the artists in the popular music section, but I knew a lot of them in the country and western section. Garth Brooks, Willie Nelson, Hank Jr., Randy Travis, Dolly Parton. I wasn't sure if Claire liked songs about cheating and loving, so I didn't buy any country music. In the self-improvement section, I settled on a tape: How to Expand Your Vocabulary.

I stopped at the lavatory in the record store. As I dropped my worn out jeans and sat down, a single piece of graffiti greeted me on the closed door: *What do you do when the world is too real?*

"I don't know," I whispered. "Don't know."

The night before we were leaving, Claire stayed out late, studying at the library. I ran alone that night, five miles, as hard and as fast as I could; I hoped the run would expel some of my nervous energy, but it didn't.

Tossing in bed, I felt every lump in the mattress, every crooked spring. If I had been preparing to take a trip to the moon, I would have been less nervous. On the moon, if the need to escape becomes over-whelming, you can float off in weightlessness, just drift away, know-ing that the lifeline is strong enough to pull you back.

Chapter Eleven

I was not a person who got carsick, but as we packed our things into Claire's car my stomach was churning. My watch said it was four o'clock p.m. We would be in Seattle about ten. Outside it was overcast, threatening to snow.

Claire's car was a Toyota Corolla. I didn't know how old it was—it didn't have a single bump on its maroon exterior. Inside, it had a tape deck and cruise control. I had seen the car parked on the other side of the street and thought it belonged to the folks living there. They had a real house, with two cars in the garage. They never once looked at the mansion as they left their house, not once. They probably thought the mansion was a crack house, if Willow had such a thing.

"This is your car?" I asked.

"Yes."

We both got inside and started the long drive to Seattle. "This car does not fit the mansion, Claire."

"You're right," she replied. "It doesn't."

I looked at her with my head cocked. "You can afford such a car?"

She took us out of Willow, onto the highway. "It's not that new."

"It looks new."

"A friend gave it to me."

"A friend gave you a car?" I asked.

"And an engagement ring. We were planning on getting married."

"When was this?"

"I was a student at the University in Seattle—that was before I decided on a degree in speech pathology. The program at Willow is run by a woman, Debra Olsen, who's very highly respected. When I finish my degree, I'll go on for my Master's." She smiled as turned the car around a bend. "I was engaged to Jim, and he had buckets of his parents' money."

"Did you meet his parents?"

She laughed. "And then I broke the engagement."

"Were they mean to you?"

"God no, they adored me, like Jim did, absolutely loved me. The four of us would make one happy family, one *rich* happy family."

"Did you tell Jim about your...your sexual...I'm having some problem coming up with the right word...Your unique sexuality?"

She smiled. "My sexual preferences."

"That must be the right word," I said, returning her smile. "Your sexual preferences."

"I explained it to him—that I was gay and had always been gay, that I had slept with a few women and a lot of men, and then I met him. Despite the fact that he was very good looking, and very rich, I just couldn't do it anymore. I came out to him and to myself. When I folded the engagement ring in his hand, he asked me if there was any chance I might be wrong." She moved her head left and right. "I told him that he had better take the car back, but he wouldn't. He said that the two of us had kissed in that car, and then he left." She moved her right hand off the wheel and patted the space next to her legs. "I have never been able to kiss a woman in this car."

As I looked at her driving us to Nowhere, I imagined what it would be like to kiss her, in this car. I imagined the feel of her lips pressing against mine, the taste of her tongue. I imagined it so strongly that my body began to want her, long before my mind could accept it. I crossed my legs, but the tingling sensation worsened. I felt like a person making a commitment to God: if You do this, if You take the thoughts of Claire's lips from my mind, then I swear I won't say Fuck anymore, or drink myself silly, or ask Mike or Hank to beat me again—if You could please take Claire's lips from my mind, could You do that please?

All my prayers did not work. Deep down, deep in the bluejeans I was wearing, sweaty deep at the crotch, I was a woman looking at Claire and imagining just what it would be like to feel her body next to mine. My skin was on fire. Even when I moved my position— crossed my feet, uncrossed my feet—everything that I knew about me was getting reorganized. I had to wait until all the small change was handed out, every last nickel, every last penny, and count it all out.

"Your mother," I asked. "She knows?"

"Mamaso believes that if I'm happy, she's happy. Jeannie's the same way—she'd love me even if I slept with snakes. Kim is still adjusting to it."

I crossed my right leg over my left. "Did you find other people like you were?"

"Yes. Then I met Angela and we moved in together. I thought Angela was coming with me, to go to the University at Willow, but at the last moment she wanted to stay at the U in Seattle. When you're committed to each other, the relationship has got to come first, and if Angela was staying then so would I. My degree could wait until Angela was done with hers. But she talked me out of it. She would stay in Seattle, I would travel to the eastern side of the state, and we would make it work. Long distance phone calls, trips back and forth—we were certain we could stay together. But we didn't."

"Love—you loved her?"

"I did, very much."

My response was so old, so entirely used up, it didn't seem to encompass what I was feeling inside my gut, a boring hole of pain. "I'm sorry, Claire."

"So was I, Alexandra, so was I." She looked at me and smiled softly. "She's with Etta now."

"Etta?" I said, disbelieving. "Etta? Back in Pike, we had a woman who worked in the Post Office, you know, a Nazarene; she had her hair in a bun and wore tennis shoes beneath her skirt. Her name was *Etta*."

"Etta and I used to date."

"You went out with *Etta*?" I asked. "I mean, did you go out like the two of us go out, like to a spaghetti feed or jogging around town, you know—*went out*. Or did you go out in another way?"

She tapped her hand against the steering wheel. "Are you asking me if I slept with her, Alexandra?"

I nodded.

"Do you want an answer?"

I nodded again.

"Then ask the fucking question, please."

"Did you and Etta—I can't believe her name is Etta—sleep together?"

"Yes, we did. Any other questions?"

There we were driving down the highway and she stared at me for a long time; I didn't care if there were no cars, it was too long to be staring at me. "Watch the road, Claire."

Facing me, she lifted her brows. "No."

"God damn it." I reached past her and took the wheel, and drove us steadily down the highway. In the blare of her car lights, all I could see was darkness everywhere, shiny white marks on the blacktop. I scooted toward her, keeping my hands on the steering wheel. "You know, there's absolutely no reason for you to be such a shit."

She laughed. "Me? I'm a shit?" When the car hit 61 m.p.h., she set the cruise control on and relaxed in her seat. Her hands were folded on the back of her head.

"You haven't been with many women, have you?" I asked.

"Have you?"

"Me?"

"You."

My mother came to dwell inside me, saying: *Don't let anyone tell you this is wrong.* "I'm not talking about me. You. We're talking about you."

"I slept around with a lot more men than I have women. Jim tried to tell me I was bisexual, but he was wrong. When I sleep with a woman, I am a lesbian, and when I sleep with a man, I am a lesbian sleeping with a man."

I took her hand and placed it on the wheel, regained myself with my arms crossed next to the door. "You need an L stuck on your forehead."

"L for Lesbian?"

"L for Lucky." I took the map from Claire's glove compartment and a flashlight, and followed the green line of I-90 west, getting my bearings. On the map, Seattle seemed very far away. "That's where we're going," I said. "The other side of the state."

"Yes."

"People put their pants on one leg at a time," I said. "Even in Seattle." Reflectors on the roadside sent back spasms of light. I stared at their flashing beams, a froth of light into the darkness. "Going with you... I'm a little bit scared, Claire. I don't meet people very well... Back home, folks thought I was stuck up. But I wasn't. If you don't have anything worth saying, it's best to keep your mouth shut. But your brain, it's always working."

I was quiet for a long time, until Claire broke the silence. "What's in your brain now, Alexandra?"

Her eyes were luminous, dancing from the road to me. "I think you are a very beautiful woman, Claire. That's what I'm thinking." I studied the changes occurring in her eyes—light blue, gold surrounding the irises, then a dark insistent blue moving up and down my face. I pressed on my head, far in the center of my brain where my mother's voice resided. "It's not good, what's inside of me."

"Alexandra," she said softly. "It's not—"

I cut her off. With my eyes closed, I said, "My brain is working overtime, but my mouth has taken a vacation."

"You are *letting* your mouth take a vacation."

I turned my head and stared at her. "All right," I finally said. "I'm *letting* my mouth take a vacation. Now I'm going to read this map, to find out where we're going and where we've been."

"I don't think you'll find out where you've been on a map."

"Claire." I gently touched her arm. "Please, don't."

She stared at the highway for a long moment before she nodded. "We're coming into Moses Lake. To the right, you'll see the water."

But I wasn't checking the map for Moses Lake, I was looking at Pike. A red highway line headed north toward the border of British Columbia. Pike was marked on the Washington side in minuscule type, identified by a tiny white dot. Mt. Abercrombie, where Stevie and Dad hunted, stretched above the other mountains and peaks. The blue line of the river snaked northward toward Lake Sullivan. Stevie and Dad had brought home some fine trout from that lake. The shaded green of the Colville National Forest enveloped the entire area. Within the green, white squares and triangles signified privately owned land. The smallest white square on the map marked my mother's mountain.

I got lost in the map for a long while, studying the familiar names: Mount Baldy, Calispell Peak, Old Dominion Mountain, Metaline Falls, Gypsy Peak. The town of Colville was to the west. Near there, unmarked on the map, was the shack where my mother was born, the forest where my grandfather lost his head, and the rabbit hutch where my grandmother lost her mind.

My eyelids filled with lead as I stared at the fuzzy words on the map. I tried to stay awake, but no amount of blinking could keep my eyelids from falling down.

When I woke up, the first thing I noticed was my hands between my legs, comfortably relaxed. "I fell asleep," I said, crossing my arms to my front. "How long?"

"A couple of hours."

I felt hot in my groin, burning up hot. It was a feeling that was new to me, waking up and feeling the tingling inside. "I don't think I dreamed," I said. I looked at her, but she was watching the road as we passed a semi. "Big truck...I don't think I dreamed."

Claire leaned forward and hugged the steering wheel with both hands, with her head resting on top. She looked at me from the corner of her eye, a tiny smile playing on her lips. "You don't," she said.

I started to blush, huge red flames burning across my face, as I looked at her. I had dreamed, and it was a dream with Claire inside of it. Claire and me, me and Claire—the two of us riding in this car—Claire and me, me and Claire—and I laced my hands near her breasts, on her breasts, and kissed her in this car that she has never kissed a woman in—Claire and me, me and Claire—I kissed until her breasts became alive beneath my tongue.

"If your dreams are any indication, you must be wonderful in bed, Alexandra." Staring at the highway, she ran her fingers through her hair. "Jesus."

"I dreamed...of you."

"I know." She nodded. "You said my name."

"Well, I guess that's that."

"*What* is *what*, Alexandra?"

"It means I'm processing—that's what it means. For example, I look at a sunset and don't have a name for it, or a feeling to describe it; it is a sunset only, a sunset *period*. But then later, after I haven't even thought about it, I can describe that sunset. I can talk about the way its colors bleed together. Do you know that long before we had names for the colors—rust, maroon, green—those colors abounded in the sunset...iridescent colors. The way I process things is like looking at a sunset. I don't even know things have happened, but they have, inside my mind. Patchins, Teresa and Mike, Hank, the mountain, and my mother—all of it is in there. *This* is in there, all of it, every bit of it. You, me, the ride to Seattle, all of it."

She focused on me, like the lens of a camera. "I am not your mother."

"No, you're not."

"Do you mean that? Can you look at me and hear my voice, and mean that?"

"You are Claire Thomas. You are not my mother. Claire Thomas."

Through a smile, she replied, "Thou doth protest too much."

"God damn Shakespeare...is it Shakespeare?" She nodded her head. "When you are five years old, like I was when my mother died, you can believe all sorts of things, but you can't believe that any Power will bring her back. How can you believe in a woman who's dead?"

"She is not dead, not inside you."

"Oh, but she is."

Slowly, she shook her head. "There is no one who can touch you and not feel her."

I held to the dashboard until my knuckles became white. "I'm working on it, Claire." Claire looked at me, but I did not return her glance. The spasms of light held my eyes; it was like being hypnotized. Emptiness stretched ahead. No trees, no buildings, no towns. My mouth felt dry and my stomach churned. "We're a long way from nowhere."

"We're coming to George."

"George, Washington?"

George, Washington, sprouted up at the side the highway. Near the exit was a roadside restaurant—Martha's Inn. In the streetlight, a woman who looked like she could have been Widow Kyle's sister was leaving Martha's Inn; she had the Widow's bulky stature, purposeful stride, and mouse-colored hair.

"That woman there," I said to Claire. "She looks like a neighbor of mine in Pike, name of Widow Kyle. She wasn't really a Widow, her husband wasn't dead or anything. He just left her in the night. One time, the Widow got the idea she'd sell Avon. She wasn't the kind of woman you'd expect to come to your door selling Avon things, but she needed extra money so could buy a goosedown parka from the Ward's catalogue." I pressed my hand into my stomach; talking, like a teaspoon of soda in a glass of water, was making the nausea subside. "Since she was selling the makeup, she thought it was only right that she wear it, but she couldn't wear it without feeling cheap. She only lasted a week selling Avon. She had to wait a long time before she got the parka, buying it with her Social Security money."

I rested the side of my head on the window of my door, stared at the snow-covered wheat fields. With the moon cascading off them, they nearly burned my eyes. White. My mother wore white on the mountain. Why white, I didn't know. Could it have been that she just liked the color of white? Could it have been that simple—she liked white?

Claire reached for the thermos of coffee that she'd prepared for the trip. I took the lid off and poured her a cup. "Here," I said. "I can do it."

I had a whole reservoir of stories I could have told from back home, but I didn't feel like talking anymore. I flipped the radio on; mile after mile, we listened to songs sung by people I'd never heard of. Now and then Claire would hum along with one of the songs. It was nice, listening to the sound of her voice. Her voice—hers.

As we approached Snoqualmie Pass, the road grew worse, covered with slick, hard-packed snow. A blanket of fog stretched ahead of us, and then we were within it. Claire gripped the wheel and leaned forward, close to the windshield. In the dense fog, the only way to follow the curve of the road was to keep the dim red tail-lights of the car ahead in view.

"Jesus, I hate this," Claire said.

As we reached the summit of the pass and began to descend, the snow line receded. On the sides of the highway, the wind whipped the loose snow in tight spirals. Finally, the studded snow tires began to hum as they connected with the black tar of a clear highway.

The radio buzzed and cracked, and probably had been doing so for a long while without our being aware of it. I flicked the radio off. "I brought a tape along for us to listen to," I said. I reached into the back pocket of my Levis for the tape. My good clothes, my new clothes, were locked in my suitcase. I hadn't wanted to wrinkle them by wearing them on the drive. "It's a tape about improving your vocabulary."

When I turned the tape deck on, the announcer explained that the key to vocabulary expansion lies in having the persistence to introduce new words into daily conversation. Within this tape, a word would be introduced, its dictionary definition provided, and then the word would be used in various sentences. A pause would follow the introduction of each new word, allowing the listeners time to construct their own model sentences and recite them aloud.

One of the first words given was loquacious: talkative. In the pause when we were to supply our model sentences, I said: "Sometimes, loquacious people use up a lot of words but don't really say anything that's worth saying in the first place."

Another good word was sagacious, which meant gifted with discernment, having practical wisdom. My model sentence was, "I want to be sagacious."

Claire's model sentence was, "In a lot of ways, you are sagacious."

The tape had some more good words on it, like insouciant, obfuscate, obsequious. But it also had some words that seemed ridiculous, like rubiginous; it was defined as ruddy, used in reference to a face.

"It seems to me that if you mean ruddy, you should just say ruddy," I began, tossing a smile at Claire. "It doesn't cut it to say that the drunk passed out on the couch has a rubiginous complexion."

Since we'd been on the clear road with very little traffic coming in either direction, Claire had assumed a strange position behind the wheel. Her right foot was resting near the brake pedal but her left foot was balanced on the dashboard.

"What's that word you used," she asked. "For the colors of the rainbow?"

"Iridescent," I replied. "I learned that word when I was young. Every once in a while my mother would lay out a new word for me. Tributary. Heroine. Iridescent. Dead." When Claire turned to me, I managed a small smile. "Big words for a little child."

As we approached Seattle, she put both feet on the floor. I was thankful that I wasn't behind the wheel taking the car into bumper-to-bumper freeway traffic. I'd never seen so many cars in one place before.

"If you look, way out ahead, you'll see the Puget Sound."

"I don't see it." I rolled down my window and breathed in the moistness of ocean air. "Better view this way." I pulled my upper body out of the window and sat down in the window frame, holding onto the hand grip above the inside of the door. We were going at least 45 m.p.h., but cars were going by me, passing left and right. Now and then, people waved.

I looked in at Claire through the door. "*Seattle.*"

She smiled and grabbed my ankle. "If we run into any policeman, you're paying the ticket."

Everything was lit up around me—small stores and massive skyscrapers, the malls, the Space Needle, the street lights, the bars, the houses—everything was lit on fire. On the mountain, you know when it's night because darkness falls around you and there is nothing to replace it. But in Seattle, darkness falls and lights come on. Lights everywhere.

I nudged Claire with my foot. "Where's the Puget Sound?"

"There." She pointed straight ahead.

You could barely see it, a dark blue vacuum of water. In the distance, a ferry boat pulled toward the shore. Its edges were surrounded by embers of red on the blue water. Out beyond the vision of my eyes was the Pacific Ocean. Columbus must have had angels with him, diving across the seas until he found a continent. My mother said that we were like Columbus, having discovered the isolation of the mountain as our own. It was our America.

I got out of the window and into the car. "In the darkness—everything is light." I touched Claire's arm where the light from a passing car had illuminated it. "Light."

"That's our exit ahead," she said.

I wished my tape had introduced a word that was like 'nervous' but bigger and wider, more encompassing; I needed a word for the feeling of anxiety that was growing inside my stomach as we drove down the hilly streets and stopped in front of a box-shaped house.

Stiff from the drive, it took Claire a moment to straighten her back when she got out of the car. Her mother came out of the house and wrapped her arms around her, their upper bodies rocking side to side. She was wearing a pair of spandex leggings and an oversized jersey that came to the top of her knees. The leggings were red and the jersey was purple. She looked at me over Claire's shoulder.

"It's good to meet you, Mrs. Thomas."

"Do you see my mother around?" she asked Claire. Claire smiled, and lifted one shoulder in a half shrug. "Do you see her?" she asked me.

"I...I don't think so."

"Well, if she does show up, which is quite unlikely since she's dead, you can call her Mrs. Thomas. But call me Doris."

"I'm Alexandra."

Her lips were barely smiling. "You're the one who's always listening through the walls?"

My hands were crossed behind me. They moved up and down. "Well...yeah."

She broke into a broad smile. "I like her," she said to Claire. "But she is rather shy. Aren't you?"

"Me?"

"And she has difficulty responding to questions. Yes, you."

"I…I, uh, no, not shy."

When they went in the house, I got my suitcase and followed behind them; I stood on the threshold and stared inside. Doris' house had a comfortable, lived-in feel. A two-seater couch was in the living room, an afghan draped across its back. A recliner chair was placed in direct line of vision to the television set. The weather channel was on the TV screen. She pushed the knob in with her toe, turning the television off.

"You're letting all the cold air inside," she called to me. "If you want to stay out, close the door. If you want to come in, close the door. Either way, the door stays closed."

As I came inside and closed the door behind me, Doris rustled Claire's hair. "Kim is spending the night at a friend's. She said to give you this." Doris gave Claire a big old kiss on the cheek. "She'll be back tomorrow in time for turkey."

Claire placed her hands on the small of her back and leaned backwards. "Christ."

"Here," Doris said. She sat Claire down on the couch and folded her collar back, brushed her hair aside, and began to knead her neck and shoulders. "It's ten-thirty, you know."

"We said we'd be here at about ten o'clock," Claire replied.

"Next time, say ten-thirty."

"Whatever I say, you just add a half hour onto it. That'll solve the problem."

"Whatever you feel like saying, then *you* add a half hour onto it," Doris said. "And that'll solve the problem."

"We're half an hour late, a half hour."

I stared at the two of them and wondered which one would give, but it didn't look like either of them would. Stubborn mother begot stubborn daughter, and both of them had smiling eyes.

"Are you two hungry?" Doris asked, as she folded Claire's collar into place. "You probably left at four-thirty—"

"Four," Claire said.

"And probably didn't have dinner. I ordered a pizza and have three-quarters of it left." She squeezed Claire's shoulders. "Jeannie and Ruby will be here at supper time." She was standing behind the couch and Claire tipped her head backwards to see her. "You know," Doris began. "I would never have left you home with your father, had I known." She placed her hand on Claire's forehead and brushed back the hair. "Never." When she looked at me, I felt naked beneath her eyes. She had that way of looking that makes you feel seen. "You know?" she asked me.

"Claire's father—she told me."

"Well..." She looked at the carpet. "I kicked him out in November." She pulled her shoulders back. "So come on, then, let's go eat the pizza." The moment Claire rose up, her arms went around her mother. "Oh Christ," Doris said, holding her. "Thanksgiving makes me think of it all over again. *On top of the door!* God damn Thanksgiving, fucking holiday."

Claire's voice said, "Fucking piece of shit Thanksgiving."

"Fucking piece of asshole shit Thanksgiving."

"Fucking piece of asshole shit-eating bastardizing Thanksgiving."

"Fucking piece of asshole shit-eating bastardizing god damn Thanksgiving." Doris pressed her head into Claire's shoulder, then pulled away. "God damn stupid holiday." She and Claire exchanged a smile, and began to walk toward the kitchen. Doris turned to me. "Are you hungry?" she asked.

"I would like to go to the bathroom, please."

"Down the hall," she replied. "To the right."

I didn't look at Claire or her mother as I grabbed my suitcase and left the room. Inside the bathroom, I locked the door and sat on the edge of the bathtub, slowly rocking. Claire had a mother, and that mother was Doris, and Doris could touch Claire in a non-sexual way, and Claire could touch Doris in a non-sexual way.

I pushed myself up and washed my face, feeling the sting of cold water hitting my skin. From my suitcase, I removed another t-shirt, took mine off which was sweaty on my chest, and put the other on. I joined Claire and Doris at the kitchen table. Except for residual lines around her eyes, Doris' face was ageless. The lines creased as she smiled.

"Everything come out all right?"

"Yes, thank you."

"All these thank yous and pleases are making me nervous, Alexandra." Swinging open the refrigerator, she said: "The choices are mineral water, apple juice, beer, or wine."

"Beer, please."

Doris set a bottle of beer in front of me. "So what do you do on the east side of the state?"

"I'm a grocery checker."

"Do you like it?"

"I don't have any real complaints."

Doris leaned over me as she set the pizza on the table. "You smell delicious," she said. "What is that?"

For the first time in my life, I was wearing perfume. I'd bought it at the store that sold women's wear, and put it on when I changed my shirt. I glanced at Claire, feeling the red lines shoot across my face. "They call it nature oil."

Doris served a huge slice of pizza onto my plate. Before I could say anything, she bumped her hip against the side of my body. "You're welcome."

The pizza was vegetarian style and I had never tasted anything so good. The thin crust melted like a wafer in my mouth. We ate the pizza until only one slice remained, but Claire and I couldn't finish it. We made a domestic chain gang as we did the dishes; Doris washed the dishes, I dried them, and Claire put them in the cupboards.

In the living room, I sat next to Claire on the couch and Doris got comfortable in the recliner, her legs draped over the arm. On the end table in front of me was an issue of *National Geographic* magazine. While they talked about management problems at Doris' bank—she was working sixty hour weeks for the past month—I focused on an article about Pygmies until I blocked them out. As I read to the bottom of the page and flipped to the next, the sounds coming from them stopped being distinguishable as words. Their voices hummed in the room; that was all I heard.

I was reading an article about the genetic storehouse contained within a rain forest when the humming sound took on a lighter cadence. I looked up to see Claire laughing. "She did," Doris said. "In Ernst Hardware. One minute Ruby was next to me and the next minute she was peeing in the demonstrator toilet. As far as a three year old knows, a toilet is a toilet."

The room was dark, with only one lamp on, to my left. In the dim light, Doris' red leggings were fluorescent, swinging in an arch. She smiled as she looked at me. "Remind me to give you some back issues of *National Geographic* to take home with you." She flipped her legs over the arm of the recliner and stood, stretching her arms over her head. "You two sleep well." From the hallway, she called, "Lock up."

Claire rested the side of her head on the back of the couch. Half-moons of gray were beneath her eyes. "You'll be sleeping in Jeannie's old room," she said. "Mamaso set extra blankets out for you."

"You look tired," I said.

"The drive."

"Let's call it a night."

Claire locked up and showed me to my room. Leaning into the door frame, she folded her hands into her hair, pushing it off her fore-head. "Nature oil," she said. "You aren't turning femme on me, are you, Alexandra?"

Smiling, I shook my head. "I don't think so."

***

Thanksgiving day, we worked well into the afternoon preparing the meal. There was no football game in the background; Doris set the radio to a station that was playing opera music. She cooked from scratch—the cranberry sauce was prepared with fresh cranberries, the rolls were made with wheat flour and sunflower seeds, and the baked tomatoes were stuffed with a filling of sliced garlic, bread crumbs, provolone cheese and broccoli. She moved her hips as she cooked, left and right. Claire explained it, with a smile, as "operatic dancing."

"Here," Doris said to me, as I leaned against the wall watching her. "Do you want to peel some potatoes?"

"Yes."

"Peel enough for an army. Claire—you do the green salad. And when you're done with those, I wouldn't mind if you put the decorations up. We can't have a holiday without decorations, can we?"

Claire got the decorations out—cardboard cut-outs of turkeys and Pilgrims, and orange and brown crepe streamers. Claire grinned at me. "Are we having fun yet?"

In the living room, Claire and I wove the streamers into a single orange and brown strand. We stood on kitchen chairs to reach the ceil-ing and criss-crossed the room four times with the strips of crepe. We were finishing up, taping the cardboard decorations to the picture window and the door, when Doris came in and studied the room. She held her flour-coated hands away from her body like a surgeon and nodded approval.

159

"It looks like someone's going to have a party here," she said, and returned to the kitchen.

"Is it like this always?" I asked. "I mean, do you always put up decorations, things like that?"

"She says she does it for Ruby, but it's for herself. When she's a hundred, she'll still hang hearts on Valentine's day."

The front door opened. "Hey, hey, hey...Claire's home."

"Kim!"

Kim looked like she just walked off the Miss America pageant— she was wearing a fancy shirt with a fancy jacket on top of a fancy skirt. Claire waved her streamers at her, still standing on the chair. Kim ran to her and hugged her knees. "My, I've shrunk," Kim said, looking up at Claire.

Claire stepped down and held Kim tight. Her hands went up and down Kim's jacket. "This is what got you into trouble?" she asked. "You got this jacket with Mamaso's Visa Card?"

"Of course." Kim looked me over, from the soles of my tennis shoes to the top of my black head of hair. Both of us smiled at the same instant. "I'm Kim."

"Alexandra," I said.

She blinked three times, as if she had a gay-germ in her eyes—if she blinked long enough, maybe she could make Claire straight and make me go away. But Claire wasn't going for it. As politely as possible, she made a reference to the Gay Pride Association's Thanksgiving Dinner, held today in a Unitarian Church, and mentioned that her friends April and Sue would be serving there. "Gay and straight, some students, some not," she said. "They're cooking three turkeys."

"Not as good as Mamaso's," Kim replied. Claire squeezed Kim's hand, then dropped it. When Kim looked at me, her eyes were coated with mascara; they looked like daddy longlegs. Kim looked down, trying to get the bearings she'd entered with. She walked in like Miss America, but inside she was still a child.

Claire leaned toward her and wrapped an orange streamer around her forehead. "Could you wear this?"

"I certainly could."

"For an hour. Could you do that?"

When she flung back her head, the tail of the streamer crossed her shoulders. "Want to bet? One dollar."

"You're on." While Kim joined Doris in the kitchen, Claire

watched her leave the room. "Tennis player, class president, cheerleader, debater, trumpet player, and thief." She taped a turkey on the door. "He invited Kim to Alaska, on summer vacation."

"Is she going?"

"I don't know." She sat down on the couch and crossed her arms to her chest. "He stopped sending birthday cards to Jeannie and me—probably because we didn't write back—but he still sends them to her. And every birthday and Christmas, he gets a card from her. The last letter, he invited her up."

"What does your mother think?"

"She says that he has no rights to any of her children. Jeannie doesn't care about him; she doesn't care if he's living, and she wouldn't care if he's dead. That's how she protected herself—by looking at him and seeing nothing."

"What do you think?"

"If she does go, then I'm going with her. Mamaso would probably beat me to the Alaskan ferry. Better three of us than one." She stood up and began to walk toward the bathroom. "Jeannie and Ruby will be here soon. I'm going to clean up."

While she was getting ready, I went to my room, opened my suitcase, and removed my new clothes—the black wool pants, the cream-colored rayon blouse—and put them on. I stood in front of the mirror and brushed my hair until it fell down my back like a shiny black cape, licked my index finger and ran it across my eyebrows.

Claire was coming from the bathroom, dabbing a towel to her face, when I stepped out of my room. She cocked her head toward me. "You bought new clothes."

I nodded. "My own clothes."

From the kitchen, Doris yelled: "It's Thanksgiving, Ruby!"

"They are here." She laced her arm through mine. When she approached the kitchen, she ran toward Ruby. "Look at you," she said to Ruby. "You've grown an inch." Ruby was standing on the kitchen counter, looking like she owned the world. Claire and Ruby stared eye to eye. "I've missed you." Ruby smiled and popped an olive in Claire's mouth. "And you too," she said to Jeannie. Claire and Jeannie hugged so tightly there was not an inch of space left between them. "You're going to have to come visit me." She put her hand on Ruby's head of black hair. "You and this one."

Doris said, "Tell her your average, you know, your grades."

Claire smiled at Jeannie. "She's impressed if I get above a D."

Doris said, "3-6. Can you believe that?"

"Wow," I said, leaning into the wall.

"Alexandra," Claire said. "Meet Jeannie."

"Pleased to make your acquaintance," I said, as I shook her hand.

When she smiled, tiny lines creased around her eyes. They were the same kind of lines Doris had, but not as deep—the kind of lines that people who smile frequently develop. "You're her neighbor?" she asked.

Doris thrust her hands into the salad and tossed it around. "The one who likes to listen through the walls." She lifted her brows to me. "Hum?"

I smiled. "Yes, ma'am."

"Ma'am?" Doris said. "Ma'am?"

Jeannie's hands were covered with rings, in strange locations. A gold band was on her thumb. On her index finger, below the knuckle, was a silver band; on the same finger, above the knuckle, was a ring embedded with a red stone—ruby? And on her pinkie finger she wore a band made of turquoise and coral. Her hair was pulled back from her face in a French braid, and she was wearing Mamaso's smile, the kind of smile that gets passed down through the generations; the lips rise up—free—to break open in laughter. Claire, Jeannie, and Ruby had that smile, but Kim did not. She had a smile, but it was a smile worn by Brownies. Back in Pike, I remembered hearing the Brownies sing together as they walked home from school. I'm sure they had names—Debra and Lisa and Francis—but to me they were a group of Brownies waiting to become Girl Scouts, singing that stupid song: *There's something in my pocket that belongs across my face. I keep it very close to me in the most convenient place. I'm sure you couldn't guess it if you guessed a long long while, so I'll take it out and I'll put it on, it's a great big Brownie smile.* I wondered if Kim had been a Brownie and that's where she learned how to smile—something that comes on and off.

From the counter, Ruby spoke with the kind of clarity that comes from hearing people speak to you—not at you—the clarity that comes when you are invited to speak back: "Grandma made a pie." I had read once about old souls coming back in the bodies of the newly born, bringing with them all of the pain and joy of the previous life. Ruby didn't seem to be an old soul. A three year old baby with brown eyes and dark hair, she seemed absolutely new.

I leaned into the wall as Claire, Jeannie, and Kim began to flutter about the kitchen. It was as if a signal, inaudible to me, sent them in unison to their different chores. Kim set the table, Claire poured the wine, then positioned the candles in their holders and lit them, and Jeannie took the potatoes from the stove and whipped them. Nobody said, 'I'll do this and you do this'; they just started into action.

A piece of turkey was bundled in Ruby's fist. She held it toward Claire, saying: "You like bite?"

Claire took a small bite and drew close to Ruby, nuzzling her neck. "I'm going to gobble you up, Ruby-Girl."

My eyes began to burn as I watched Ruby—her laughter was so clear and pure. I wondered if I, whose mother had worn white on the mountain, had ever laughed so.

When Doris sat down at the head of the table, Jeannie tapped her spoon against her wine glass. "Thanks to the cook."

Doris raised her glass. "And to the turkey."

Ruby sat on pillows on a chair, between Doris and Jeannie. She gripped her spoon and ate, but some of the food ended up on her lap. "Damn," she said, as a spoonful of mashed potatoes fell.

Jeannie replied, "Heck." She retrieved the mashed potatoes.

"Heck," Ruby repeated.

"Oh, heck," Doris said, helping Ruby with another mouthful of food.

As I watched them, I remembered following in my mother's heel prints to the mountain. She pointed out a buck that was sleeping under a tree one hundred yards from us. "Oh," she said, holding me to her front so I could see it. "It's fucking beautiful." With the sound of her voice, the buck evaporated into the landscape. I looked at her. "Fucking beautiful," I repeated. She slapped me. I held my face as she claimed that cursing is saved for adults, not for children, and she didn't want to hear such language coming from me. What I was taught, I taught to my brother. When he cursed, I told him to wait a couple of years and he could curse like crazy; he wasn't a curser, except for the times he was walking down the street and thought I had my head too far in the clouds to hear him curse the world—god damn sidewalk, fucking streetlight, bastard of a tree, Oh Jesus, Oh Christ, Oh Jesus Holy Christ.

As I watched Jeannie wipe her napkin across Ruby's face, I felt a part of me was not done at all, I felt raw. Claire was talking about the activities of the GPA in Willow, how they were having a dance on New Year's Eve. Kim met my eyes, then quickly averted them. She wore the orange streamer on her forehead and down her back. I wanted to say to her, *You need help, There is a ton of things you've got to work on.* I wanted to say it to Kim, because I could not say it to myself.

"Why don't you go with her?" Doris asked me.

"With her where?"

Doris tossed her napkin at me. "To the dance."

Claire was smiling at her mother. "You've got no class, Mamaso, no class." There was so much conversation going on that I couldn't keep track of it. Kim was saying that Doris went to watch her debate—a practice round—and while Kim was debating on abortion rights, she was continually interrupted by her mother who clapped constantly.

"That's right," Doris said. "It's my body, that's why. *Pro-choice.*"

To my right, a piece of turkey fell off Ruby's plate. Jeannie said, "Gosh darn."

"Oh," Claire said. "Heck."

Kim said, "Gosh darn heck."

And Doris finished it: "Oh heck heck."

Ruby's eyes were traveling from her aunts to her grandmother. "Heck," she replied. Her lips curled up in a smile.

Oh, back home, Thanksgiving was not like this. When we actually had a turkey, that was all we had; we could not afford cranberries or French bread. Widow Kyle always wanted us to come eat at her house with her thousands of relatives, but we never did. After we ate our fill of dinner, leaving enough turkey for the week, we would find a pumpkin pie set on our doorstep—Widow Kyle. Stevie and I would say a prayer before Thanksgiving dinner; it consisted of one word: "Grace." Grace for the food bestowed upon us by the will of Landy who stole twenty bucks from the wallet of her passed-out father.

There was conversation going on all around me, but I didn't pay any attention to it. I kept watching the diligent way that Ruby pressed her spoon into the pieces of the baked tomato. She got nearly cross-eyed as the spoon approached her mouth, and if the food dropped, her mouth would stay open for a moment in disbelief until her head ducked as she gazed at the food in her lap. She looked at me and smiled.

"Who's up for a game of Pictionary?" Doris asked.

I didn't know what Pictionary was, but I nodded because everyone else was nodding. We got the table cleared, did the dishes, and sat down to play.

"I need some directions," I said.

Claire explained that it involved drawing out clues that were given on cards, under the pressure of a time constraint. She, Ruby, and I were partners, playing against Jeannie, Kim, and Doris.

"All right," Doris said, as her pencil was poised. "Go." She began to draw, and Claire began to draw. Ruby sat on Claire's lap. She had her head nestled against Claire's neck, staring at the sheet of paper which was getting covered with a sketch. I watched her eyes move across the sheet, then turn to me.

"I don't know," I said, as I stared at the sheet. "Do you know?"

"No."

Claire began to point at what she'd drawn. "You can't talk, huh?" I asked. She shook her head. "So, you can't talk. That's interesting, isn't it? A speech pathology student who can't talk." She grinned and tapped her pencil into the drawing. "Do you have any ideas, Ruby?"

Ruby stared down with her head cocked. "No."

"Well...that looks like it might be Africa."

Claire looked down and then up at me.

"Well," I said. "It's not, huh?"

She shook her head.

I looked at Ruby. "Have you ever seen your aunt this quiet?"

Her two lips pursed together as she grinned. "No."

"We should play this game more often."

Claire smirked. "Shut up."

"You lose," Kim said, smiling at us. "You talked. You can't talk, and yet you talked. Tsk, tsk, tsk."

Claire set her pencil down. "And you, little sister, owe me a buck."

"No, no, no." Kim turned her wrist watch to Claire. "It's been over an hour. You owe me a buck."

Jeannie was still concentrating on what Doris was drawing, even though she'd already won because Claire had talked. "I have no idea," Jeannie said. "No idea."

Ruby looked at Doris' drawing. "Cotton candy," she said to me.

"Do you think so?" I asked, trying to make out Doris' drawing.

"Could be cotton candy, I suppose." I looked from Doris' drawing to Claire's. "Bush?" I asked.

"Um huh." She tapped the pencil into the other sketch, which appeared to be a flame streaking toward the bush.

"Burning," I said. "Bush burning...bush burning?"

Claire put her head on the table top. "Heck."

"Burning...the burning bush?"

"Tah dah," Claire yelled. "The burning bush."

Bush burning made a lot more sense to me than a burning bush. Bush burning is what you do after a clear-cut to remove the trash lumber before the tree planters come in. "What kind of a clue is that?" I asked Claire. "The burning bush?"

"You don't know the reference?" When I shook my head, Claire explained that it was a Biblical reference from the Book of Exodus. God spoke out of the burning bush, telling Moses that he was to lead the Israelites to the promised land. When Moses asked God for his name, God's reply was, "I am that I am."

A pencil in each hand, Jeannie was doing a drum roll on the table-top as she focused on Doris' drawing. "I see the flame, but where's the bush?"

"Cotton candy," Ruby said. When I studied the sketch, it looked like cotton candy to me. Ruby and I stared at it, then nodded at each other.

"It's slang," Doris said. "Use your imagination."

Claire tipped her head back, laughing. "No one but you would have thought of that."

The feet of newborn crows creased around Jeannie's eyes. "You drew pubic hair for a bush?"

"It seemed to make sense," Doris replied.

"Oh Mamaso," Kim said, whacking her on the shoulder. "Geez."

We played for a while longer, until Ruby was sleeping in Claire's arms. "She's so beautiful," I said. With her eyes closed, I traced my fingers across her brows. "She's so young." Claire lifted her carefully and set her on the couch in the living room, wrapped a blanket over her. The rest of the family came into the room. Jeannie settled next to Ruby, Kim to her right. Doris got into the recliner and Claire was at her feet.

A family, not my own.

"I'm kind of tired," I said softly to Claire. "Do you mind if I just go to bed?"

Claire met my eyes. "You're welcome to stay."

"I'll see you in the morning." I waved at Jeannie as I was leaving the room. "Nice to meet you," I said. "All of you...the food...the company...your beautiful baby girl...all of it has been wonderful. I just want you to know that I appreciate it." Before they could respond, I walked with my head down out of the room, and by the time I reached the bedroom the tears were streaming down my cheeks.

Wiping the tears from my eyes, I folded my clothes neatly into my suitcase and pulled on my sleeping shirt. I propped my hands behind my head as I lay in bed staring into the darkness. In my mind I saw Ruby's face. I had been younger than Ruby when my mother first started taking me to the mountain.

I pressed my palms against my eyes, but had no power to make any of it go away. Even if I'd had six hands—two to cover my eyes, two to shield my ears, and two to mute my mouth—I couldn't have blocked the evil that occurred on my mother's mountain. I sang a song quietly to ease the pain, to make it go away, a Christmas song: "Oh Little Town of Bethlehem." Over and over, I sang it to myself, falling into a deep and silent sleep.

I awoke in the darkness. Blindly, I got out of bed, searched for the light switch, and turned it on. My wrist watch said it was two a.m. For a long while I sat on the bed, rocking. My mother's voice came inside me: *Don't let anyone tell you it's wrong.*

I went into the hallway, to Claire's room. Knocking softly on her door, I called her name and entered her room. She rose up on her elbow as I stood at the foot of her bed. "Do you think I could stay with you for a while?" She lifted the covers and I slid into bed next to her. Tears were on my lips; as I tasted their saltiness, my stomach recoiled. They were like the taste of my mother—wet salt.

"I can't imagine anyone asking of Ruby the things my mother asked of me," I said. "She'd ask me to hit her, Claire. And I'd do it, anything she asked of me, I'd do it." Claire didn't avert her eyes from mine, even as I said: "I slept with two men and I did just like she did, I asked them to hit me."

I turned on my side, my back to Claire; it was as if parts of me were shedding away, like a hollow wooden doll that gets smaller and smaller, a tiny doll held within its core. "She would sing me nursery rhymes...'Hush little baby don't say a word, Mama's going to buy you a mockingbird, and if that mockingbird don't sing, Mama's going to buy you a diamond ring, and if that diamond ring don't shine, it's surely going to break this heart of mine.' Silver mine—it's supposed to be a silver mine at the end of the song, isn't it?"

"Yes."

On the center of my chest, my fist was clenching and unclenching, like a heart beating outside of my body. "I called her lady, Lady God. But she wasn't a god... The last time—she touched me, Claire, she had never touched me there before. Always, I had been the one...touching her. But then, she touched me. I tried not to, but I cried, I couldn't stop crying as she touched me. The next day she killed herself."

The furnace clicked on and warm air sifted from the vent beneath the bed, toward my face. My tears broke free; I cried and cried, and Claire held me. "She would tell me, 'Don't let anyone tell you this is wrong.' But it is wrong, she was wrong, all of it is wrong." Through my tears, I raised up and stared at the wall. "I don't need to stay here," I said. "I don't need—"

"Do you want to go to your room?"

"No."

Claire was on her side, her front to my back. "Then stay."

As I settled in beside her, our bodies spooned together. I concentrated on the rhythmical pattern of her breath and soon my breath joined the pattern of hers, deep and steady. Her legs were soft against the back of my own and her hand was light upon my hip.

"I didn't always hate it," I said. "I wish I had, but I didn't. That's the worst thing." Claire's knee, nudging the back of my own, was like the nod of a head. "She faced down a black bear and she won. She always won." I held Claire's hand to my waist, staring at the darkness outside the window. "But I don't think she can win anymore," I said. "Not anymore."

Chapter Twelve

On the way back to Willow, Claire drove through the maze of the Seattle freeway system and then I took over behind the wheel, following the line of I-95 east. She was dozing as I drove over Snoqualmie Pass, so she didn't see that we nearly went into the ditch in the dense fog. Holding tightly to the wheel, I kept us steady.

As we descended from the summit and reconnected with the clear highway, I let my eyes leave the road to look at her. She was sleeping sideways on the seat, facing me. Her mouth was open slightly and a needle-thin strand of spittle was on her lip. She looked beautiful to me.

We carried our suitcases up the mansion stairs and unlocked our separate doors, but it felt strange to part from Claire. I didn't want to do it. I put my suitcase on the floor and sat atop it, looking over at her.

"I could make us some sandwiches from your mom's leftover turkey," I said.

"I'll be over," she replied, "As soon I get unpacked."

My room was frigid. I plugged the space heater into the socket near the window and stared at the picture of my mother resting on the windowsill. I tried to see past the darkness of her eyes, to understand, but her eyes gave no answers.

I took the picture from the sill and placed it in the box where I kept my rent receipts, check stubs, Social Security card, and coupons. From my closet, I removed her gown, wound it into a ball and put it in the box. As I walked from one end of my tunnel-like room to the other, I realized that nothing in the room was mine. The broken down couch wasn't mine, the bed wasn't mine, and the wobbly kitchen table wasn't mine. The kitchen table had no chairs to go with it, mine or otherwise. I had lived in this room for six months without taking the effort to make it mine.

In the kitchen I unwrapped the slices of turkey Doris had sent back with us and called to Claire through the wall: "Is mustard okay?"

"No," she called back. "Mayo."

"Lots or little?"

"Little."

Claire perched on the arm of my couch as I brought the sandwiches in. Strands of her hair clung to her forehead and droplets of water were on the front of her shirt. I didn't need a vocabulary tape to give me a word for what I felt as I looked at her—love, that was the feeling inside me; pure and simple, I felt love for her.

"Seattle was good," I said, "But it feels kind of nice to be back, doesn't it?"

Claire nudged my foot with her own. "Thanks for driving," she said.

She had a test coming up and was planning to go to the library to study for it; at my door, she paused for a moment, glancing at the empty windowsill. When she met my eyes, I nodded, and that was all we had to say about the fact that my mother was no longer enshrined in the window of my room.

In the morning, when Tiny let me in the door of the IGA, he pumped my hand up and down as if I'd been gone for weeks. With all the shifting going on inside me since the night Claire and I had molded together, back to front, it felt like weeks to me too.

"You tell me if you need time off at Christmas," he said. "I got plenty of folks who'd be more than happy to get the extra hours."

"I will, Tiny."

During the holidays, time always had a way of moving fast—Christmas just a breath away from Thanksgiving, New Year's right behind, and all the New Year's resolutions to be made. I didn't want to wait until New Year's day to make mine. My resolution was to get back home and make things right with Stevie and Dad, to get back home and make things right with myself by going to whatever was left of my mother's mountain and saying good-bye. When I left the mountain, the logger stood in the way to my mother's grave. I hit his jaw and felt stone. Even if he hadn't blocked me from the lilac tree that marked her grave, I probably wouldn't have been able to say good-bye, not then. See you, I probably would have said, not good-bye.

I wandered Main Street after work, looking in the windows of the stores. The women's wear shop had a lingerie sale going on, with markdowns on things I had no need for—silk brassieres and lacy black panties. The furniture store next to it was having a sale too. I sat down on every chair there, trying them out, recliners, rockers, easy chairs. One chair was a perfect fit; it was light brown and had firm cushions for support. I felt like a queen sitting in it. When the salesperson said it could be delivered that evening, I wrote out a check and still had enough money in my account to buy three more of those chairs if I'd wanted to.

My boots crunched in the snow and my breath made clouds around my face as I walked past the Saddle Inn on the way to the mansion. When I saw Hank's car in the lot, I sat on the fender and decided this was as good of time as any to say hello.

Hank was behind the bar, drawing a beer from the tap. I pulled out a stool at the far end of the bar, away from the other folks gathered there. Hank looked at me for a long moment before he came over.

"What'll you have, Alex?"

"Just a moment of your time, please."

He came around to the other side of the bar and leaned against it, next to me. "How've you been?" he asked.

"I've been fine." I saw my reflection in the mirror behind the bar and shook my head. "That's not the truth. I haven't been so good. That's what I wanted to tell you." His hand rested on the bar. No wedding ring was on his finger. "I was having a rough time and I'm sorry I brought you into it. I'm sorry I said those things that I said. It's been bothering me and I wanted to find you and apologize."

Hank sat on the stool next to me. "I didn't want you to leave," he said.

"I couldn't stay, Hank."

"And now?"

"Now?"

He nodded. "Now."

"I'm not sure I understand."

"I'm asking if you'd like to take in a movie," he replied. "Maybe go to dinner."

His eyes were the color of good earth, a rich fertile brown, meeting my own. "I'm sorry, but I'm going to have to say no."

"All right," he replied. "But could you give me a reason why?"

His hands were folded on his knees. I turned them over and looked at his wrists—I liked his wrists, liked the way you could see the blood rushing through his veins. "There are a lot of reasons, but none of them have to do with you. I think you're wonderful, but I'm going to have to say no."

Leaving the bar, I walked up the hill toward the mansion. The snow, crusty from the night chill, glittered beneath the streetlights. Behind me, I heard footsteps and turned around to see Teresa running toward me, Mike lingering behind.

Teresa said, "Jesus Christ, you walk fast."

Mike stopped a few paces back from her. Tilting his head toward the sky, he averted his eyes as he said: "We were in the Saddle when you came in."

"But we couldn't catch your eye," Teresa added. She was wearing a coat with a fake fur collar, or at least I thought it was fake. Everything about her seemed fake—her blue-coated eyelids, her platinum blonde hair, her scarlet fingernails. Her voice was lilting and simple, as if she were trying to talk down to me, but she couldn't, for I was more than a head taller than she was and a lifetime smarter. "Don't you have anything to say to us?" she asked. When I shook my head, she tossed me a saccharin smile. "Since you apologized to Hank, we just assumed we'd be next on your list. You weren't whispering, you know." As I turned away, Teresa grabbed the tail of my coat. "Come on now, Alex. Let it go. Come on up to our place, just like the old times. Before you know it you'll be having more fun than the day the pigs ate your brother."

I stared at her teasing eyes and knew that by playing the hillbilly I'd be playing right into her hand; but I'd give her what she wanted, one time, and then it'd be over, forever over. "You got it wrong," I said. "The pigs ate Duffy Hannigan."

Laughing, Teresa glanced at Mike who stood away from us, his arms crossed to his chest, his head tipped to the sky. "Duffy," she said. "Perfect."

"He had a heart attack inside their pen. When Mrs. Hannigan found him, the pigs were rooting into his body."

"What'd they do with the pigs?" Teresa asked. "Lynch them?" When I turned my eyes on her, she said: "So they butchered them? And did Mrs. Hannigan realize that when she ate her morning bacon she was actually eating her own husband?" Smiling, she opened her hands. "Can't you see, Alex? Everything is relative."

When I started up the hill, she grabbed my coat again. "Mike?" I said. "I want you to take her away from me." He lowered his head, facing me. His right eye was swollen shut. "Jesus, Mike, what happened to you?"

"You gave us the idea," Teresa replied. "I guess we got into it a little more than we should have."

"You let her hit you, Mike?"

The line of silver streaking from the corner of his mouth broke open as he smiled. "Good times, Alex, get them where you can."

Teresa had not released my coat tail. "Take her," I said to Mike. He stepped toward her and folded her hands behind her back. She didn't fight to free herself. Leaning into him, she winked at me as I turned away.

"Alex*andra*," she said. "Alex*andra*."

***

My new chair got delivered that evening. I heard them on the staircase: "All right, now, take it up. Good, good." When I opened my door, two young men, about my age, had their hands wrapped around my chair and were lifting it up the staircase.

"It goes in this room," I said to them.

They were having a difficult time getting it up the stairs. There wasn't enough room for both of them on the staircase, so one guy was on bottom and the other one was on top. They lifted my chair a step at a time.

"I didn't think it was that heavy," I said.

"Nothing we can't handle," the guy on the top said.

The guy on the bottom was bearing almost the entire weight of the chair. His biceps, small as they were, bulged. The other guy was trying to take some of the chair's weight off of him, pulling it forward, but you can't change the law of gravity; what goes up must come down.

"Here, let me give you a hand," I said.

"Nope," the guy on the bottom said. He looked up at me with his face drenched in sweat. "We can do it." They set the chair down inside my door and started walking down the stairs.

"Thank you."

One of them was out the door, but the guy whose tiny biceps had bulged looked up at me from the bottom of the stairs. If I stared at him with one eye, my right, he looked like a midget.

"You know, I could have helped you," I said.

"See my back?" I saw the slogan written on the back of his jacket: *Brown's Furniture—We Deliver*. He walked like a penguin out the door.

In my room, I pushed the chair to my window—it didn't seem that heavy to me. I propped my feet on the windowsill and stared for a long while at the falling snow in the streetlights. The longer I stared, the more I found myself wishing; I wished I'd never met Mike and Teresa, never raided gardens with them, never had the opportunity to feel fondness for them. But as soon as the thought became clear to me, I knew it wasn't the whole truth. They had been important to me once. Even if I tried, I couldn't hate them now. I could choose not to be around them, but I couldn't hate them.

The *National Geographic* magazines that Doris gave me were stacked in the corner of my room. I picked one up and started to read an article about the manatees who lived in the causeways in southern Florida. I'd never seen a manatee before, but I fell in love with them the moment I looked at their punched-up snouts and gentle eyes. The article said that, due to their mass, the manatees couldn't move quickly enough to avoid the speedboats in the causeways. The boats' propellers would rip into their flesh as they tried to dive beneath the surface of the water.

The magazine stayed open on my lap as I leaned my head back, the tears streaming down my cheeks. Since the night I spent in Seattle, huddled in Claire's arms, I found myself crying over everything; from manatees, to a baby girl sitting in a cart at the IGA, to the newly fallen snow when it captured my footprint, to an aged man who gave me five dollars and two pennies when his order was five dollars and twenty cents, to the majestical beauty on Claire's face, and to me, for all that had occurred on my mother's mountain.

The tears were long since dry on my face when Claire came up the stairs. She knocked on my door once and then opened it. "Hey," I said, lifting my hand to her. "I've become a furniture owner." Rising, I patted the seat. "Sit."

She propped her feet on the windowsill, just as I had done, and folded her hands behind her head. Gold flecks, pure gold, flashed in her eyes. "I want it," she said.

"Can't have it," I replied. "But anytime you want to come on over and sit in it, you can."

"Mamaso called me," she said.

I nodded, sitting on the windowsill. "Yeah?"

"It seems Kim is not going to Alaska this summer. She's been picked to be a group leader of cheerleaders camp. She'll be paid for it, and it runs all summer. Kim's excited. Mamaso is ecstatic." Claire stared out the window and into the whiteness of snow. "Eventually Kim is going to see him. She says that his back is bad. An old man with a bad back...her father...my father."

"My mother, your father," I said, giving a small smile. "That makes us soul mates."

She met my eyes and nodded. "I've got a test tomorrow," she said. "Why don't you go take it for me."

"Does it have anything to do with white-tails, coyotes, bobcats, bears, or anything else related to Pike?"

"No."

I smiled. "Sure, I can take it." When she stood up to leave, I said, "I would like you to stay."

For a moment she searched my face. "I have to study, Alexandra."

"In your room, right?"

"Yes."

"Tell me, your room is probably frigid, isn't it?" When she nodded, I said, "That's because the radiators don't work. And Patchins hasn't even got the storm windows up yet. In here, you'll have a nice heated place to study. Unless you like to study in the cold?"

She came back to my room with a huge book that would have made a great doorstop. Kicking off her shoes, she folded her legs beneath her on the chair, opened the book and glanced at me where I sat on the floor reading a book I'd gotten at the county library. It was a book on the Pacific Northwest—the rain forests and the canyons, the mountains and the deserts, the sweeping variety of trees: pines, maples, oaks, firs, willows, and redwoods.

"No," she said, looking up from her textbook. "I can't do this."

"What?"

"Sit in your new chair," she said. "Here, get off the floor. Trade me places."

"I have a strong back," I replied. "Sitting on the floor doesn't bother me at all."

"Well, it bothers me." She put her hand out and I took it. "Try out your new chair." When I opened my mouth to speak, she put her hand over my lips. "It's useless, Alexandra."

When she drew her hand away, I wanted to take it back and kiss her fingers. "All right," I said. "Read, Claire."

We fell into an easy quiet as we read, the silence broken only by the flipping of the pages. Claire's head lilted to the side and her eyes moved slowly across the lines. When she glanced at me, both of us smiled, then returned our eyes to our books. I glanced up and Claire was watching me. She didn't avert her vision even as I sat with my head cocked, staring into her eyes. "If you had any idea of your own beauty—" She closed her book and stared at the ceiling. "I've got to go to the library."

I smiled as she turned her eyes on me. "At the library you won't have me for company."

"Maybe I'll actually be able to concentrate on what I'm reading."

As she was heading down the stairs, I called, "Hey, Claire." She leaned into the railing. "I don't want to interrupt your studies or anything like that, but I just kind of wanted to tell you that I think it's about time you'd better initiate your car into your sexual preferences...that's what I've been thinking, Claire. Of course, I don't want to upset your studies, but I would be willing to break your car in."

"With whom?"

"Well, maybe with myself, although kissing a rear view mirror doesn't sound like fun." I put my hands into my pockets. "Well, you know, I just thought I'd tell you that as you go off to study."

She smiled up at me. "Goodnight, Alexandra."

I waved my hand into the air. "Claire."

That night, I don't know if she had sweet dreams, but I did. In my dreams we shared the same bed and in my dreams we did not sleep. The dreams stayed with me like a song you can't get off your mind through the day as I rang the keys at the IGA, bagging the groceries, sending the customers home.

***

Claire and I went jogging in the evening, running together down the dark streets. "Did you know," I said, smiling as I jogged next to her, "that we have hummingbirds back home. One time I was at the mountain, and a hummingbird stuck his beak up my nose."

She began to laugh. "No, you never told me that."

"I stood still for a long time, waiting for it to come to me. And it did. You could get cross-eyed staring at it." I smiled. "I sneezed."

She stopped outside the mansion and stretched her legs out by leaning against the telephone pole. She watched me out of the corner of her eye as I opened her car door, and got inside. I was silent, my heart beating inside my chest, as a moment passed, then she came inside. Frost covered the windows of her car, and she was a shadow.

"Oh, Alexandra," she said softly.

"First, let me talk, just let me talk." I rested my hand, palm up, in the space between the two of us. My hand felt like a lightening rod, taking in the crackling energy which traveled between us. "I know there's a lot of stuff inside that I'm probably going to be trying to understand for a long time. But one thing that's not a mystery is how I feel about you."

Her eyes shifted across my face, slow and progressive, taking me in. "It doesn't usually happen this way for me," she finally said.

"How does it usually happen?"

"It normally starts with a kiss," she replied. "With a kiss—" Her words disappeared as I kissed her lips. For a long, long while her lips were soft and open, meeting my own. "Are you sure you want this?" she asked quietly.

"More than I've wanted anything in my life...I want you."

Resting her head on my chest, she said, "I've never met anyone like you."

"About that dance your mother was talking about, New Year's Eve." I kissed her lips. "Go with me."

She smiled. "First you want to fuck me, then you'll ask me out?"

"I don't want to fuck you," I whispered. "But I would like to make love with you." When I got out of her car, Claire followed. In the darkness, we walked arm in arm to the door of the mansion and went upstairs to my room.

"I seem to have lost control of this relationship," she said.

"I don't think you ever had control," I replied, as I pulled the sweatshirt over her head and kissed the nape of her neck.

"If I tell you to take off your shirt, would that mean I'd regained it?"

"I don't think so."

"Take off your shirt anyway," she said, pulling it off my body.

One by one, a piece at a time, our clothes fell to the floor.

I loved the taste of her, the scent of her, I loved her plum-colored nipples reaching toward my tongue. I loved the sounds she made as my lips moved across the ridges and valleys of her body. Most of all,

I loved the way she laughed as she rolled me over and kissed the moistness of her body from my lips.

"Do you plan to make this a habit, Alexandra?"

"Yes."

"Good."

Her fingers roamed across my skin, reading me like braille.

Chapter Thirteen

I asked Claire to bring home a college catalogue so I could see what kind of courses were offered. I had no immediate plans to enroll, but it was something I thought I might do someday. Sitting in my chair with my feet propped on the windowsill, I thumbed through the catalogue. The heater buzzed and sent a red light toward my legs, but I still felt chilly. When I got up to look for my wool sweater, I couldn't find it in my room or in Claire's. Since we'd assumed joint custody of both rooms, it was harder to keep track of things. I found a pair of her shoes in my room, a pair of my socks in hers, but no wool sweater anywhere.

Claire was wearing the sweater when she came home that night. She dropped her backpack to the floor as she walked across the room to me. Kneeling in front of the chair, she slid between the V of my legs.

"Hi," she said.

"The sweater looks good on you."

She slipped her hands into the hip pockets of my jeans. "It belongs to a friend of mine." Beneath the sweater, her skin felt hot. My hands enclosed the sides of her ribcage and I could feel the pressure of her breath as she flicked open the buttons of my jeans. "It is time," she said, "to consecrate this chair."

That night, as we lay on her futon, the scent of our bodies lingered beneath the blankets; it was the most powerful scent I'd ever known, fecund and earthy. Claire's head rested upon my chest. Freeing a strand of hair from the side of her mouth, I said, "I've been thinking that I'd go back to Pike for a day or so. I left so quickly I never said good-bye to my Dad and my brother. I'd also like to spend a little time at my mother's mountain."

Claire's lips brushed across my forearm. "When?"

"Soon." I held her hands to my mouth and blew on them. "I would like you to come with me." I smiled. "Otherwise, I'd have to hitch." When she nodded, I turned her hands over and kissed the skin. "Mostly, I'd like you to see the place that's made me. That's why I want you to come. We could go this weekend, if you've no plans."

"This weekend is fine," she replied.

"One other thing I've been thinking about." I placed her hands on the sheets. "There are a lot of things rolling around inside me. I think it's time, Claire…It's time for me to see someone who would listen to me…That's what I think. A therapist."

She held me to her front. Her room was not so cold with the two of us in it, not so cold at all.

***

This time of year the snow would have made the road leading to the mountain impassable, so I rented two pairs of snowshoes from the outdoor store on Main Street. They'd keep us from sinking into the drifts.

"Do you know how to use snowshoes?" I asked, closing the door of my room behind me.

She nodded. "April and Sue like to spend Christmas at the cabin; it's April's parents', but they're road warriors, driving the RV across the nation. Last year they invited me. We snowshoed in." She locked her door, and I locked mine. "April and Sue would like to get to know you better. I told them to wait until the honeymoon is over." She smiled as she strolled down the stairs.

"Honeymoon." Carrying the snowshoes, I followed. "Honeymoon."

"You drive," she said to me. "I'm a tourist."

Dressed in our warm clothing, I got in the car and had to adjust her seat to make room for my legs. Driving at a steady fifty-five, I took us past the snow-covered wheat fields of eastern Washington, northward, toward the wilderness.

The railroad, running parallel to the highway, told me we were getting closer to home. On the far side of the railroad tracks the river twisted like a huge black snake. The highway crew had forgotten to remove the sign that went up each summer: "Box Canyon Dam Is Open—Extremely Dangerous To Swim."

Only a madman would test the currents when the dam was open. If that were true, I wondered what kind of word you would give to a mother who would toss her own child into the waves. Madwoman came too easily to the tongue and didn't encompass the whole of her; it did nothing to capture the look in her eyes as she pulled me from the river and wrapped me inside her jacket. Shame blanketed her eyes as she asked that I forgive her for not having the courage to baptize the two of us on the river's floor.

The river shed its skin behind us as we approached Pike. A welcome sign marked the city limits: "Greetings from Pike, Washington. This town is like Heaven to us. Please don't drive like Hell through it."

We didn't veer from the highway to enter the side streets where the folks I used to know lived—the pasture where Bell ate Parson's feed, the rundown Ramstead shack, the chicken coop where Widow Kyle snatched eggs from her hen, the house where Stevie and Dad lived on a street called Hollywood—some mayor's idea of a joke, Hollywood Boulevard.

The highway took us to the road leading to the foothills of my mother's mountain. I parked the car and Claire came to stand beside me as I stared at the skyline. I couldn't believe how small the mountain seemed. No huge head rose to meet the sky.

"I thought it was bigger," I said. "It always seemed bigger to me...but it's not so big." Zipping up my fatigue jacket, I pulled on my stocking cap and got the snowshoes from the car. "If you need to rest, tell me."

We put our snowshoes on and started the climb. Trees encased in a crystalline layer of snow bordered the road. Our breath became labored as the road steepened. It made a fog around our faces and broke free, returning every time we breathed again. We did not talk, saving our breath, yet as we passed an ancient cedar tree where strands of silver hair marked the nesting place of a deer, I used my breath to say: "Deer's bed."

Our snowshoes slapped against the snow like beavers' tails. The sun cast shadows on the road, reflecting the long thin outlines of the trees. At the top of the mountain the shadows disappeared and the white was broken by piles of charred lumber breaking through the snow.

"The fuckers clear-cut," I said, stopping at the edge of the meadow. "They clear-cut the whole thing." If a meadow was an open space surrounded by forest, this was no longer a meadow, for no forest surrounded it.

A mound of charred lumber thrust through a snowdrift beside us. Claire sat on a limb catching her breath while I tried to put the markers back on the land—the deer blind, the patch of Indian paintbrush, the lilac tree—but without the frame of the forest, I couldn't place anything.

"There used to be a lilac tree here, to mark her grave. There's no reason why they had to cut it down." I pulled my stocking cap off and rubbed it across my face. "This was a stupid idea. It's stupid and it's a waste of time."

"Where was the lilac tree?"

"What's the point?"

Claire's hand made a square across the four corners of the meadow. "Was it there? There? There? There?"

I tossed my head. "Out there." Walking past the piles of black wood, I stopped in the center of the meadow. "It was here somewhere." When I realized I may have been standing on my mother's grave, my legs felt rubbery. The snow trapped the edges of my snowshoes as I backed away, tossing me to the ground.

I had no energy to right myself. As I stared at the sky, an ache pounded behind my eyes, the same kind of ache I used to wake with, sweaty and trembling, in my bed. It was like waking from a dream as I sat up and pointed toward a spot where a gnarly black pine had once stood and saw my mother hanging from the tree that was no longer there.

"There," I said. "She hung herself there." Claire knelt behind me. "You can't see it," I said. "It's not there." It was not there, but still I saw it—even in my worst dreams I had never before seen anything so horrible as the circles of white that were her eyes.

"I found her here, hanging from the tree." Claire's breath caught in her throat and her body pressed against the back of my own. "She left me at the Widow Kyle's. She said I couldn't come with her. As soon as the Widow turned her back, I ran away. She was here…she was hanging from the tree." I pointed at the tree that wasn't there. "I found her walking stick at the foot of the tree and slung it over a branch to pull myself up. But I couldn't get the rope off. All I could do was sit on the branch and hold her head…Do you know how I could leave her, Claire?"

Her head shifted against the back of my own.

"Because I believed she'd be there the next day, I believed she'd be in the tree waiting for me. In my mind she wasn't dead. She was in the tree waiting for me to come back." Claire's hands were locked together at my front. Holding to her forearms, I said, "The Widow found me on the street and wrapped me in a blanket on her couch. She asked me where I'd gone to, but I didn't tell her. It was like our secret, my mother's and mine, like all of our secrets."

"Dad—he went looking for her that night. I was on the Widow's couch when he came back. I'd been quiet for so long the Widow thought I was asleep. I never saw such a look on my Dad's face before, like he was holding his grief in so tight it was turning his blood into ice. He asked the Widow to call Parson and send him to the mountain. He told the Widow to have Parson bury my mother where she fell...That's when I knew she wasn't going to be there the next day or the next. She'd fallen out of the tree and she wasn't going to be there anymore."

The silence around us was even deeper than our own as we held one another, front to back. For a long while neither of us had the power to move.

"Maybe she thought dying was the only way it was going to stop," I finally said. "Maybe she was right."

I walked to the center of the meadow where, beneath the snow and earth, my mother was buried. Folding my hands behind my back, I stared at the ground. "I can't kneel to you." My snowshoes dipped into the snow and steadied. "I wish you could have loved me differently, Mama, I wish you could have." My knees began to buckle as I backed away, but I did not fall. "Good-bye."

Claire laced her arm through mine as we followed the paw prints of our snowshoes down the mountain. I didn't feel there were any words left to say as we leaned into one another at the foothills.

When we pulled up to my house, there were no lights on inside. As I was getting out of the car, I saw the Widow sitting in front of her picture window. The next moment her door flew open and she was striding down the walk.

"I knew you'd pop up someday, I kept telling your father you would." Glancing at my house, she said, "That's why they made telephones, Landy, so you can call first and find out if anyone's home before you drive two hundred miles. They're in Reno playing the slot machines."

"Reno?"

"Couldn't believe it myself, but I guess Daniel figured he was due some kind of vacation after all these years." Counting on her fingers, she said: "It's Dan and Stevie and his girl Shannon, Shannon's sister Mary and Mary's husband Dean. They even took Hepburn with them." The Widow slapped me on the behind as she turned to Claire. "Who'd you bring with you?"

"This is my friend," I said. "My friend Claire."

"Are you and your friend hungry?"

"Sure," I said. "Sure we are."

The smell of calamine ointment and lavender bath powder filled her house. Claire and I sat at the table while she fed us roast beef sandwiches and vanilla milkshakes. All those years I'd tried to escape from her, it felt good to be sitting with her now.

"You do intend on staying the night, don't you?" the Widow asked.

"I haven't gotten so far as figuring out the night time yet."

"Seeing as how it's dark outside, this might be the time to decide," she said. "Sensible thing is to stay on over at your folks house and then get up bright and early and come over here for some bacon and eggs to send you on the road. That'd be the sensible thing to do."

"Do you still have that mean old hen?"

Nodding, the Widow said, "You'll be eating her eggs in the morning."

If I'd been more alert, just looking at the snow on the Widow's walk would have told me that Dad was away. If he were home, the walk would have been clear. I found the shovel at the side of the Widow's house and made a path through the snow.

There had never been a time when our house was locked, and even a trip to Reno wasn't enough for Dad to lock it. The house was chilly, but Claire and I got warm as we climbed the stairs to my old room and slid beneath the covers of the bed. The radio was on the bedstead. When I flipped it on, the country music station from Colville came in strong.

"This was my room," I said. "This was my bed. That was my radio. This was my home." As Claire curled against me, I rested my hand on her shoulder, staring at the white walls of my room. Always white, as long as I could remember, white.

"I've been thinking," I said. "I think I'd like my old name back. It's a good name, there's no reason I shouldn't use it, and there's nobody else I know who has it. Folks who know me well call me Landy."

Claire's eyes were astonishing—so very alive. "Landy."

"Could you get used to it?"

"I believe I could."

Lesa Luders received an MFA degree from Eastern Washington University. She teaches writing at the University of Idaho, and lives with her partner in Moscow, Idaho.

Other titles from New Victoria

ALL THE WAYS HOME PARENTING AND CHILDREN IN THE LESBIAN AND GAY COMMUNITIES—A COLLECTION OF SHORT FICTION.
Includes well-known writers, Beth Brant, Ruthann Robson, Jane Rule, Julie Blackwomon, Jameson Currier, as well as budding young authors writing about being part of lesbian and gay families.*"This is a powerful, inclusive collection, and oh so very real. We've been waiting a long time for a book like this."*—Irene Zahava, editor, *Lesbian Love Stories.* **$10.95**

EVERY WOMAN'S DREAM by Lesléa Newman
Lesbian life and love. As always, Newman brings a sharp yet playful style to these tales of sex, monogamy, fantasies, the future, and the possibility of lesbian motherhood. Who else can write about lesbian life through the story of a travelling sock? **$9.95**

ICED by Judith Alguire
The author of the classic sports novel *All Out*, now offers readers a look at life in the fast-growing world of women's professional ice hockey. Ex-player Alison Gutherie is now coach of the Toronto Teddies, trying to mold a professional team despite the owner's sexism and her attraction to Molly Gavison, an enigmatic young player. **$10.95**

SPARKS MIGHT FLY by Cris Newport
In this romantic first novel by Cris Newport, Philippa Martin, a former child prodigy grown into an exceptional concert pianist, discovers that her music and her muse are gone—from her hands and from her heart—driven away by her lover Corinne's unfaithfulness. No longer able to play, she returns home in shock and despair. **$9.95**

A PERILOUS ADVANTAGE THE BEST OF NATALIE CLIFFORD BARNEY
Edited and translated by Anna Livia with a foreword by Karla Jay
Finally, the writings of one of the century's most notorious lesbians is available in English. Barney, a woman blatant about her lesbianism at least 20 years before *The Well of Loneliness* was published, believed romance should be lived as well as written about, and began her last lesbian affair when well into her 80s. **$10.95**

LESBOMANIA by Jorjet Harper
Examine the scientific evidence that lesbonauts visited the Earth in prehistoric times.Cruise down the Nile with Ancient Egypt's lesbian Pharaoh, Hatshepsut! Lesbomania takes a humorous look at life within the lesbian community, its subculture, issues that divide us, sex and romance, coming out. With cartoons by Joan Hilty **$9.95**

**Available from your favorite bookstore or direct from
New Victoria Publishers**
PO Box 27 Norwich VT 05055-0027 **1-800-326-5297**